She's Not the Type

Also by Elaine Soloway

THE DIVISION STREET PRINCESS

GREEN NAILS AND OTHER ACTS OF REBELLION: LIFE AFTER LOSS

BAD GRANDMA: AND OTHER CHAPTERS IN A LIFE LIVED OUT LOUD

Dear Lisa.
Thanks for coming & buying!
Love,
Elaine

SHE'S NOT THE TYPE

A Novel

Elaine Soloway

She's Not the Type: A Novel

Originally published in ebook format in 2011.

ISBN: 978-0-692-09470-9

Book design by Sarah E. Holroyd (http://sleepingcatbooks.com)
Author photo by Ron Gould Studios
Cover image used under license from Shutterstock.com

For all of my friends who also are not the type.

One

Ann could remember almost every detail of the evening she received the phone call.

It was after dinner, a Friday in May. She was seated at the kitchen table reading John Dewey's "Human Nature and Conduct," preparing for an exam the following morning. Grease and garlic from her mother's broiled chicken perfumed the air; the preferable sweet scent of strudel had disappeared.

"One piece is enough," Sylvia had said when she pulled the dessert from Ann's fingers and wrapped it in aluminum foil. "Don't forget that tummy," she added, nodding towards her daughter's waistline.

Ann's eyes traveled downward to the area her mother highlighted. By now, she should've gotten used to Sylvia's teasing about the small drooped belly easily seen if Ann faced foreword before the bedroom mirror. But when she turned sideways and sucked in, the small roll would completely disappear. That was enough to convince her the problem lie in her poor posture and not her love of sweets.

As always, Ann kept silent at her mother's taunt. She wasn't sure why she never spoke up, never got riled and returned with a strong, *Hey, Mom, that hurts my feelings.* Never suggested Sylvia focus instead on her only daughter's positive features, like her brain and quick wit. No, those rebuttals would remain tucked safely behind Ann's cowardly tongue.

She feared any backtalk would turn her mother against her, or worse, wound Sylvia. Either way, Ann wasn't willing to chance it.

Fortunately, 21-year-old Ann Simon had opinions of others to boost her self-image. She brightened when complimented on her fair skin sprinkled with a tablespoon of freckles, her coppery red hair, and her green eyes; a "cutie pie" she was often labeled. And if she were to shed the extra 10 pounds that vexed her mother, or added five inches to her height, or left her black-rimmed eyeglasses and thick lenses on the nightstand, then she might even be tagged "a beauty."

But alas, in that year of 1959, with Richard J. Daley as the city's mayor and Dwight D. Eisenhower the country's president, within Ann's small circle, the coveted beauty description was reserved for one of her best friends at Chicago Teachers College, Lois Golden.

To her classmates, Lois was known as the Jewish Elizabeth Taylor (that was before Liz married Mike Todd and really did convert to Judaism). With her porcelain skin, inky black cap haircut and spit curls, dark eyebrows, and *shiksa* nose, Lois could be the Hollywood star's double.

Many of the girls were jealous of Lois' beauty, but what Ann really coveted was Lois' boyfriend, the lanky Joel Robins whose Southern accent—brought to Chicago from Charleston, South Carolina and smoothed by his teenager desire to fit in—only added to his luster.

Ann's secret longing for the boy was only shared with her closest friend, Leah Shore (soon to be Leah Friedman once she wed her fiancé, Ken). "Isn't he adorable?" Ann would swoon whenever Joel was spied picking up Lois at the college's exit doors.

"Down girl," Leah would warn. "He belongs to another."

When the telephone call came in to the Simon household that evening, Ann's mother didn't have to shout to call Ann to the phone because the apartment the women shared was so small, one of them could have whispered in the living room and be easily heard in the bathroom at the end of the hall.

A garden apartment, that's what the real estate listing had called it. Basement was more like it. Because Ann was only four-feet ten inches, and her mother barely five feet, neither of them had to stoop when they stepped down into the living room during their first tour of the place. But others, any taller than the petite occupants, would've had to lower their heads to avoid a bruised forehead. The apartment's tight quarters didn't dissuade Sylvia, and since she could swing the $95 monthly rent on her switchboard operator's salary, a lease was signed.

Sylvia had a knack for decorating and soon transformed the dark and occasionally damp space into what visitors called "a doll house." Needlework (handcrafted by Sylvia herself!) with Asian scenes hung on walls in the living room and in the one bedroom. Each glass-topped end table held a lamp with a brightly painted Geisha girl as its base, and on the shelves of the circular coffee table, stood half a dozen figurines—boys and girls in country frocks, ceramic baskets painted to look woven, and other cheap statues Ann had to dust every Saturday morning.

Despite Sylvia's beautifying, the apartment was more subterranean than floral. Their back door, which should have led to the outdoors, opened instead into the apartment building's laundry room. In the morning, when Ann woke early for school, she could hear the appliances already rocking the concrete, and would try to match their rhythm as she brushed her teeth.

In the living room, when she sat on the plastic-covered couch and looked out the window on the opposite side, Ann could see the feet of other tenants as they walked past. By now, she knew the sturdy ankles bundled in bobby socks belonged not to a teenager, but to the landlady, Mrs. Mandelbaum. And the slim legs and high-heeled shoes that tapped across the pavement were of course, Sylvia's.

The kitchen table that doubled as Ann's desk was rectangular and gray Formica. To accommodate the tiny room, one of the longer sides was pushed up against the wall. Three chairs surrounded it and the one where Ann was seated had a series of small cracks in its cushion that caused her to fidget and lose her place in the textbook.

Ann heard the telephone ring, but didn't rush to answer it because the reading assignment was essential if she was to ace the next day's test. (Ann never received less than a B in high school and was determined to match or beat that record in college. So far, she was on track.) Besides, the caller was likely one of her mother's relatives checking up on their widowed sister.

"It's for you," Sylvia said to Ann. She hunched her shoulders up toward her clip-on earrings to signal *this caller is unknown to me.* A Swirl housecoat covered the white nylon blouse with a deep V-neckline and polyester blue dotted skirt Sylvia wore to work that day. Raven-haired, blue-eyed, and shapely, she could've been crowned a beauty queen, if women in their 40s were encouraged to compete.

"Be right there," Ann said. She scraped her chair backwards along the linoleum, barely missing the enamel stove behind her. She turned her book upside down to save her place and capped the pen to lay it aside the notebook paper. Then she stood, rubbed the back of her leg where the chair had left a mark, and took six quick steps towards her mother.

"Thanks, Mom," Ann said as Sylvia handed over the black receiver. The phone was mounted in the hallway, a tunnel so narrow that one of the women had to turn to the side to let the other pass.

"Hello?" Ann said.

"Hi, it's me, Joel, Joel Robins."

Ann wondered what prompted this call. Had he been searching for Lois and believed she was at Ann's place studying for the Dewey exam?

Although she had never heard Joel's voice on the phone, there was no mistaking its soft Southern lilt; a melody she wished would last longer whenever they met face to face. Sometimes, she'd run into him at school, when he came to pick up Lois. As he waited for his girlfriend, they'd make small talk in the hallway. When he spotted Lois, and turned to leave to catch up with her, Ann would fight the urge to reach a hand to his shoulder and stop him. More, she wanted to say, more words. But she never had the nerve to say it out loud.

"Listen, I've got to talk to you about something," Joel said on the other end of the line. "Can you meet me tomorrow? Maybe the park across from your house?"

"Sure, but can you give me a hint?"

"No, no. I'll tell you tomorrow."

"So?" Sylvia asked after Ann returned to the table. "Who was that?" Supposedly, she was putting away the dishes Ann had dried and left standing on the sink's drain board. But was she also eavesdropping? If so, she was still mystified by the caller's identity.

"Joel Robins," Ann said.

"What did *he* want?" Sylvia knew the name was attached to Lois, as in Lois and Joel. Ann could tell by her mother's expression she had hoped the mystery man might be calling for her unattached daughter. It was her mother's wish that Ann join the enviable circle of engaged coeds.

"I'm not sure," Ann said. "He wants to meet me tomorrow to talk about something. Maybe because I work at Feldman's, he wants my advice on an engagement ring for Lois?"

Ann enjoyed her part-time job at the jewelry shop on Milwaukee Avenue. Although her role—typing invoices and filing certificates—kept her in the back, whenever she heard the doorbell's ring signaling customers, she's slip from behind her desk and peek at the pair as they gushed over the glass display case.

"Wouldn't that be wonderful if that was it?" Ann said to her mother. "If Joel wanted my advice on a ring for Lois?" She was fudging, of course.

"Wonderful," Sylvia said, banging a dinner plate atop its stack.

Ann arrived in the park first. That was her habit: Forever early. She couldn't remember a time when she was ever late for an appointment. Even before the professor opened her classroom for the morning, Ann could be found standing outside the door. If she were especially early, she would dig into the novel tucked inside her tote bag. But if she could hear the professor's footsteps coming down the hall, she'd use a textbook to fill the minutes and prove her earnestness.

While waiting for Joel to join her on the park bench, Ann closed her eyes. She inhaled the spring air, the grass freshly mowed by the Chicago Park District, and lilac bushes. Compared to Ann's *garden* across the street from the park, these smells were the real thing.

"So?" was Ann's first word as soon as Joel took his place next to her. "Why the big secret?" She looked up at his face, which she was surprised to see anguished, rather than excited with big news of a planned engagement.

Even seated Joel was a good foot taller than her. His eyes were hazel, his hair light brown, which he wore slicked back like Gary Cooper. And like the movie actor (Ann loved him in "High Noon"), Joel's forelock would occasionally fall onto his face. If it weren't for his eyeglasses, the slim young man to Ann's left could've been a stunt double.

Joel was silent for a moment, but the park was noisy with the whoops and hollers of children playing on swings and slides, birds greeting each other from branches of towering trees, and shouts of "go, go, go," from the nearby baseball diamond.

Joel looked up from his hands that were splayed on beige slacks covering his skinny legs. "I have to stop it before it goes any further," he said.

"Stop what? What are you talking about?"

"Lois, my thing with Lois. Everybody thinks we're gonna get hitched, but it's not gonna happen."

"What? Why not?" Ann asked. "I thought you two were in love. I thought you called to ask my advice on an engagement ring."

"See. See how far it's gotten?" He looked exasperated. Then, he took hold of Ann's hand. "It's you, it's you I want to be with. You're cute. You're funny. You're smart. You're the one I love."

Almost immediately, Ann felt terrible about Lois. How would Lois ever handle the disappointment, the embarrassment? But slowly her emotions shifted from sympathy to happiness. *She* might be the one to wind up with that diamond ring. Maybe Feldman would even give them a discount?

Like an innocent bystander at the scene of an accident, Ann rejected any responsibility for what she had just heard. She couldn't help it if Joel didn't love Lois anymore; it wasn't her fault he loved Ann instead. Maybe this was fate working its magic. She certainly wasn't going to stand in the way of her destiny, and Joel's, and poor Lois'.

To be honest, Ann wasn't totally surprised. Although his choice of Ann was a shocker, and Lois was sweet enough, Ann didn't think Lois was right for Joel, despite both their Hollywood good looks. Lois didn't seem to appreciate Joel's humor. Ann noticed this when they double dated and took Joel's dad's Chevrolet Impala. While in the back seat untangling herself from her schlub of a date's attempt at a sloppy kiss, Ann would pause mid-wrestle to laugh at some quip Joel made from the driver's seat.

But Lois hardly ever reacted.

"I have to break up with her," Joel said. He released Ann's fingers, which he had been squeezing throughout his excruciating confession, and put his head in the palms of both his hands.

He dug his loafers into the dirt below, while Ann's shoes swung from the bench, never reaching the ground.

"She'll be crushed," Ann said. She wanted to peel off the hand that seemed to be holding up one side of his head and return it to its clasp of hers, but she didn't. Instead, she placed her abandoned hand on his shoulder, like any good friend would do. Even though by now, she had advanced several levels beyond friend.

"I know, I know, but I can't help it." He was as tormented as a 22-year-old pre-law student could be. "You'll go out with me, won't you? You like me. I can tell. You chuckle at my jokes."

Ann sat up taller on the bench. She wished Sylvia could see her now. Big deal about the tummy; handsome Joel had just revealed *she* was his heart's desire, not the stunning Lois. Brains and wit *do* count for something. Suddenly she felt powerful, but knew she'd have to play her hand carefully. One false move, and she could lose the jackpot.

"I like you, sure. But I've never thought of you *that* way," she lied. "I don't know, I don't know. Lois will hate me, she'll never forgive me."

"But if it's not right, not meant to be…if *we're* meant to be together, shouldn't that be what counts?"

"I suppose so," Ann said. "But you have to tell Lois first. Leave me out of it. Once things cool off, we can see each other. Maybe in a few weeks; but not yet, not for awhile."

"Hot dog!" he said, revived. He kissed Ann on the cheek and continued, "I'm going straight to her house so I don't lose my nerve."

Ann watched Joel spring to the Chevy parked at the curb. He looked as valiant as the Western film's sheriff, Will Kane. She closed her eyes, took in a deep breath to capture the park's fragrance, then stood and skipped across the street.

"So, what was the big mystery with Joel?" Sylvia asked. She was seated on the couch, her knitting needles firing across one another. Ann dropped into the stuffed, checkered-patterned armchair that squatted in a corner of the room. It didn't match anything else in the space and was really too large, but Sylvia had it moved from their last apartment to save money. ("We'll get it recovered when I save up for it," Sylvia had said when she first saw how the chair overpowered its roommates.)

But Ann loved the armchair and hoped Sylvia would never replace its covering. This was her father Gene's chair and Ann could remember his overweight, diabetic body sinking into its cushions. She could see him there dozing, the ash from his Camel lengthening and sagging until it joined other scorches from his three-pack-a-day habit. Just last year, at the age of 48, Gene had a massive heart attack that left his favorite chair empty and his daughter in mourning. As for Sylvia, the beautiful widow? She continued on, lighter than ever. Ann wasn't surprised Sylvia rallied—she had continuously squabbled with Gene—but a little prolonged grief wouldn't have been so bad.

"He's breaking up with Lois," Ann told her mother. "He wants to date me."

Sylvia stopped her knitting and stabbed the needles into the ball of yarn at her side. "What? What did you just say?"

"He's breaking up..."

"Oh my God," Sylvia interrupted. "What will happen to Lois? That's a terrible thing to do to someone."

"What about me, Mom? Aren't you happy for me?"

Sylvia rose, stuffed the yarn and needles into the canvas bag at her feet, and said, "She'll hate you. Your friends will hate you. How can I be happy for that? And what about me? I play mahjong with her mother once a week. She'll hate me; the girls at the table will hate me."

"I know, I know," Ann said. She closed her eyes and rested her head into the hollow left by her father. She took a deep breath and inhaled, trying to capture scents that still clung to the fabric: cigarettes, Old Spice, Brylcreem. Soon she relaxed, and found comfort—even strength—for the rocky days sure to lie ahead.

Two

In her dream, Ann arrived at school terrified. (Was it Chicago Teachers College or Senn High School? She couldn't tell.) She was to take an exam that morning, but she hadn't studied for it, nor had she ever attended one class the entire semester.

Heart beating, she raced to the principal's office to explain her plight. Instead of finding the expected head of the school, she saw her dad Gene sitting in his chair.

"Daddy, what are you doing here? You're supposed to be at Waldheim."

"I'm subbing," Gene said, taking a drag of his cigarette. He flicked his ashes on the polished floor. She immediately thought, *oh, oh, Daddy's going to get in trouble.*

Then Gene morphed into her boss Gershon Feldman, with a jeweler's loupe pinched into one eye. "You're in quite a fix, young lady," he said.

"I know, I know," Ann sobbed in the dream. She slouched down in the hard wooden chair opposite the principal's desk (which by now had shifted to a park bench filled with chopped off tree limbs). "But I can't take the test if I don't even know what book I'm supposed to read."

"That's no excuse," the man said. Was he Mayor Daley now!

Thankfully, she woke up.

On the bus ride to school, Ann tried to review the Dewey text, but her mind kept snapping back to Joel and his declaration of love the day before. Was that a dream, too? No, the tumbling feeling in her stomach, a mix of dread and excitement, confirmed all its reality.

"Wait up!" It was Leah, catching up as Ann stepped off the bus. "My God, you look awful." Leah grabbed Ann's arm and swung her around. "Didn't you sleep? It's only an exam, for Christ's sake; not the end of the world."

Ann let Leah's arm remain on hers and led her off to the side, away from the crowd of students streaming into the school's double doors. "I have something to tell you. But first you have to swear not to tell anyone else, and second, promise you won't hate me."

"Shit, this has got to be good," Leah said. She extracted a Winston from a pack in her jacket pocket, lit and inhaled, and puffed out a wisp of smoke. "I'm all ears." Tall and skinny, with dark hair and blue eyes, Leah had a lady-like Audrey Hepburn look. But the tobacco and her occasional salty language clashed with her otherwise elegant image.

Ann started with the phone call and ended at her knotted stomach. (She had wanted to include the nightmare, but the details had evaporated smoke-like into the air.) "I think I need one of those, too." She reached for a cigarette, but instead of Leah's smooth maneuver and the expected calming affect; Ann coughed so hard her friend had to pound her on the back.

"I don't think smoking is your forte," Leah said. "And perhaps stealing someone else's boyfriend isn't your talent either?"

Still gasping, Ann tried to say, "But I didn't...it was his...not my idea."

Leah laughed. "I'm only kidding, sweetie pie. I believe you. But that's not going to stop Lois and the rest of the girls from wanting to hang you from the nearest tree."

"I know, I know," Ann said, catching her breath.

"Play dumb," Ann urged Leah as the two of them strolled into the lunchroom. Students occupied the long tables, oblivious to the soap opera underway. Crumpled napkins, half-eaten sweet rolls, and plastic coffee cups lay discarded alongside piles of textbooks. It didn't take long to spot Lois surrounded by a half dozen girls. Dressed in white cotton blouses, or short-sleeve sweaters with white peter pan collars, the coeds looked like first-year nurses gabbing about a hapless patient.

"What a bastard!" said Rose, her hand on Lois' shoulder who sobbed into a soaked ball of Kleenex.

"What's going on?" Ann asked innocently. She clutched her books to her chest.

"Yeah?" Leah repeated, playing second banana. "Did somebody die?"

"Didn't you hear?" Rose looked from one blank face to another. "Joel broke up with her." She lowered her voice, as if they *were* in a funeral parlor paying respects. "We were all expecting an engagement, a diamond, then he goes ahead and does this."

"I hadn't heard," Ann lied. Then she turned to her cohort and said, "Maybe she tried to call when I was on the phone talking to you? What a bastard," she finally said.

"A real asshole," Leah agreed. She took Ann's elbow to lead her away from Lois and her posse. "We'd better get going," she said. They took the stairs two at a time until they reached their classroom.

Before walking through the open door and taking their seats for the Dewey exam, Ann put a hand on Leah's arm. "You're really a friend for sticking by me. I wouldn't blame you if you joined the other side. Once it's all out in the open, you could be found guilty by association."

"Listen, kiddo, you'd do the same for me."

"I'd like to think so," Ann said. She let Leah enter first, and then followed behind her. Their seats were in adjacent rows, which made it easy for one or the other to look up and roll her eyes at the textbook questions, or at the drama underway in real life.

As Ann told Joel, for the time being, she refused to see him in public. But that didn't stop her from taking his nightly phone calls. She'd sit on the floor in the garden apartment's narrow hallway, her back against the wall and legs extended. Each night they'd chatter on about some topic or another: their upcoming summer jobs, their worry about the building Vietnam War and the draft that might scoop Joel out of law school; and then, Ann would report on Lois.

"She's still taking it hard," Ann told Joel one night. She wrapped the black cord around her fingers and studied her nails, which had been abused daily by her teeth.

"I'm sorry," he said, "there's not a gal-darn thing we can do about it. When can we go out?"

Ann was a bit put off by Joel's quick dismissal of Lois, the girlfriend he had squired for the past year.

If it were Ann, and she had just traded in one boyfriend for another, she'd have some leftover feelings of sadness, guilt; maybe even regret. But Joel was evidentially eager to move on, even as Ann tried to slow the moving train.

"Not yet; a few more weeks. Maybe she'll get over it by then," Ann said. She untangled the cord and splayed the fingers of her left hand, imagining one of Feldman's stones on the ring finger, next to the pinkie. Definitely, the chewing had to end.

And then, the following month, Ann spied Lois tearless and chatting with Barry, Rose's older brother, a pre-med student. He had parked his Buick at the college's exit doors and was waiting to give his sister a ride home. Leaning against its fender, Barry was smiling at Lois, and Ann could swear Lois returned the soft grin.

It was safe, Ann figured, so Joel and the girl he deemed funny, smart, and cute, could be public. Saturday nights they were seen snuggling at the Terminal movie theater; then sharing hot fudge sundaes with whipped cream, maraschino cherries, and chopped nuts at Buffalo Ice Cream Parlor; and at other locales favored by young people falling in love.

"Some friend you are," sniffed Rose one Monday morning. Evidentially, the five Saturday nights in a row, plus their details (including the flavor of the scoops) had traveled along north side telephone lines, reached Rose and eventually Lois. "You didn't even have the decency to tell your supposedly good friend you were dating her ex," she said.

This was true, but decency wasn't the issue. It was cowardice, plain and simple. Every time Ann thought she would just call Lois and apologize, ask for forgiveness and understanding, she got cold feet. And for whatever reason on Lois' part—perhaps she was too nice or too hurt—she also never sought out Ann for a confrontation. So it was left to comrades like Rose to mete out punishment.

"But Lois is okay," Ann protested. "I saw her with your brother. They were holding hands. Besides, I didn't have anything to do with the break-up."

"I don't care," Rose said, "it still stinks."

❧

And then, one-by-one, like fair weather fans of the Chicago Cubs, Ann's friends dropped away, until it was only she and Leah left in the stands.

Even Sylvia was affected, as she had feared. "I'm leaving my mahjong group," she said one evening when Ann was on the phone with Joel, and Sylvia had to step over Ann's legs to reach the bathroom. "The cold shoulders I get could freeze Miami Beach."

"But Mom," Ann said, "Lois has moved on, she's practically going steady with Barry. Can't your friends move on, too?"

"At our age, we're not so forgiving," she said.

After weeks of being shunned at school, and at home (thankfully at work, Feldman was clueless), Ann's resolve evaporated and she called Joel. "I can't take it anymore," she said. "I'm ending this; us."

"Give it time, give it time. It'll blow over," Joel protested. "For pity's sake, sugar, we have our whole life ahead of us. Don't chicken out on me now."

"No, no, I'm not cut out for this." She hung up the phone. She didn't say a word to Sylvia, but the upturned corners of her mother's red lips as she sat knitting, reminded Ann how easily sound traveled in their tiny flat.

Ann lasted two weeks without Joel. She missed his nightly phone calls, their lingering kisses wedged behind the Chevy's steering wheel, their hand-holding walks through *their* park, the double dates with Leah and Ken; and most of all, Ann missed Joel's Southern endearments. She was certain there'd never be another boy to call her *sugar*, or to swear she was the prettiest little thing his eyes were blessed to see.

"I miss you. I love you," she finally confessed into the phone. "We'll just have to let Lois and the whole world hate us."

They were engaged in September (10% was all Feldman could swing), with plans to marry the following June. Leah, only Leah among her friends, offered *Mahzel Tov*, and cooed over Ann's small diamond.

❧

As the familiar notes of "Here Comes The Bride" sounded, 75 guests interrupted their chatter to swivel in the seats of their white folding chairs. All eyes focused on the closed double doors behind them. Any moment, here in the Lilac Room of the Evans Hotel, on the 19th day of June in the year 1960, Ann Simon would wed Joel Robins.

Behind the doors that would open onto the cloth-covered path leading to the *chuppah*, Ann attempted a relaxing deep breath, as recommended by Modern Bride magazine. But her dress's tight bodice prevented even a subtle sigh. How she hated this dress! Why had she let Sylvia talk her into this castoff?

"Christine wore it for the ceremony only," her mother had said, describing her co-worker's claim.

It was three months before the wedding and she and Ann were in the bedroom of their garden apartment. The door was closed so they could see the full-length mirror that was nailed to its back.

"She swore she changed to a party dress right after her vows, and hung it in its Field's garment bag," Sylvia had said, as she stood behind Ann. They were both staring into the bargain-basement glass and Sylvia's hands circled her daughter's waist, pasting the dress to her as if Ann were her cutout paper doll.

"You can't even see a wrinkle," Sylvia pushed.

"Okay, I'll try it on," Ann said, stripping to her underwear. She slipped the dress over her head and wriggled into it. "Zip me." Then she held her breath, in case the metal's teeth hungered for flesh.

"Ugh," Ann said at her image.

"What? What's wrong with it? It's lovely. And she's only charging us $50."

"I look like a marshmallow topped by a cherry."

"You're crazy. Try on the veil."

The veil did seem to lift a viewer's eyes away from the unfortunate boat neckline (tugboat was more like it), but the hemline was wrong, too. Okay, full-length would've been over the top for an afternoon wedding, and mini—which would've displayed her legs, her best feature—would've been tacky. But this dress cut her off mid-calf, a particularly ugly spot.

As usual, Sylvia prevailed, so here was Ann, in the cheap dress on the day of her budget wedding, behind the paneled wooden doors. She refused to let the dress or the modest venue bring her down. She was overjoyed to be standing where she was, fortunate to be rescued from an old maid future, and about to marry a man she truly loved.

She felt a mixture of excitement and butterflies and tightened her grip on the small bouquet of Lilies of the Valley she held close to her waist. The hotel's wedding consultant opened the doors, and then smoothly stepped aside. The bride began her march, walking slowly to match the music, and sinking her white dyed-pumps into the runner with each pointy-toed step.

All was a blur in Ann's line of sight. To assure glamour photographs for the album that would be delivered to the Robins' in two weeks, both bride and groom ditched their spectacles for the ceremony.

Somehow, Joel made it safely down the aisle, and when his parents on either side grabbed an elbow of his white tuxedo jacket for the final three feet, they looked like elderly, overdressed scouts shepherding a blind man across the street.

(Fortunately for Ann, Manny and Pearl Robins' affection for Lois had easily transferred to her. "We're so very pleased to meet you, dear," Pearl had said at the first introduction. "You've made our son as happy as a blue jay." She took both of Ann's hands in hers, and then kissed her cheek. "Welcome to the family, sugar," Manny added, repeating his wife's gesture.)

The bridesmaids and their escorts were in place, too: Leah and Ken Friedman; Danny and Julia Simon, Ann's older brother who had flown in from Denver with his sour-faced wife; and Claire and Ted Alexrod, Joel's sister and brother-in-law.

Thank God for Leah. Not only was she the only non-relative in the bridal party, but also the only friend who would be preserved in the plastic pages of the gold-stamped Simon-Robins wedding album.

As Ann neared the altar, where silver-haired Rabbi Morris stood dead center, Ann could see her mother coming into focus a few feet from the *chuppah*. Sylvia's oldest brother, Fred Fisher, had escorted her down the aisle and the two of them looked as solemn as sentries. When she was hidden behind the door, open just enough to hear her music cue, Ann detected murmurs of "gorgeous" and "such a shame" as the widowed mother-of-the-bride walked the aisle.

As she got close enough, Ann's vision improved, and she echoed the viewers' sentiments: Sylvia did look gorgeous in her lilac dress with lace top, three-quarter length sleeves, tight-belted waist, and full organza skirt.

Ann imagined the wedding guests likely pinned Sylvia's stoic expression to Gene's death, as well as the loss of her roommate daughter. But Ann knew there was something else that barred her mother's usual lovely smile: She hated Joel.

As Ann neared Sylvia on the cloth-covered path, she flashed to a scene that had taken place in their garden apartment.

"Aren't you happy I'm finally engaged?" Ann had asked her mother. She spread her left hand and lifted the quarter-carat diamond up towards Sylvia's face. "You've nagged me about a ring my entire senior year. 'Everybody's engaged,' you said. 'When are you going to find someone?' you said. Isn't that what you wanted?"

"I didn't mean you should steal someone else's fiancé. You couldn't find someone else?"

"I didn't steal him. They were never engaged. Don't you remember, *he* left Lois."

"How do you know he won't do the same to you?"

"He won't. He was young; Lois had been his first serious girlfriend." She drew her hand away from her mother and planted it on her own hip. "How do you know I wouldn't do that to him?"

"You're not the type."

Her mother was right. Ann was the classic good Jewish girl. Always on time, homework handed in the day it was due, never talking back to an elder (or to anyone else for that matter), still a virgin at nearly 22, and hardly the sort of person who would cheat.

"I want you to be happy for me," Ann said, "I want you to love your future son-in-law."

"Okay, I'm happy for you," Sylvia said.

After Sylvia and Fred delivered Ann to her designated spot, the bride finally relaxed and took in the breath she had attempted at the start of the ceremony. Her slow, blurry march, tense as a tightrope walker, had finally ended, and now Ann stood alongside her tall, handsome groom.

As Rabbi Morse recited the vows, and the young couple promised to abide by them, Ann looked up at her new husband's face. Happiness—as long as we both shall live—awaits us.

Joel lifted his rented black dress shoe and drove it down onto the napkin that covered the ritual wine glass. As his foot caused the glass to shatter, cries of *Mahzel Tov* rang out. With her veil above her head, and her vision clearer, Ann's eyes circled her bridal party, the best friends, her brother and his wife, her new in-laws, her mother and uncle. The faces of the little group lit up with smiles, and their voices echoed the good wishes of the assembled guests.

All but Sylvia's, whose expression hadn't changed since her march down the aisle. Only her red-tipped manicured hands, which were twisting the soaked ball of Kleenex in her fist, showed any movement.

Three

It wasn't fair. It seemed as if every woman who came into Ann's view was either pregnant, pushing a baby carriage, or dragging a bawling infant by its pudgy arm. Bellies that looked as if they were concealing pillows, or stomachs resembling basketballs, were at bus stops, in supermarket checkout lines, or on her school's faculty. What was wrong with her? Why couldn't she conceive?

It was their third year of marriage, and they were living in a third floor, one-bedroom apartment in Rogers Park. The rent was an affordable $200 per month and the neighborhood was safe, although Ann would never enter the courtyard on her own after dark. It was that desolate U-shape, like walking into a canyon with no escape, which made her tremble.

Their building was older and their apartment had been painted over many times. Even the window frames held layer upon layer of paint, which made it difficult for Ann to raise on hot summer days. After struggling, she'd call Joel to the rescue. She liked that part of marriage—having a tall, strong man at the ready.

Actually, there were many things Ann liked about her role as wife. At times, she felt as if she were playing house, mimicking Sylvia's grocery shopping, cooking, and cleaning. But when it hit her, when she realized this was *her* house and she could decide on her own which dishes to prepare (the simplest), which supermarket to frequent (the Jewel closest to their apartment), and how often to dust (every other week was enough), she was even more delighted to be Mrs. Joel Robins.

They were a happy young couple, eager to see each other at day's end and to cuddle spoon-like in bed each night. Unlike the squabbling of Sylvia and Gene that Ann had grown up with, or the silent treatments Joel told her about between Manny and Pearl, their marriage was sunny and loving.

Up till now, they postponed pregnancy so Ann could work while Joel finished law school. After he passed the bar and was on his way to becoming the breadwinner, the time was right to start a family. They both wanted children, two—a boy and a girl—sounded just about right.

So Ann tossed her contraceptives in the garbage, coaxed Joel to bed earlier than usual so sex could be wide-awake rather than a sleepy possibility, and added parenting magazines to her pile of reading material.

At first, the switch from playful sex to purposeful coupling left Ann with a sense of loss. But the result would be worth it, and surely, once their child was born, they could return to the lustful romps of their earlier years.

But nothing happened. No swelling of the tummy, no morning nausea, no little boy the image of his father, or bitty girl with her mother's red hair. Ann thought the problem might've been caused by the years of birth control, for hadn't she read somewhere a woman's reproductive system could be knocked off balance by continued use of contraceptives?

Early on, the diaphragm had been her first successful attempt at barring the door. With her gynecologist taking her step-by-step through the process of insertion and removal, Ann learned how to hold and load the rubber circle with spermicidal gook, use a hand mirror to insert it into her vagina, and afterwards, how to reach in and pull out the slippery disc.

In their first year of marriage, Ann and Joel wouldn't let a night pass without having sex.

Everything about this marital bonus (Imagine, a willing partner right there at your side!) was a marvel to them. Joel would wait in the double bed while Ann tucked herself behind the door of the bathroom to perform her messy ritual.

By the second year, when the novelty of sex and its ready availability had worn off, when Ann's teaching schedule and stack of papers to grade took precedence, when Joel's studying was more important than orgasm, the diaphragm spent as much time in the medicine cabinet as it did inside Ann.

That didn't mean young Mr. and Mrs. Robins lost any of their desire for lovemaking.

Every so often, in the middle of the night, when Ann could sense a rustling taking place on Joel's side of the bed, she'd reach for her eyeglasses, speed to the bathroom with its flaking white paint and rusted fixtures, locate the diaphragm among the aspirin, cough syrup, shaving cream, and Aqua Net, then do her squirt-insert-double check, and race back to bed before her husband fell into a deep sleep.

Finally, the miracle of science brought the Robins spontaneity and peace of mind. Oral contraceptives, The Pill, had changed the landscape. Now, an unwanted pregnancy could be thwarted by a doctor's prescription and adherence to a scheduled dosage. Women no longer depended upon a man's use of a condom (Joel turned this down.), the messy diaphragm, the rhythm method, or other means of birth control. To the relief and joy of women everywhere, and to its manufacturer, the Pill became a landmark in pharmaceutical history.

All Ann had to do now was twist the plastic circle, align the calendar disc with its designated 10 mg. dose, drop the tiny pill into her hand, swallow, and let the chemical set up its blockade. No longer would she have to guess if tonight was the night, no longer did she have to endure those stumbles in the dark; she could be ready whenever the mood struck.

But six months after she had let her prescription for Enovid-10 lapse, to allow Joel's seeds an easy swim towards Ann's eggs, something unexpected happened. Every 28 days or so, she'd feel the telltale leak. She'd rush to the bathroom at home or in the Women Teachers Lounge, pluck a Kotex from her stash, then return—head bowed and tears stinging her eyes—to whatever she had been doing before the heartbreak.

A visit to a fertility doctor sent them home with assurances there was nothing physically wrong with husband or wife, along with instructions for identifying the optimum time for intercourse. Ann would obediently take her temperature, check the calendar's date, and leave a note in Joel's lunch bag to remind him of the evening's task. Still, nothing.

"Maybe it was all the contraceptives I used?" she said to Joel one night. She was putting into words what had entered her mind.

"Maybe the combination of science and technology messed up the natural order of things? Maybe we pissed off Mother Nature?"

They had just finished eating dinner (broiled chicken from a recipe Sylvia had given her, and sweet potato casserole courtesy of Pearl) when she brought up the subject. Ann was clearing off the dishes and Joel was waiting to replace the plates and silverware with his textbooks. In a minute, she would join him in their routine of studying and grading papers after the meal.

When space became available, Joel set his stack on the table, and put his arms around Ann. He drew her close so her head was pressed against his chest. "Don't be silly, sugar, give it more time. You were meant to be a momma, it'll happen. Just give it more time." He clicked open his fountain pen, and spread the pages of "American Law in the 20th Century." This was Ann's signal to take her place at her end of the table, uncap her red pen, and one-by-one review the shaky or bold penciled answers of her adorable, round-faced, African-American third grade students.

When Ann got her assignment to teach at Bauer Elementary her first reaction was fear. The school was located in a tough west side neighborhood (Leah had won a place in a north side school with middle class families.). Ann had read enough newspaper stories to worry about her safety. But she loved children and the thought of being with little ones and instilling in them a passion for learning was enough to overcome any misgivings.

Miss Robins, that's what her children called her from the first day she entered Bauer, a squat, plain-bricked building. While Bauer's faculty was a mix of black and white, the student body was 100 percent black and at the low end of the poverty scale.

Each morning Joel dropped her off at the lunchroom doors on his way to law school. She'd kiss his cheek before popping out of their Volkswagen Beetle to knock and signal Bertha, one of the hair-netted ladies. Ann loved this start to the day: catching a ride with her husband and being greeted by a large, friendly black woman who seemed as eager to see her as she was to announce to Ann the menu for the day.

"My babies are going to have a choice of pizza, macaroni and cheese, or meatloaf," Bertha might say. "Take a guess which dish is going to disappear first."

"Thanks, Bertha," Ann would say, as Bertha held the door. "I'll put my money on pizza."

After this small ritual, Ann went to her classroom on the second floor. She paused to take in the aroma of chalk, crayons, and pencil shavings that were linked to every other Chicago public school, as well as to hair pomade specific to Bauer's students. Her homeroom: 203. She had only to scan the walls to confirm that it was in fact her terrain.

There was her Palmer penmanship on the front board, listing vocabulary words of the day. The bulletin board on the wall opposite the giant permanently locked windows was papered with student assignments, or cutouts of turkeys, Santas, snowflakes, or sunbursts, depending on the season. After she erased the previous day's words and listed a new batch for the children to copy, recopy, and be tested on at the end of the week; and once she unloaded her tote bag and placed the graded papers on their matching desks; and when the books in the room's small library had been straightened with their titles facing out; Ann felt satisfied and prepared for the opening bell. With time to spare, she'd go down to the teachers lounge and chat with others who had already performed similar tasks.

From the very beginning, Ann looked to the faculty for advice. Although she had completed the required four-year course of study and did her stint as a student teacher, this was the real thing. Ann felt as unsteady as an ingénue.

"Don't take any nonsense from day one," Clarissa Jackson had said during Ann's first week at Bauer. Like the other welcoming teachers, Clarissa took on a mothering role and patiently advised Ann on classroom discipline. Just a few inches taller than Ann, and slim, Clarissa held a thermos in one hand and slapped it into her other as she spoke. "If they see you're a pushover, that's the end of order and respect."

Florence Blum, who was Jewish and one of the oldest members of the staff, had other wisdom to offer. "Don't go overboard with the tough stuff," Florence had said, putting a hand on Ann's arm as if to demonstrate tenderness. "These children come from broken homes. They've got lots of siblings to deal with; uncles [she removed her hand to use her fingers to draw quotation marks in the air] who come and go. Sometimes, there's so much tumult in the house they can hardly get any sleep."

Clarissa moved her head back and forth, signaling either disgust or disbelief, and said, "Spare me your white liberal sob stories." Then turning to Ann, she added, "What most of these kids need is a big swat on their behinds."

Then, other teachers weighed in and offered suggestions ranging from candy bar bribes to isolation in the coat closet.

Fortunately, in her first years of teaching, Ann could use affection, gentle persuasion, and copious praise to tame her 35 students. She had her favorites, too. Like smart little Patty Nicholson, whose black hair was separated into two puffy balls she wore on each side of her perfect head. Patty had perfect attendance, and came to school with all of the supplies needed for the day and with her homework completed.

Patty was one of the little girls who rushed to Ann each morning for a welcoming hug and repeated the gesture on their way out the door at 3:15. Ann believed this practice of wrapped arms, body-to-body closeness, smell of pomade on student and citrus shampoo on teacher, felt so good that neither could imagine a day without it.

Ann's favorite among the boys was Ronald Williams, who was not as well behaved or as smart as Patty, but at nine-years-old, was already a lady-killer. With the prettiest eyes and longest lashes Ann had ever seen on a boy, Ronald was so adorable, that Ann forgave his clowning around or forgotten homework.

It wasn't only her children who captivated Ann; she was similarly taken with the African-American teachers. "Black people are so easy going, so smooth, so comfortable in their skin," Ann told Joel one evening after returning home from a Bauer staff party. She and Joel were in bed. She pulled in closer, enjoying the familiar smell of his skin—a combination of Ivory soap and Mennen Skin Bracer—the feel on her body of his freshly washed cotton pajamas, and the soft sound of his voice as it trailed off to dreams.

"The women don't obsess over a few extra pounds, and the men seem to enjoy all females no matter their size," she continued. (If only Jewish men were so generous, Ann wouldn't have to add to her collection of diet books every time a new one was published.)

"Hmmm," Joel said, yawning. Then, something must've triggered a memory, because he loosened himself from her clutch, sat up and said, "I guess you could be right. In my daddy's shop, one of the shoe salesmen was a guy named Cedric Brown. Big, beefy like a football player. The women customers loved him.

"They'd walk right by my daddy, or any of the saleswomen, and head for Cedric. 'What do you think?' they'd ask him. Then, they'd spin around in a dress they were trying on. And no matter the shape of the customer, skinny as a beanpole or chunky as Cedric himself, he'd say, 'Lordy, you look like a movie star in that dress.'

"Then, depending upon the customer's color, he'd add Dorothy Dandridge or Lana Turner. And the thing of it was, he really meant every word. He just loved the ladies, and it didn't hurt Daddy's cash register either."

Ann laughed as she pictured the scene at Manny's dress shop, one of several he had owned in Charleston before moving north. "But, have you noticed how tough they are on their kids," she asked. "In school, if any students talk back, the African-American teachers, mostly the men, but I've seen a few women do it, too, grab the kid by the shoulders and shove him against the wall. The best I can do is threaten to send the loudmouth to the principal's office."

By then, she was talking to the bedroom ceiling as Joel had returned to his pillow and was snoring.

But everything seemed to change in her third year at Bauer. The incoming kids seemed to have gotten rowdier, tougher, and less moved by hugs or praise. Some, like DeShawn Jefferson, her particular nemesis, challenged her from the Pledge of Allegiance to the ending bell.

While the majority of Ann's third grade students were age eight or nine, DeShawn, having flunked several grades, was eleven. "DeShawn, please sit down," she'd say safe behind her desk. When he'd ignore her request and continue to roam the aisles, slamming shut children's school books, pushing pencils off their desks, or shoving a child from his seat, Ann would catch up to him and attempt a tougher tone.

Looking up as he towered over her, with her voice as strong as she could muster, she'd say, "Go back to your seat right now!"

"Who's going to make me?" he'd say, staring down at her with his thick arms crossed against his chest. Then he'd laugh, and a few of his cohorts would join in. It *was* a comical sight, a teacher who'd need a stepstool to reach his height. He clearly outmatched her.

But she stood her ground and eventually DeShawn would weary of the standoff and then saunter back to his seat. Some of the children, clearly disappointed there'd be no bloodshed, could be heard uttering, "Shit."

That was another problem with this year's crop, many of them swore. Third graders! Children! When she was lining her class up for a trip to the assembly hall, let's say, she could easily hear, "step lively, motherfucker," or "get your big-assed feet off my shoes." Instead of confronting the foul-mouthed (boys, and girls!), she'd pretend as if she hadn't heard a thing. But sometimes, when the insults would lead to punching, or hair grabbing, or arm-twisting, she'd have to intervene.

"Stop that!" she'd yell, rushing towards the fight. Often, that'd be enough to dampen the dust-up; but other times, she'd have to rely on Jim Morris, one of the African-American teachers.

His classroom was across the hall from hers and they would often be marching to the auditorium the same time as she and her rowdy group.

"Oh, oh, here come Mr. Morris," someone in Ann's group would warn. And like a hero riding to the rescue, Jim (he was one of those black men who seemed to have a soft spot for any female, no matter their size, or race) would walk purposely to the troublemakers, and with a hand on each one's shirt, yank them out of line.

He held their collars, but now lifting them off the ground. "What would you like me to do with these future jailbirds, Mrs. Robins?" he'd ask. The rest of the class would start to giggle until a hard look from Jim would bring their own hands across their mouths to shut themselves up.

"Thanks, Mr. Morris," she'd say, straightening her shoulders to find her own backbone. "I think they've gotten the message." He'd wink at her and bring his right hand to his temple, as if he were saluting a high-ranking officer. She'd laugh, her children would look at each other and smirk; and then they'd all—teacher and students—march along.

One night as she was getting ready for bed, Ann looked into the bathroom mirror to see red spots decorating her torso. "Honey, take a look," she said to Joel. She lifted her nightgown and exposed the bright design that was now beginning to itch.

"Whoa," he said. "Measles?"

"No, can't be, I've been immunized," she said. "I have an appointment with Dr. Cohen on Saturday. I'll ask him to take a look."

"Definitely not measles," Dr. Cohen said. "Looks to me like it could be stress related. Anything bothering you lately?" He removed his stethoscope from where it was hanging around his neck and laid it atop her patient file. Then he sat in his chair, folded his arms across his chest, and wheeled away from her.

"Well," she said, retying her paper gown that had been undone for the examination, "Besides the fact that I'm not getting pregnant, and the kids at school are driving me crazy, and more guys Joel's age are being drafted, I guess I'm doing okay."

"I think you've just made the diagnosis," he said. He pulled some papers out of her folder, and once more reviewed their findings. "You know we've done all the tests, and they've all showed there's no physical reason you're not conceiving. And Joel's tests confirm the same thing. I bet if you quit teaching, you'd get pregnant."

"From your lips to God's ears," she said, reaching for her clothing that was hung on the back of the examining room's door. She wondered if she'd ever be blessed to see on that hook a pair of slacks with an elastic waistband, plus a tent-like top that would flow over a swelling stomach.

A few months after her medical exam Ann came home from work to find Joel at the dining room table. He was studying a stack of official looking papers and a few colorful brochures. She couldn't tell from the expression on his face—it looked like a mixture of concern and excitement—what was going on. "What's all this?" Ann asked, taking a seat next to him.

She dropped her tote bag on the floor and didn't bother to pick up the pile of papers that had slid out and scattered at her feet.

"Everyone says I'll have a shot at getting sent to a better Army base if I enlist, rather than wait to be drafted," he said. "So now that law school and the bar exam are over with, I think we should do it. Here, sugar, take at look at these pamphlets."

This was a lot for Ann to absorb. First, there was the dread attached to the word *Army*, like: enemy, shot, killed. But they would surely be stationed stateside, so Ann relaxed. She'd be an Army wife, with an officer's salary, and no need for her to work. Perhaps all of her attention could now be focused on the bigger job of getting pregnant.

"You mean I could quit teaching?" she asked, suddenly feeling as if she had been granted a pardon just hours ahead of an execution. Before picking up the brochures, she dropped down to the floor, gathered up the assignments with the shaky or bold penciled answers of her horrid, troublesome, dangerous third graders, and stuffed them all back into the canvas bag. Then, she stood up and threw the filled bag into a corner of the room.

"Let me see, honey, let me see," she said. Her face was all smiles as she put an arm around her soldier's neck and plucked one of the brochures from his hands. As she turned the pages, each displaying either an earnest soldier or an Army base that could double as a college campus if you ignored the tanks and weaponry, Ann relaxed. Yes! There it was, a photograph of an Army family complete with bright-eyed children. She could almost feel the pattern of raised, red dots on her torso dissolve until she looked, once more, like her old self.

Four

Ann was in the passenger seat of their Volkswagen Beetle trying to read the wrinkled paper that was unfurled in her lap. But the moving car, combined with the map's tiny print and squiggly lines made her queasy, so she turned instead to stare out the side window. She laid her head on the back cushion, and relaxed as flashes of fat trees or outstretched farms appeared and disappeared before her eyes.

She and Joel were on the road from Chicago to Massachusetts, where Joel would fulfill his Army requirement and Ann would enjoy the life of Officer's Wife. As the sky darkened, somewhere in New York state, and the passing scenery became obscured, she studied her reflection in the side window. "My breasts look even bigger than normal," she said. "That's supposed to be a sign of pregnancy. Isn't it?"

"Maybe the doc was right. You've stopped teaching, maybe your body is finally cooperating," Joel said.

"From your lips to God's ears," she said, repeating the wish she had revealed to Dr. Cohen.

In her daydreams during the long road trip, Ann pictured herself already ensconced in her military life. She could see Joel, tall and handsome in his officer's uniform (Gary Cooper in "The Court-Martial of Billy Mitchell?"). She could feel his kiss on her cheek before he left for his peacetime duties on base. Peace was the dominant theme in her musings; there'd be no firepower, no talk of war, and no threat of her young husband being snatched away from her so early in their married lives.

As for herself, Ann would keep busy on the base by emulating other wives of officers. There'd likely be a service club where women with time on their hands could prepare care packages for enlisted men in international danger zones.

Perhaps, with her teaching background, she could volunteer to instruct unschooled wives in Basic English. She smiled as she imagined the grateful women who would surprise their returning infantrymen with better grammar and spelling.

It was important to Ann that she do something useful outside the home. Although she mimicked her mother's domesticity, in truth she held no love for cooking and cleaning. Unlike Sylvia, who took pride in her brisket or her strudel, Ann was uncreative and followed recipes to the letter, as if they were scientific experiments that would blow up the house if she erred even one step.

She dusted and mopped in the same half-hearted but obedient way. She kept a clean home because that was what was expected of a Jewish woman. She never shared her true feelings with Joel because on the one hand, he'd likely feel tricked by marrying a woman who wouldn't hold up her end of the bargain. And on the other hand, if Joel asked her what she'd rather be doing than being a homemaker or schoolteacher, she hadn't a clue.

One thing she was certain of was her desire to be a mother. In those car ride daydreams, her mind would travel to a longed-for place: the birth of a son, Greg (short for Gregory and named after Ann's father Gene). She knew she shouldn't be dwelling on a baby when the possibility was still remote. Her larger than normal breasts could be a figment of her imagination, or wishful thinking. But it was impossible for her to block that vision.

She could see Captain Joel Robins rushing back home at lunchtime and after work to coo over their first child. If she could stretch her daydream further, she'd see little Greg with an oversized catcher's mitt in one hand, reaching up for a ball thrown by his father. That last scene would take place in Chicago, for Ann's thoughts wouldn't extend any more than two years spent away from her real home. Now all she needed for this dream to become real was for nature and the base gynecologist to cooperate.

⁂

"Yes, you're pregnant," confirmed Phil Sherman, M.D. She had made an appointment with this Fort Maxwell gynecologist after a second month had elapsed without a visit from her bathroom enemy. "Expect a March baby," he said. "Remember, you have to keep your weight down. Eating for two is an old wives tale. I don't want to see you packing on the pounds by your next appointment."

"Thanks! Thanks so much for the wonderful news!" Ann said. She was referring to the positive test results, rather than his diet directive. She had assumed pregnancy would allow her to enjoy foods prohibited first by Sylvia (*You don't need that.*) and sing-songed by Joel (*My sugar loves her sugar.*). Now her own doctor, supposedly on her side, was getting in on the act. She wondered if there would ever be a time in her life when she could let herself go. Eat whatever she wanted; be fat and uncaring of what anyone else thought. She doubted it.

The minute Joel walked in the door from his morning spent at the Judge Adjutant General's office, Ann dropped the American Baby magazine she purchased at the PX store and jumped from the couch.

"Hooray!" Joel said. He left the door open and his face had a wide grin. "I just saw Phil and he told me the good news."

Ann's face fell in disappointment. How could *her* doctor spoil this moment! She had it all planned out. Just like in the movies, she'd ask Joel to take a seat. At first, he'd look worried and plead for a quick answer as to what was going on. She'd smile to calm him down. Then she'd say—softly, almost a whisper—*we're having a baby.* That would be Joel's cue to leap from his chair, lift her in his arms, and kiss her head as he whirled her around the kitchen.

Instead of that scenario, she just stared at her husband. He still had his charming Gary Cooper smile, but his Army crew cut robbed him of the lock of hair that once fell on his forehead and needed Ann's touch to brush away. His Southern drawl was mostly gone, especially here on base where good ole boys might be considered rednecks.

"No, no," Ann said. "Hasn't he heard of doctor-patient confidentiality? I wanted to be the first to tell you." Did Dr. Sherman also spill the beans about added poundage? She hoped he wasn't that much of a traitor.

"Sugar," he said, reaching for her chin to bring her face into view. "That doctor-patient thing belongs to TV shows. What difference does it make who told me first? The important thing is, we're having a baby!" Finally, he lifted his wife off the floor, twirled her around, set her down, then went straight to the telephone to give his parents the news.

She supposed he was right—what difference did it make who brought him the news, as long it was as wonderful as theirs. But after trying to become pregnant for nearly a year, after all of those disappointing trips to the bathroom, after detesting the sight of any woman with a swollen belly, she deserved the right to be the first to tell her husband. She guessed there was nothing left to do but forget about her theatrical scene and focus on the future. And, that's just what she did.

"Guess what, y'all!" She could hear Joel on his end of the line, reclaiming his accent for appreciative listeners. "That's right. Yes, yes, 'course we feel blessed. Wait, I'll put little momma on the line."

"Hi, Mom, hi Dad," Ann said. She could just about see Pearl and Manny sharing the receiver, their faces lit up in smiles, perhaps even tears of happiness. "Couldn't be more excited," she agreed. As soon as Joel got back on the phone and signed off with, "y'all take care," Ann dialed her mother. "Guess what!" she said. She had another scene in mind for Sylvia: a few wild guesses, a build up of suspense, and then *boom*, the big news.

"You're pregnant!" Sylvia shouted. Had Dr. Sherman gotten to her first? Her in-laws? Of course not, this was the news everyone in Ann's circle had been waiting for.

"Yes!" Ann said. "And the baby is due in March." Once more she dropped her sketched out dialogue and focused on the good news at hand.

"Is *he* excited?" Sylvia asked. *He* was Joel, who remained unnamed even after four years of marriage.

Although it was Sylvia who had started the skirmish, once Joel suffered her darted looks and caustic remarks, he returned fire. Ann had given up hope of a love match between mother-in-law and son-in-law, but perhaps now, with the impeding birth of a grandchild Sylvia and Joel would call a truce.

Sometimes, though, the two enemies fooled her by joining sides—unfortunately, at Ann's expense. Like the time they were all at the going-away party Manny and Pearl had hosted to see Ann and Joel off to Massachusetts. Her in-laws had put on quite a spread in their posh Winnetka home. The dining room table held trays of pungent smoked fish, corned beef, and pastrami, while the china buffet served as dessert bar. Here, the mouth-watering smells of sugar, butter, and chocolate lured sweet-toothed fans; like Ann.

"Did somebody die?" was the question asked by Ted, Joel's brother-in-law, as he entered the dining room. "The table looks like it's set for a *shiva*."

"Hush now," Pearl said, putting her hand over his mouth. "That's a terrible thing to say to a body going into the military."

"Only kidding, Mom," Ted said. Then, being the glad-handed salesman he was, gave Joel a playful punch. "We don't have to worry about this guy. He's going in as a captain, gets to live in officers' quarters, work in the JAG office, and probably be on the golf course more than the target range."

"I don't see a blessed thing wrong with that," Pearl said. "Do you?"

While all of this was going on, Ann snuck to the buffet table. As she was about to grab a second slice of cake, she felt a hand atop hers, halting her mid reach.

"You don't need that, sweetheart." It was Sylvia, smiling as she took the plate from Ann's hand.

Joel, who had overheard Sylvia's scold, laughed. "I try to tell my little sugar, she's going to be wider than she is taller if she keeps eating sweets, but, well, you know your baby girl."

Ann turned around to glower at her husband, who was now winking at Sylvia. Oh well, Ann thought, at least they've found something to agree on. But the minute they left the room, Ann made a beeline for the cake.

Despite occasional bouts of homesickness, their stint at Fort Maxwell, which began in 1963 and wouldn't end until '65, was as pleasant as Ted had predicted, considering they were on an Army base and the country was dipping its combat boots into war in South East Asia.

Ann and Joel took advantage of the childless months remaining to occasionally drive to Boston, or dine in hundred-year-old inns with creaky floorboards discovered in their countryside jaunts. One weekend, Leah and Ken Friedman (as the sole support of his elderly mother, Ken was exempt from military duty) came to visit and the two young couples took a road trip along the rocky shores of Cape Ann. While their husbands in the front seats groaned about Chicago sports teams, Ann and Leah compared weight gains, debated baby names, and traded advice.

"Nurse or bottle?" Leah asked. She had a few months head start on her pregnancy and had already gathered both positive and negative reviews on either choice.

"Nurse, definitely nurse," Ann said, placing her hands on her chest. "There's got to be a reason I've been lugging around these 36Ds my adult life."

Before Leah could respond, her face grew gray. Then, she gasped, "What's that smell?"

"Fish?" Ann suggested. As the VW pulled up to one of the many seafood restaurants along the coast, the two women flung open their car doors, clamped hands over their mouths, and raced to find the door marked Women.

❧

Ann and Joel's Fort Maxwell house contributed to their satisfaction in the Army assignment. It was a pleasant, wood-framed, two-bedroom duplex among a group of officers' quarters.

Their home had a front porch big enough for two plastic-webbed beach chairs, and a back yard trailing off into plush woods. The furniture they had shipped from their Rogers Park apartment filled the kitchen, living room, and one bedroom in the compact house.

By the time Joel had nailed on the walls their framed posters, family photographs, and copies of famous paintings, the place took on an agreeable, lived in look. Only the second bedroom, small—but big enough for a baby's crib, changing table, and duckling-decaled dresser—was at first empty.

Sometimes, when Ann tidied up after Joel had left for work, she'd wonder about the hundreds of other families that had inhabited the house before the Robins. She couldn't put a finger on the men; all she could envision were males of various sizes and colors in khakis. It was the women who intrigued her. Were they delighted with the kitchen and its spic-and-span appliances? Did they excel in welcoming home their soldier with fragrant meals? Or were they like her, indifferent?

As for the base itself, if she ignored the bulky rows of tanks, ear-splitting noises from the target ranges, and uniform-clothed men, Ann could pretend she was on a college campus somewhere out east. And since she had never actually been on a college campus, Ann saw the red bricked structures with white trimmed windows and arched doorways as departmental buildings. The Georgian-style homes of the starred generals could substitute for Greek letter houses, and the acres of greenery could easily pass for some university quadrangle.

Her campus fantasy even included military wives, who she sorted into sorority types and women they rejected. Ann explained her thinking during one of her phone calls to Leah.

"The generals' wives have these service club luncheons that are just an excuse for cocktail hour," Ann said. "I'm excluded because I don't drink, my husband didn't come from West Point, and although they don't say it, I'm Jewish."

"Well, what about the other wives? Wouldn't they welcome a friendly gal like you?" Leah asked.

Before answering, Ann recalled her attempts at friendliness with wives of enlisted men. One scene stuck out.

She was in the playground, lurking on the sidelines and imagining herself with her own child. A woman about her age was pushing a toddler in a swing. "How old is she?" Ann asked brightly. The woman gave the swing a hard push before answering. "Two. "

She didn't look in Ann's direction. "I'm expecting," Ann said. "Nice," was the woman's reply, and again her eyes focused on her daughter in the swing. As Ann walked away, almost with tears in her eyes, she saw the woman turn to another mother at the next swing. "Spare me the grand ladies of the base," Ann overheard her say. The other woman laughed and continued to push the little boy on the swing.

"You mean the ones married to sergeants who schlep their families from base to base?" Ann asked Leah. "Who are in constant fear their guys will be on the front lines in Vietnam? They think I can never understand their sacrifice, and resent my soldier husband who's a college grad. And my being Jewish doesn't help with this clique either."

"Aren't there any Jews on the base?"

"A handful, but I feel fish out of water with them, too."

"Maybe you should learn to swim," Leah suggested.

❧

There *was* one woman at Fort Maxwell, who, although totally different than Ann, was one of her favorites: her next-door neighbor, Jeanne, married to Bill Anderson, a Green Beret. She was a tall and thin Southerner, with blonde hair that varied from dark at the roots to lemon yellow, depending upon the number of weeks between beauty parlor visits.

Although she dressed in boxy suits (*almost-Chanels*, Ann labeled them, with their cheap wool, cotton fringe, plastic buttons, and neon colors) at the service club luncheons; at home, Jeanne wore pajamas and an untied robe no matter the hour.

"You should see her house," Ann told Joel one afternoon when he returned from the golf course. "Her groceries from the day before are still in their paper sacks sitting on the kitchen counter. She leaves them there—sometimes all day—until she finishes a book she's reading. She doesn't even get dressed!"

That scene at Jeanne's house was a revelation to Ann. Her own experience of other people's homes included Sylvia's and the tidy apartments of her Jewish girlfriends back home in Chicago.

The one time she visited Clarissa Jackson's house, the schoolteacher's surroundings were even neater than Ann's. She felt naïve the first time she saw Jeanne's house and its chaos, as if she were a traveler in a third world country. So this is how another half lives, she thought.

"Good thing Bill isn't here to see her mess," Joel said. "He might use one of his M16's to get her lazy ass moving."

"Sometimes, I wish I could be as casual as Jeanne about housekeeping," Ann continued, as she brushed crumbs from the table into the palm of her hand. "Just let things slide until I felt like doing them."

"Don't even think about it, sugar," Joel said. He rose from his chair and left his crumpled napkin, empty plate and water glass where they stood. Then, he kissed her cheek, replaced the stiff captain's hat on his crew cut and was out the door.

Along with Jeanne, another of Ann's favorites at Fort Maxwell happened to be a male, Gary Solomon. Gary was part of the small gang of Jewish officers and their wives who socialized at dinner parties or after Friday night services at the synagogue in the next town. (The Robins weren't religious, but both felt it important to support their tribe. And at a time of budding international conflict, a little extra prayer couldn't hurt.)

Whenever Ann and Gary found themselves at the same event, they managed to veer next to each other. Because of their similar short sizes, when they were face to face—discussing books they were reading or Broadway plays (Gary was a New Yorker and Ann followed opening night reviews in The Boston Globe)—he could stare into her green eyes and she his blue. Whether it was cowardice or loyalty—or perhaps her rounding tummy—their flirting never flared into full-blown conflagration.

Still, Ann had to admit she enjoyed the mix of daring and danger their accidental bumps and lingering touches stirred.

❧

If Ann didn't make it as a housekeeping zealot, snobby officer's wife, or femme fatale, the role she did ace was Pregnant Woman.

She loved everything about her condition, including her monthly doctor visits, her swelling stomach, and her awkward waddle. She even tolerated her diet restrictions. It was easy to resist sweets and fattening foods if her good behavior would help guarantee a healthy child.

Her sole bout of nausea occurred on the coast with Leah, and she was grateful for the sleepiness that forced early departures at boring gatherings. She even adored her maternity wardrobe; a small collection of tent dresses with prissy peter pan collars and smocked bibs purchased cheaply at the PX.

The only tricky thing about being pregnant, she told Leah, was driving the VW. "I have to push the driver's seat way back to accommodate my belly, but then I can barely reach the pedals with my short legs."

"So, how do you manage?" Leah asked, on the other end of the line.

"Slowly and carefully," Ann said.

Any drawbacks were easily forgotten whenever Ann felt the bird-like flutter in her stomach. "Hurry, feel!" she'd order Joel. She'd grab his hand and place it atop the soft thumping. Miraculously, all other sounds and motions seemed to disappear for her. Gone were the shouts of marching orders and soldiers' rhythmic stepping on the outdoor field near their home. The grinding and sputtering of tank motors as they started up or crawled back to their garages fell silent. All would vanish as Joel's fingers twitched atop Ann's rounded belly.

"I feel it! I feel it!" he'd shout. Then, Ann would smile, proud of her baby's accomplishment and her role in his feat.

Finally, on Passover 1964, sometime between the chopped liver and the matzo ball soup, Ann's labor pains grew stronger and stronger. She was trying to hold out till dessert, but damn it, the anvil swings in her belly were seriously interrupting digestion.

"I think it's time," she whispered to Joel as she tugged at his sleeve. He set down a zigzag piece of matzo that was still painted with the liver and onion mix, and asked, "Now? Are you sure?" Then they excused themselves from the dinner hosted by the Jewish chaplain and walked quickly to their car.

Twelve hours later, Ann woke from the anesthesia, not remembering anything after being placed on a gurney and wheeled into the operating room. She could've requested a more natural, drug-free birth when Dr. Sherman had earlier given her the option. But as much as Ann wanted to be awake to be the first to see her newborn, she knew her pain level was low. And besides, she didn't know anyone in her circle of women (Jewish Pain-free Princesses, Joel called them) who wasn't knocked out beforehand.

"It's a girl," Joel said as he leaned over her. "She's beautiful, with a head of red hair, just like her momma. Perfect. Seven pounds, fourteen ounces."

There wasn't an ounce of regret on Joel's face when he announced their baby's gender. If he missed his future sports pal, there was no evidence of disappointment. As for Ann, she was thrilled and relieved their daughter had passed all tests assuring normalcy. And truthfully, she was delighted to have a girl to shower affection on, a daughter to praise from 'morn till night, a child to love no matter her pudginess.

They named her Audrey, put a silk ribbon in her hair, and brought her home to the painted white crib with pink mattress and bumper guards, the musical mobile centered overhead, the stuffed animals that lined the wooden slats, the padded changing table, the packages of Johnson's baby powder and ointment, and the plastic-lined diaper pail. And in this idyllic, pastel environment, their daughter never stopped crying.

"Maybe she's hungry," Sylvia suggested during one of their nightly phone calls.

"I can't nurse; it just won't work," Ann sobbed. "I've tried and tried. The pediatrician says to surrender and feed her a bottle." Ann was angry with herself for her failure. All of the parents and baby magazines claimed breastfeeding was absolutely the best method for assuring a healthy child. If Audrey became ill at any point in her infancy, surely it would be Ann's fault.

"The bottle is perfectly fine," Sylvia sniffed. "I didn't nurse, and you turned out okay."

As for Joel, he managed to glean the best of fatherhood. In the hour before he left for work, or when he returned home for lunch, he'd lift a bawling Audrey from Ann's shoulder and head for a chair. Then, he'd bounce his daughter on his knee, sing to her, and make her laugh.

At nighttime, Joel left the feeding and diaper changing to Ann. He could drown out the baby's wails with a pillow held over his ears, and fall back asleep. But Ann cried along with her daughter, wishing she could defy the pediatrician's orders and feed or comfort her baby any hour of the day. But if following a regimented schedule was what it took to be a good mother, that's what Ann would do, even if it meant breaking her own heart.

Fortunately, as soon as Gerber's baby foods were added to Audrey's formula, their beautiful, redheaded baby girl settled into a routine of eating gustily, sleeping peacefully, and playing happily.

It seemed that each morning, when Ann would reach into the crib, Audrey had accomplished a new feat. She rolled over! Sat up on her own! Stood with her tiny fingers gripping the railing! She's crawling! Said dada! Ann would report these developments to all, as if they were Olympic achievements.

The Robins had always planned on another child, and because getting pregnant with Audrey was so difficult, they wasted no time in trying again. The minute her daughter could be seen sleeping peacefully in her crib, Ann would tap her soldier on his shoulder and lean her head in the direction of their bedroom. Joel quickly interpreted this gesture and cooperated.

Whether it was a second baby he coveted, or simply sex with his eager wife, he happily joined Ann in bed. While their love-making may have lacked the zest of their childless years, it was enough to satisfy Ann. This time it wasn't passion she sought, but another baby.

With this round, Joel's ammunition quickly hit its target. They were ecstatic with Dr. Sherman's estimate of a September '65 baby, when they would all be back in Chicago, away from the clouds of war looming over their Army base.

Now, Ann never missed a Friday night service at the synagogue, and a chance to catch God's ear. "A healthy pregnancy and escape from Fort Maxwell," she'd pray.

Five

Audrey was belted into her high chair giddily flinging green peas from the metal tray to the floor when Joel came in with the news. "They're sending my team to Texas," he said glumly. He flopped onto a kitchen chair and threw his cap to the nearest counter.

Ann rose from the spot on the linoleum where she had been wiping up the baby's last pitch. She placed a palm on the kitchen table to steady herself and her bulk. "Why Texas? When? How long will they keep you there?"

"I'm not sure. But if we go anywhere from Texas, it's to the Dominican, not Vietnam, so that's something positive. Looks like Johnson's playing tough guy with the Communists. He's already sent Marines to South Vietnam, now soldiers to Santo Domingo. One of the guys said they're even extending tours and some Special Forces are being shipped off to secret assignments with no clue as to when they'll return. Another rumor says docs and lawyers are being 'involuntary re-enlisted.'"

He put his head in his hands and stared at the floor. Ann couldn't see her husband's eyes, but she wondered if tears were forming in his as they were in hers. But Joel straightened up, wiped one beige sleeve across his face and stood up. Courage, he chose courage.

"Maybe my mother can come stay with me," she said.

"You can't stay here alone?" Joel asked. He returned to his seat and folded his arms across his chest. He narrowed his eyes and stared at her, as if he were an interrogator and she a defector. "I may be gone only a few days. You've got friends on the base. What're you worried about? I'm the one who could be shipped off to war."

"I know, I know, but I've got a year-old baby and I'm pregnant with another. You're about to go off to who-knows-where. Who knows when you'll be coming back? And, okay, I admit it, I'm scared to stay here alone."

Alone. She realized she had almost never been left home alone. Every since she was a child, she feared someone would break into her bedroom and kidnap her. It went all the way back to 1946 when a girl her age had been snatched from under the nose of sleeping parents, then murdered and dismembered. From that time on, Ann refused to sleep by the window and balked at staying home alone.

When she was older and a babysitter, she would tremble if she heard wind rustling the trees, or the noise of rattling pipes. Once, she was embarrassed to admit, she had to phone her uncle and aunt who were out on the town. She told a phony story of a stomachache to persuade them to come home and relieve her of watching over her younger cousins.

It was foolish she knew. Now she was an adult and lived in a house surrounded by military men. But one of them could be the dangerous type, a burglar picking off officers' homes in the dark. No, she didn't think she could handle it, being alone, and with an innocent child depending on her for safekeeping.

And now there was the added fear of her husband being injured, killed. She'd be a young widow like her mother; her children growing up fatherless. The more she thought about Joel's leave-taking, the more scared she became. She had to take a seat to calm herself.

"Do what you have to do," Joel said. "If you need your mother, go ahead and call her."

She wished Joel were more sympathetic. She was only 26, new to Army life, new to motherhood, far from her real home. Perhaps if she revealed her childhood experience, he'd understand. But this was a man who grew up in the South, with Ku Klux Klan and other Jew haters as neighbors. He'd hardly be the type to fathom her nightmares.

Ann felt guilty bothering Sylvia with her small complaints because her mother had enough to worry about with her new husband, Sam Stein. "I never want to be a burden to my children," Sylvia had explained when Ann asked why she married a man 20 years her senior.

"I thought he had money. I could quit my job, maybe live without worrying where I'd wind up in my old age. How stupid could I have been?" Sylvia said. "Sure, he let me leave the linen company; but he makes me search the papers for grocery store coupons. And I have to ask him for every penny."

Despite Sam's rap sheet, Ann was relieved when he agreed to let Sylvia fly to Massachusetts and stay with her and Audrey for the first weekend of Joel's absence. Sam came along, Sylvia explained, "because he doesn't know what to do with himself if I'm not there. And maybe he's scared I'll buy you or the baby something. Here he can keep his hand on his wallet."

When they arrived, Ann was happy to see Sylvia eagerly jump into the role of doting grandmother. She watched her rush to feed and diaper her granddaughter at first cry. And Ann smiled with relief to see little Audrey coo happily when her *bubbie* came into view. The baby would raise her two creamy arms and laugh, allowing her grinning grandma to lift her out of her crib or playpen.

Witnessing Sylvia's fawning over her new granddaughter made Ann feel a success. At last she had done something admirable in her mother's eyes; had produced someone her mother considered wondrous. (If Sylvia credited Joel for any part of Audrey, Ann never heard about it.)

As for Sam, a tall, grey-haired man, with age spots splattering his hands and forehead, he seemed at loose ends during the visit and wound up spending most of his time watching television or remarking about the cheap PX prices.

"What do you hear?" Joel asked Ann during one of his phone calls from Texas. "They don't tell us anything." She imagined her husband in camouflage, talking to her on a mobile phone, ducking behind some simulated brush. Later she learned he had excused himself from a poker game to make the call.

"According to the news on TV, things are calming down and some U.S. troops are coming back to the States," she said.

Before the weekend ended, Joel and his team were on their way back to Fort Maxwell.

But other officers from the base weren't as lucky; they would remain in the Dominican for an entire year (poor Gary Solomon). And as for those sent to Vietnam, God only knew how long they'd be away.

Sylvia and Sam packed their suitcases the same day Joel's plane touched down. "Sorry I was such a baby," Ann said to her mother when she was seeing her off at the airport. "I should've been tough enough to be by myself for one weekend." Then she hugged her mother, cuddling close to her. "I just wanted my mommy with me."

Sylvia stayed put in the hug. "It was my pleasure," she said. She stepped back and kissed Ann's cheek so that a red lipstick imprint remained.

"Tell Sam thanks, too," Ann said, leaving the mark where it was planted.

Sylvia looked around. "*Now* where did he go?" Then she spotted Sam wandering around like a lost child. Her face grew dark as she cried, "Oy vey," and ran to catch him.

❧

Departure day from Fort Maxwell had finally arrived. The Robins' furniture and belongings were already bumping along on a van headed for Chicago. All the good-byes, hugs, and promises to keep in touch had been rendered. A professional crew cleaned their empty duplex so it could pass its white-gloved final inspection.

On the road trip back to Chicago, Joel had the radio tuned to the news. Each announcement silenced whatever conversation was going on between him and Ann. They even shushed Audrey if she happened to be babbling when war news came on the air.

From all reports, it seemed as if each day more and more troops were being sent to Vietnam.

Not until they crossed the border from Indiana into Illinois, without word that Joel's unit would be called back to duty, did Ann breathe easier. All of her prayers at Friday night services were working.

And when Joel's discharge papers finally arrived in their Chicago mailbox—thanking him for his service to his country and declaring him officially a civilian—did Ann feel confident the next chapter in their life would go according to plan.

Six

"It's sort of small, don't you think?" Joel said, reaching up with one hand to try and touch the ceiling. His fingertips were a few feet shy, but considering his six-foot-height, Ann could understand his reaction.

"No, it's perfect," Ann said. She was holding Audrey in her arms as they walked slowly around the two-bedroom apartment on Chicago's near south side she and Joel had leased before they left Fort Maxwell. The law firm recruiter, who had linked Joel to his new job at Horowitz and Bernstein had touted City Shores because it was only three miles from his office. "Look, if you stand here and bend to the left, you can see the lake."

Ann didn't believe she could be any happier than at that moment. She was back in her beloved Chicago, the city of her birth, her childhood, schools, and marriage. She loved everything about this Midwestern capital: its lakefront and beaches, the fancy shops along Michigan Avenue, downtown with Marshall Field's and Carson Pirie Scott department stores, neighborhoods with bungalows and greystones, retail strips with apartments above the stores (like the one of her childhood), buses and elevated trains. What a wonderful city for her lucky children to grow up in.

The windows in the space that served as both living and dining rooms were floor-to-ceiling. From the 10th floor height, she felt as if she was in a nest, high atop a tree. She could see the sprawling Beth Israel hospital campus across from her building, the white-coated medical personnel going from work to their apartments, the occasional ambulance with a blasting siren heard from above, and a playground with mothers and children oblivious to the noisy horns.

"The kids will have to share a bedroom," Joel said. He was at the other end of the apartment, but Ann could hear every word.

"They'll love it," Ann said. "They'll never feel lonely." Yes, cozy like a nest. She remembered the bedroom she shared with her brother Danny in the three-room apartment above their father's grocery store. Not once did she feel cramped in those days, only comforted and safe with his boyish protection. (She glossed over Sylvia's tight garden apartment for that chapter was remembered only for Joel's entry into her life.)

"What if the new baby is a boy?" Joel asked. "You going to put him in the same room with his sister?" By now, he was in the kitchen, turning the stove's pilot lights on and off, as if *he* were the family cook.

Ann, still carrying Audrey because she wanted her daughter to experience her new environment in the security of her mother's arms, used one hand to open the refrigerator door.

"Danny and I shared a bed when we were kids," she said. She was peering inside the empty, lighted space. "We managed to grow up okay, and we still love each other."

"That was back in the good old poverty-stricken ghetto days," Joel said. Now he was opening kitchen drawers and banging each of them shut.

He was likely thinking of his big house in Charleston, where he and his older sister Claire had their own bedrooms, and where their eight-year age difference further separated them.

Ann returned to the windows. She felt drawn there, as she once had been by the second story window in her grandfather's apartment in the same ghetto neighborhood Joel belittled. She remembered sitting happily there, watching passersby and imagining their life stories. She'd see shoppers entering the fruit market, the kosher butcher store, the hardware store, and moviegoers crowding into the small theater.

At her City Shores' window, she couldn't make out the details of the pedestrians' faces, and the primary building in the foreground was the hospital rather than a streetscape of friendly shops.

But there was enough action in her view to give her the same sense of energy and contentment she had felt back then.

She knew the population here was different than the one she viewed in the old days. Back then, the inhabitants were Russian, Polish, and Italian immigrants. Here, the people going to and fro were white, black, and Asian. She supposed some of them were immigrants, too, but certainly more educated than the just-off-the-boat crowd she remembered. Ann liked the idea of living in this cosmopolitan place; it upped her self-image, made her feel more sophisticated—a liberal city dweller rather than a conservative suburbanite.

"What about a yard, like we had at Fort Maxwell?" Joel asked. "Y'all are going to be stuck inside all day."

"Didn't you see the playground and sandbox downstairs?" Ann said. She finally set Audrey down on the beige wall-to-wall carpeting that was standard throughout the apartment, except for the linoleum covering the kitchen and bathroom. "There were at least a dozen kids playing there, on the swings, slides, teeter totter. The mothers on the benches looked like they were enjoying themselves, too."

Ann's heart had quickened when she saw that tableau on their way into the building. She could see herself, smack dab in the middle of these young women. She could see Audrey in the sandbox, planted protectively next to her little sister (okay, maybe her brother) who was digging with a plastic shovel. Perhaps, here at City Shores, Ann would no longer feel fish-out-of-water like she did in Fort Maxwell where she didn't fit in with the wives of generals or of enlisted men. And sometimes, she had even felt out of place with the other Jewish women on the base. Maybe here, back in the city, she'd learn to swim.

❧

Ann knew some in her life weren't as thrilled about City Shores as she was: her mother, her in-laws, and Leah for example. All four opponents cited its location as its major drawback.

"Okay, I can appreciate you don't want Winnetka," Manny had said. "But how 'bout something closer in, like Skokie? Why in the god-dammed middle of the ghetto?"

"Daddy, I can be at my job in 15 minutes," Joel said. "Why in the world would I want spend an hour in the car or on the train? And City Shores isn't the ghetto, it's middle class, integrated."

Leah, also in the suburbs, had nearly the same argument as Manny, but without the prejudice. She accepted Joel's job as the reason for the housing choice, but worried the distance between the two women would strain their friendship. When Ann promised she wouldn't allow that to happen, Leah was temporarily mollified.

As for Sylvia who lived in the city, she didn't push for the suburbs but wondered why Ann and Joel couldn't have chosen a safer neighborhood on the north side. "We're fine here," Ann protested. "The only difference is there are more African Americans in this neighborhood. Is that your problem, Mom?"

"Of course not. I'm sure the ones who live in your building are perfectly nice; it's the others, on the outside, I worry about."

Ann knew what her mother meant, but wouldn't give her the satisfaction of agreeing. Like most of City Shores' residents, no matter their race, Ann stayed within the boundaries of her immediate community. Few ventured beyond its borders where liquor stores, storefront churches, boarded-up buildings, and unsavory characters were the norm.

"One heart," Joel said. Then he leaned back in his chair and collapsed the cards in his hands like a fan.

"One spade," from Claire.

"Three clubs?" Ann said. She looked across the card table to her husband, hoping for a smile. She was a poor player for she lacked the competitive spirit the game required; and she was too antsy to sit still for even one round.

But Bridge was the favorite sport of Joel's family, and ever since he and Ann returned to Chicago, they were expected to be part of the Sunday night game at his parent's suburban house.

Every time Ann entered this house she was struck by its opulence. Her past residences—the minute apartment above the store, the narrow garden apartment, the Rogers Park walk-up, and the Fort Maxwell duplex —didn't prepare Ann for the space and furnishings of the elder Robins' home.

It was Georgian style with paneled double doors opening onto a marble-floored foyer.

A polished wooden staircase with an Asian rug runner and a hanging crystal chandelier were the focal points. The living room was off to one side and it was furnished in French antiques, sofas that took up the entire room, and oil paintings with gilded frames. If Manny and Pearl were trying to escape the Russian *shtetls* of their ancestors and their own Southern roots, this House and Garden spread appeared to do just that.

The kitchen was in the back of the house and looked out onto a landscaped garden that required weekly maintenance by a crew of Mexican men. All of the appliances were top-of-the-line, white, massive, as if the inhabitants hosted lavish dinner parties that required an in-house chef.

Ann was awed by the splendor of the kitchen, but felt no envy. She never saw herself as a cook, didn't want to be known for her entertaining, and couldn't imagine being the mistress of the house directing staff. No, the kitchen in their City Shores apartment, cramped if more than two were at work there at the same time, was just fine for Ann.

The dining room of Manny and Pearl's home, where the Bridge games and dinners took place, was on the other side of the entry hall. A giant wooden cabinet with glass doors that showed off Spode china and Waterford crystal stood on one wall. And in a corner, Manny had set up a four-sided card table because the massive wooden dining table would've made playing awkward. Fortunately, there was enough space for both tables.

This night, Joel removed his glasses, closed his eyes, and rested his forehead in the palm of his hand. Oh, oh, what did I do this time? Ann wondered.

But who could blame her for a misplay with labor pains chasing after each other?

"I think my water bag just broke," Ann said, rising from her chair to inspect the seat cushion. "Oh, Mom, I'm so sorry." She saw the damp mark on the upholstered seat and went to fetch a towel from the kitchen. But Claire stopped her.

"I'll take care of that. Go, go," she said. "We'll bring Audrey home with us." Then she gave Ann a quick kiss and hustled her to the door. "Joel, call as soon as the baby is here," she shouted to her brother who was gathering up his and Ann's belongings.

"Yes, dear, go," Pearl said, waving her arm toward the door, but staring at the seat cushion. "It's Italian suede," she said softly. "Very much doubt if that'll come out."

Manny, who was about to accompany Ann and Joel to their car, put his arm around his wife's shoulders. "Sugar," he said, "it's just a chair. If need be, I'll buy you a whole new set."

❧

This time around, it took only six doped-up hours to produce another Robins. Ann woke in a private room at Beth Israel Hospital to find bouquets of flowers and Joel leaning over her. "You did great, sugar," he said, pushing a lock of red hair that was pasted to her forehead. "She's the spitting image of her sister."

And she was, except for Jessica's (soon to be shortened to Jessie) head of light brown hair that matched her dad's. But her sweetheart face and her birth weight were exactly like her older sister's: seven pounds, fourteen ounces.

Once again, Joel had been denied a son. And because he and Ann decided two was their limit, they had already given orders for her tubal ligation while on the operating table. Like his reaction when Audrey was born, Joel gave no hint at disappointment. As for Ann, she did feel a bit of a failure for not producing the ideal mix of genders. But the minute she saw her second daughter, all regret disappeared. Two girls, nearly twins! This new one as perfect as the first. She felt truly blessed.

While still in the hospital, Ann couldn't stop thinking about Audrey. A new worry overtook Ann: Would Audrey be jealous of the attention and gifts soon to be showered on the new baby? Ann should caution visitors to include Audrey in their praise, to perhaps bring a small present for her.

She wasn't sure why this troubled her so. It was as if Audrey's umbilical cord was still attached from mother to daughter and any wound or slight felt by her first born would be doubled on the mother's end.

Sylvia visited the day after Ann and her newborn arrived home from their weeklong stay at Beth Israel. (As for Joel's parents, Pearl phoned to say, "We'll wait till y'all bring her by the house on Sunday." They had already sent a new crib they had purchased and stored until Jessie emerged whole and healthy.)

"Where's Sam?" Ann asked her mother, handing the baby to Sylvia's outstretched arms.

"I left him home and took the bus," Sylvia said. She placed the baby against her shoulder, patted her back, which was as small as a pack of cards, and then kissed her head. "I could kill myself for never learning how to drive." She thumped Jessie faster than necessary to win a burp, and continued, "Every time I get in the car, I feel like I'm taking my life in my hands."

"Poor Mom," Ann said, kissing her mother's rouged cheek and lingering to inhale her cosmetics. Ann didn't think it would ever disappear, the absolute pleasure a mother or daughter gains from the other's aroma. Even in the case of Ann and Sylvia, who had had their share of ups and downs, the bliss remained. As for her own girls, Ann already would stay an extra minute over their tiny heads, savoring the smell of each girl's hair as if it were the costliest perfume.

Seven

One morning, a few months after Jessie's birth, Joel stopped at the front door before leaving for the office. "I wish I could be home more," he said wistfully. "You get to be with the girls all day and I only get them for an hour before bedtime. They'll grow up hardly knowing me."

"It won't always be like this," Ann said. She was in the hallway with him, had given him his goodbye kiss, and was about to return to their daughters' bedroom when his words held her in place. "The longer you're with the firm, the less you'll have to put up with grunt work. You'll have secretaries, paralegals, all sorts of assistants."

"No, no, you're wrong, sugar." He was leaning against the doorframe. I feel like I've been chewed up and spit out. I hate corporate law. All day, buried under paperwork the senior lawyers throw at me. I don't know how much longer I can take this."

Ann tried to listen; this was getting to be a familiar morning gripe. But this day her ears were tuned to her daughters' frequencies. She wanted him out the door, to the elevator, down to the lobby, and on a Number 3 bus to his office. She wanted to get back to her girls who had quickly leapfrogged over her husband to Number 1 in her heart.

Just last night she and Joel had a skirmish about Ann's shift of attention from husband to daughters. "Come over here, sugar, sit by me," he had said. He was patting an empty place next to him on the couch.

Ann was stretched out on the floor. Audrey was building a tower with red plastic blocks and Jessie was propped up in a bouncy seat next to her sister. Ann's elbows were on the floor and her head was resting in the palms of her hands. She was staring at her two girls, enjoying the sight of them together and the sound of their babbling. She could swear Audrey was trying to explain the tower to her baby sister. And from the delighted look on Jessie's face, Ann believed she understood every silly syllable.

"Not now, honey, I'm playing with the girls." She picked up one of the blocks and moved it towards Audrey. For that, she received a wide smile. Audrey lifted it from the spot and carefully placed it atop the tower. When the stack wavered a bit, than settled down, Audrey clapped her hands in delight.

"Wonderful!" Ann said.

"I don't think they need you on top of them like that," Joel said. He was scowling, and the hand that had been placed on the empty space was now moved to the television remote. "What about me? I'd like your company, too."

"Come down here," Ann said. She patted the carpeted floor. "You complained you don't see them enough. Here's your chance."

"No thanks," he said. Then he turned his attention to the program the remote had selected.

By the look on Joel's face, she knew she'd made a mistake. "Wait. Here I come." She pulled herself up and lifted herself from the floor. Her daughters didn't look up or protest her absence.

"Don't do me any favors," he said.

"No second chances?"

"Forget it."

So she returned to her prone position, swallowed any further discussion, and focused on her daughters. She knew Joel was angry, but she was glad he dropped his plea so she could get back to the girls. For some reason, their company—small as they were—filled her with joy, while being in Joel's presence didn't bring the same feeling. She wasn't sure if it was the crappy mood he usually brought home from work that was causing her to move away from him. Or, if it was the other way around: her growing focus on the kids was turning him into an unhappy man.

"Joel got pissed at me last night because I chose to play with our daughters rather than sit next to him on the couch." Ann said. "And when I crawled into bed at night, trying to assume our usual spoon position, he shook me off and rolled over to the far side of the bed."

She was seated in Merle Brody's living room, and engaged in one of her favorite activities: City Shores' daily mom-and-tot gathering. A half-a-dozen mothers and their children were there, with the kids tousling over an assortment of plastic and wooden toys, and the women drinking coffee and sharing stories. (All were white. Somehow Ann's appreciation of her building's diversity never translated into friends of color.)

What Ann didn't own up to with the women's group was her reluctance to confront Joel in bed. She should've said something, maybe even apologize for dismissing his request to sit next to him on the couch. She should've opened a discussion, asked for patience while she learned the ropes in this balancing act of wife and mother. But instead, she took his cue, turned away, and rolled over to her side.

At least she and Joel weren't yelling at each other like Sylvia and Gene had done in Ann's childhood. Perhaps it was Manny and Pearl's silences they were emulating. If this was what Joel wanted, she'd go along. His bedroom rebuff gave her another excuse to dote on her daughters rather than her sour husband.

"Don't worry, it's like that with all husbands," Merle, her next-door neighbor, said. "They get terrified their wives will deduct an ounce of attention from them. Then they act out in the only way they know how—denying us affection, sex. They're all big babies, worse than our children."

Merle was slightly taller than Ann, with curly blondish-brown hair, pretty brown eyes, and almost a drawl in the easy way she spoke. She wasn't from the South like Joel, just the sort of person who didn't rush her words. Ann on the other hand, had a habit of speeding through a sentence to forestall any interruptions.

"You should think about having an affair," Marilyn Christensen suggested, taking a Fig Newton from the plate she held out to Ann. Tall, Marilyn's tone was commonplace; as if the dark-haired beauty had suggested Ann try a new variety of baby food. "That would jazz things up. You'd get some excitement, hot sex, and you could let your husband do his pouting without bringing you down, too."

"Having an affair sure solved my problems," Sally Fitzsimmons said. She always dressed nicely for these get-togethers—a skirt and blouse, rather than the peas-and-carrots-stained pullovers and stretched slacks of the other women. Her voice was quieter than Marilyn's; perhaps wanting her confession hidden from the children playing at her feet. "Duncan never found out about my lover, and it actually improved our sex life. I was hornier at home, so he didn't try to find out what caused it. I guess he was afraid to ask, worried it might disappear as quickly as it came."

"I could never do that," Ann said, "cheat on my husband." Then, she reached for another cookie. For a moment, she remembered Gary Solomon from Fort Maxwell. She wondered what would've happened if she wasn't pregnant at the time. Perhaps they might've fallen into an affair. Maybe it *would* be nice to have sex with someone else, someone who wouldn't give her grief if dinner wasn't ready on time, or grow angry if he wasn't the center of attention. Someone she wasn't legally attached and beholden to.

"You're naïve," Marilyn said, interrupting Ann's musings. "Never say 'never.' You don't know what you'll feel like after years of marriage, after your husband is totally engrossed in his law practice, after he starts sleeping with his secretary."

Ann shook her head a tentative "no" while the other women in the group nodded in agreement with Marilyn. "You'll see, Ann, you'll see," they said.

Marital problems weren't the only subject discussed by their chatty group; they covered politics, too, and Vietnam was always a hot topic. The women all sided with the anti-war protestors, but as far as Ann knew, their solidarity rarely went beyond signing petitions.

"Did you see the picture in today's Trib of the kids being dragged from the draft board?" Sally asked.

"Thank God Joel has his Army stint over with," Ann said. "I can't imagine either one of us gusty enough to defy authority." Merle and Marilyn nodded in agreement as both of their husbands had already served in the military, too.

"My brother says he's going to Canada if his number comes up," Sally said. "Earl's not going to sacrifice himself for a war we never should've gotten into in the first place."

Watching televised scenes of anti-war protestors made Ann feel ancient. Although she was just 10 years older than the longhaired boys, or plain-faced girls (their bravery extended to being filmed without makeup!), she felt generations apart. That's what the responsibilities of marriage and motherhood will do, she thought. Surely no one expected a homemaker and mother of two babies to engage in street demonstrations. It would be irresponsible to forgo her grocery shopping trips, weekly laundry, cleaning, and carrying for her daughters to join protestors, no matter how much she believed in their cause. At least that was her excuse when City Shores' activists tried to recruit her.

The members in Ann's circle were also sympathetic to the plight of African Americans who were trying to promote voter registration in the South. And when the discussions first turned to civil rights, Ann told them about Joel's experiences in Charleston. "He said some members of his synagogue were very vocal about the mistreatment of blacks, while others were glad they were around to absorb some of the prejudice that would've been aimed at Jews. Joel said his family fell somewhere in the middle."

When Ann thought about her days at Bauer Elementary School, and the African-American faculty and kids she loved there, she'd say, "Injustice, such injustice," and shake her head. Then she'd return to sipping her coffee, nibbling Fig Newtons, and joining in on the discussion ten floors above the street.

The Robins were ending their second year at City Shores, and about to sign a new lease on their apartment, when Joel rushed through the door waving an envelope and grinning like a million dollar prizewinner. "Sit down, sugar, sit down, I've got big news," he said.

"I got an offer to be in-house counsel for a hospital in Arlington Heights! It'll be easier work, and great dough, enough to afford mortgage payments on a new house in the suburbs. And I've already talked to my folks. They'll lend, well, really give us, the money for a down payment. All we have to do is pick the house."

Ann looked at her husband's excited face and realized her expression was nowhere near his. The suburbs? Leave the city? Her heart began to beat fast. She felt, well, frightened. Certainly not like the times when she was a child and refused to sleep by the window. But being snatched from the comfort of her cozy nest at City Shores had a similar feel. Back then she worried she'd never ever see her parents again if the criminal had his way. Now she feared the city life she loved would be ripped from her.

"I didn't know you were looking elsewhere for a job, or that you wanted to live in the suburbs," Ann said. She supposed if they talked more, rather than perfecting their silent treatments, she would've learned his plans. "I thought you knew I didn't want to leave the city." Then she grabbed a daughter in each arm as if to protect her from abduction.

"You're being selfish," Joel said, his face reddening. "Everybody in our situation, with kids, live in the suburbs. It's only natural to want a house, a yard, good schools, peace and quiet. You're crazy as a loon to turn all that down." Then he pulled Audrey from Ann and hoisted his first-born up on his shoulders. Calmer and fortified now, he continued, "It'll be much better for the girls. They'll have their own bedrooms, plenty of kids their own age. I'll have an easy commute to work. You'd be closer to Leah, to my folks. What could be sweeter?"

She released Jessie who was wriggling away to join her dad and sister. Her family was smiling as if they could already see the backyard swing set, the den with color TV and shag carpeting, the driveway and attached garage, lawn chairs wobbling on fresh sod, a skinny sapling rising out of fresh earth, white families bonding over barbeque grills, and every other feature pictured in Sunday suburban real estate ads.

While Joel was waiting for Ann's answer, she walked to the large windows and took in the view she had grown to love. She thought about the mom-and-tot group and the conversations that both comforted and stimulated her. When she saw the Number 3 bus idling on the corner to pick up passengers, she thought about downtown and her visits to Fields and the big public library. And the playground, the sandbox, the happy gathering places for both mothers and their children. She'd have to give all of that up. But family is the most important thing in the world, isn't it? And Joel was the breadwinner after all.

What right did she have to insist they stay in the city when she didn't contribute a cent to their income? He was the head of household; she was merely a dependent, not unlike their daughters. His word should rule.

"You're right," she said. "Of course you're right. The suburbs will be great. I'll grow to love the suburbs. Let's do it." Her back was to the windows as she joined her husband. He was grinning now, in that charming way he had once used to woo her on a park bench.

Eight

Six months after the moving truck had unloaded the Robins' possessions, and hauled everything into their three-bedroom bi-level in Spring Grove, Ann was seated in her friend Leah's kitchen staring out the bay window. As she watched Leah march to the swing set to replace a jacket her older son had shucked and tossed to the ground, Ann shook her head and sighed.

Instead of wood or chain link, infant trees and miniature bushes served as fences between homes, giving the appearance of greater acreage. Add a barbeque grill (small or massive depending upon the husband's occupation and grilling talent), four chairs with padded seats tucked under a round table shielded by an oversized umbrella, a small plastic inflated pool, and you'd have more or less the same picture in every Spring Grove backyard.

Inside Leah's kitchen, paintings and accessories that echoed a Spanish theme surrounded the two women. Flamenco dancers, a mustached man strumming a guitar, a clock with chili peppers counting the minutes, all hinted at faraway places, instead of the suburbs 30 miles northwest of Chicago.

If they had been in Ann's kitchen, the décor would've been more modern: white everyday dinnerware, white clock with black numerals, straight lines, absence of curves—except, of course, for the bay window that jutted out the back of her home and every fourth kitchen in their housing development.

When Leah returned to the kitchen, she took one look at Ann's downhearted face and said, "Enough already. Give it up. You can't still be missing the city?"

Ann didn't answer, just continued staring into the open space with tears forming in her eyes. Leah pressed on, "You've got to get involved in some stuff out here. You're not even trying. How about my synagogue's women's board?"

Ann shook her head. The idea of becoming part of a group where every woman was her replica (same age, religion, household income; but likely not the same level of dissatisfaction) sounded stifling, rather than comforting.

"Okay, no synagogue," Leah said. "What about our musical theater group. You'd get to meet more people; and Joel, he likes to sing, doesn't he?"

"Yeah, he has a great voice in the shower. I suppose it couldn't hurt," Ann said. "We've both been feeling pretty down; Joel with his boring job, me with my boring life."

Then Ann told Leah about the conversation she and Joel had had that very morning: " 'I should've stuck it out at my old job,' he says to me. And then he adds, 'Not only do I have doctors chasing me down worrying about malpractice suits, but I've got CEOs, board members, and even the head of volunteers on my back.' "

"Sounds dismal," Leah said. She put two Mrs. Fields chocolate chip cookies on a plate and pushed it towards Ann. "Here."

Ann took a bite of one, then set it back on the plate. "Yeah, it hasn't helped our love life either." This was uncharted territory for their discussions, but Ann thought she'd dip in a toe. She missed the intimate conversations that took place in her City Shores mom-and-tot group.

Leah took her chair, paused to look out the window and check on the kids, perhaps to be certain they weren't in eavesdropping distance. She picked up the other cookie and said, "Have you tried talking to him about that? Ladies Home Journal says you should never go to bed angry."

"Easy for them to say. Harder to bring up the subject." Ann was thinking of the wall of silence that had been building between her and Joel ever since the birth of their second child. "Maybe I should have an affair? That's what the girls back in City Shores suggested."

"God forbid!" Leah said. She stood up, folded her arms in front of her and glared at Ann. "I know you're not big on religion, but you made a vow when you married. How can you even think of violating that?"

Ann felt reprimanded, as if she were one of Leah's trouble-making kids. "Calm down. Calm down," she said, raising and lowering her right hand as if to guide Leah back to her seat. "I was only kidding."

Ann thought it wise to change the subject. Her toe dipping evidentially wound up in hotter water than she expected. "The other thing that's bugging me are our neighbors. Not you of course [although Leah's sanctimonious attitude wasn't helping]. The women around here only want to discuss what they're cooking for dinner. Our neighbor, Helen? She spent an hour telling me how she chose carpeting for the living room."

Leah smiled. Calmed, she stirred her coffee and said, "Okay, so Helen's a dimwit, but Spring Grove isn't exactly dullsville. You've got to give it a chance."

"But listen to what she says to me next," Ann interrupted. "'You must be grateful to get out of the city,' she says. 'We heard you used to live in a black neighborhood before you moved here.' And she whispers *black* as if the word itself was dangerous. "I tried to explain we were in a nice, middle-class neighborhood that happened to be integrated. But she just shook her head and said, 'thank God you got out alive.'"

"I wish we never left the city," Ann said. Her eyes again started to tear. "I can't figure it out. I should feel at home here, right? Among my own people. A house in the suburbs, isn't this where we're supposed to be? But instead I feel like an oddball, fish-out-of-water again. What's wrong with me?"

"Give yourself time," Leah said, putting her hand on her friend's shoulder. "Anyway, it's not you, it's not Spring Grove, everybody's down in the dumps. The newscasters are calling '68 the worst year of the century." Then using the fingers of her right hand to keep count, and starting with her thumb, said, "in April, Martin Luther King gets assassinated; then in June, Bobby Kennedy gets killed. We've still got half million troops in Vietnam. And Tricky Dick is running for president. No wonder you're depressed. The whole country's depressed!"

"Don't forget about Mayor Daley and the Democratic convention," Ann said. "Ordering tear gas on the protestors. Maybe you're right. Maybe it's not just me. I suppose even if we were back in City Shores, the news would still bring me down."

❧

Sometimes, though, when Leah's consoling didn't work, Ann would take a 90-minute bus ride back to downtown Chicago.

She'd schedule these outings for Thursdays when Betty was there to clean the house and watch over Audrey and Jessie. Their housekeeper, Betty Reynolds, with her short grey hair tight as a steel wool pad and her sturdy slim body, was one of the middle-aged African-American women who were retrieved each morning from the Spring Grove train station by their suburban employers.

Betty was born in Mississippi, had a son who'd been incarcerated, and funneled her frustration and anger into the vacuum or mop she banged around the Robins' wall-to-wall carpeting and wood floors. But Betty was kind to Ann's daughters; and that was more important than abused household tools.

Ann kept her Chicago outings from her mother because Sylvia had been ecstatic about the move to Spring Grove. "It's time you got out of that neighborhood," she had said to Ann. When she saw the suburban house, Sylvia ran her fingers across the brand new GE appliances in the kitchen and laundry rooms, and walked from the house directly into the two-car garage that would shield from rain and snow a Honda and a Volvo, bicycles with training wheels, and a lawnmower.

"This is all I've ever wanted for you," Sylvia said.

As for Joel's parents, they had puffed up like peacocks on the day their son led them through the Spring Grove bi-level.

"Could be a mite thicker," Manny had said as his fingers grasped the front door.

"That's standard, Daddy," Joel said. "We'll get it replaced eventually."

Manny reached for his wallet, but Joel put his hand on his father's arm before it touched his trousers' pocket. "Stop already," Joel said. "I said we'd take care of it."

"Now don't go and get your feathers ruffled," Manny said, moving his hand away from the bulge.

And although they gave their blessings to their son's new home, Sunday dinners and Bridge games were still held in the elder Robins' Winnetka house.

Ann knew her dismissal of Spring Grove made her seem like someone who had been kidnapped from her native land and refused to learn her new country's language or adopt its customs.

Sometimes, Ann would imagine she was one of those costumed figurines hermetically sealed in a museum diorama, like the ones grade school teachers pointed out on class trips. Just as those dusty pioneers or Indians were frozen forever in time and place, Ann often felt as lifeless in suburban Spring Grove.

Nine

"So, how about it?" Leah asked. "Have you thought about our musical theater group? The one I suggested the other day?" She issued the questions as soon as Ann entered the kitchen and took her usual seat at the table.

Before responding, Ann spied on her daughters who went straight to the backyard where the Friedman boys were tousling over a plastic car molded to look like a BMW, even down to the hood ornament. Benjy had beaten his younger brother to the child-sized vehicle, hopped into its planked seat, and was about to pedal away when Adam caught up with him. As Adam wailed and pounded his small fists onto Benjy's shoulder, Audrey and Jessie appeared in the yard. This was enough of a distraction for Adam to immediately turn off the waterworks and let Benjy pedal off.

Boys, Ann thought, as she watched Leah's kids in their aggressive play. Better her than me. I'll take girls. Ann imagined herself in the future, with Audrey and Jessie—a trio of feminine friends. She doubted Leah would have the same pleasure with sons, for weren't boys more likely to separate from their mothers as they grew older?

Ann turned from the window and answered Leah, "Sounds like a good idea. Now, all you have to do is to convince Joel."

Leah looked outside, then flung open the door, jogged to the yard, and blocked Benjy's path. "You have to learn to share," she could be heard saying. Adam, in the meantime, with nary a tear on his adorable face, raced to join the girls on the swing set. When Leah realized her interference wasn't needed outside, she returned to the kitchen and to her plan for improving Ann's life.

❧

Leah waited until their Friday night bridge game to broach the subject. "We need a tenor for our next musical theatre show," she said to Joel. Her voice was casual, because she probably didn't want to appear pushy or alert him to the conspiracy. "You'd love it, Joel, it's Rogers and Hammerstein. 'Oklahoma.' One club."

"Yeah, Joel," Ken agreed, studying his cards. "Nice bunch of people, and a chance to get out of the house and dress up in silly costumes a few nights a week." He hadn't been in on the scheme—the women thought it best to keep him in the dark so he wouldn't overplay his hand. Ken already knew about his friend's job blues, and perhaps that was enough of a clue to add his encouraging words.

"Do it, honey," Ann said, as she watched Joel fan out his cards. "You've got a great voice, and you've got that whole cowboy thing going. Maybe I could work backstage, or help with tickets." Then she rose halfway from her chair, reached across the table and pushed back a lock of hair that had fallen across her husband's forehead.

"I'll think about it," he said, shoving away Ann's hand. It was little gestures like that that saddened Ann. Once upon a time—B.C., Before Children, she called it -Joel would smile at her touch, even hold onto her hand for an extra beat. A nostalgic time when they'd give each other a quick peck on the cheek if either was departing to another part of the house. But lately, with the wall building between them, especially its position down the center of their king-sized bed, all those niceties dissolved.

Joel surprised everyone by agreeing to audition for the Spring Grove Players, and then winning the role of Will Parker. As for Ann, she joined the Ticket Sales Committee, and sat in on weekly meetings where its chairperson, Francine Wolf, was as serious about the group's task as if they were charged with filling up Chicago Stadium.

Ann's new activity temporarily restrained her mind from snapping back to the city and she was relieved to see Joel happily attending twice-weekly evening rehearsals, carrying his marked-up musical score as proudly as he did his leather briefcase. And soon, Ann could hear his strong tenor voice rise to reach and hold a high note as he practiced the melodies each morning in the shower. She hoped this lightened mood would continue and eventually extend to her. But thus far, his smiles (which she had sneakingly caught when the bathroom door was ajar) went to the mirror as part of the character he was playing on stage.

"Ann, this is Larry Bennett," Leah said, as she pulled Ann toward a black-haired man who was surrounded by a handful of people. The two women were in the mostly empty auditorium of Spring Grove High School waiting for the dress rehearsal to begin.

"Larry teaches drama here and he's directing our show," Leah said. She was showing him off as if he had flown in from New York for this bumpkin assignment. (Ann figured Bennett considered his time too valuable to waste with behind-the-scenes personnel like her committee, and that's why their paths hadn't yet crossed.)

A Johnny Cash look alike was Ann's first impression: About 5'10", broad shoulders, blue eyes, dark complexion. Not black or Hispanic. Italian? Definitely not Jewish. Thirty-five? Forty?

One of the men in the group of Spring Grove players raised a hand to ask Bennett a question, shy as a freshman in that very building. "A minute," the director said, patting the questioner's shoulder. Then he turned to Ann, "Very pleased to meet you," he said, with a smile as bright at the nearby footlights.

He took Ann's hand, gave it a shake, and held onto it. She did not pull it away. "Would you mind taking notes?" he asked.

All of the actors had already gone backstage to change into their costumes, and any spouses who accompanied their husband or wife that evening had scattered themselves throughout the rows of the cavernous space. As for Leah, she was backstage, performing multiple roles of stage crew, costumer, make-up artist, and set designer.

"No, of course not," Ann said, pleased to have been given an assignment that involved paper and pen. She was the sort of a person who enjoyed making lists, preferring office supply stores to boutiques. And being useful to this good-looking, intriguing guy didn't seem too hard to take either.

She took the seat next to Larry and together they watched as the cast entered the stage and assembled in their places.

"Sorry," he said, as his arm (a lovely male arm) bumped hers on the armrest they shared.

"No problem," she said. She wondered why he left his arm there, and more importantly, why she didn't move hers.

As the singers lifted their amateur or trained voices in solos and choruses, Ann's bare arm and Larry's just-the-right-amount of hair-covered arm, remained next to each other for the entire evening—almost as if they had been welded together.

Did Larry feel it, too? But his eyes were fixed on the stage; neither he nor Ann turned to search the other's face for clues as to what was going on that night as they sat in Row One of the darkened Spring Grove High School auditorium.

Casual as could be, Larry kept his left arm, Ann her right, locked in place. The small orchestra of adults (long removed from their own high school bands, but game to unearth instruments from attics and crawlspaces), plus teens from the school's music department, gustily played Rogers and Hammerstein's score.

The actors shouted their lines to the rear of the empty house. The singers' voices sped or slowed depending upon their roles. And as a classic American musical played out on stage, a B-movie, with its tawdry plot, was just starting—front row, middle seats.

Ann's arm never lifted from its glued spot except when Larry asked her to record something on her pad of paper. "Laurie needs to move to the right. She's blocking Curly," he'd say. Or some other correction whispered to her right ear.

That whispering didn't help either: soft wisps of air toasting her face, the heat from their fused arms. At times, she had difficulty following his directions, for she felt too weak to lift her hand to move his pencil across the paper. (His pencil! Previously nestled in a pocket next to *his* body, handed over to her shaky fingers from *his* moist ones.)

When the rehearsal ended, and the amateur actors left the stage to fetch wives, husbands, or belongings they had tossed aside on front row seats, Larry and Ann rose, separated their arms, and greeted the actors coming towards them.

"Thanks," Larry said, turning to her with that smile. "See you tomorrow night?"

"Sure," she said, and wondered: was it her secretarial skills he coveted, or something else? Ann surprised herself by hoping for the *else*. Then, she turned to locate her husband among the cast members who were exiting from backstage and entering the auditorium, still humming tunes they boomed earlier.

"Hi, honey, I'm here. You were great," Ann shouted to Joel. She stood on tiptoes and waved her arms to make herself more visible.

"No, no, I was terrible," Joel said when she caught up to him. "Did you see I forgot my line in the first act, and missed the high note in my solo?"

"Didn't catch it," she said. Then she stretched once more, this time to attempt a kiss on a cheek scented with makeup remover. "I'm sure no one else heard it either. You'll be perfect Friday night. Remember, a bad dress rehearsal means a great opening night. Not that you were bad..."

But Joel ignored her flattery and turned to Ken, repeating the same question, "Did you see I forgot..." Ann didn't listen for Ken's response, for she knew Joel's fellow cast member would offer her same reassurance. She felt like a rebuffed stage door fan. Actors and their egos, she thought, even in this community theatre production.

Ann and Joel drove the short distance between the high school and their home in silence. Was he able to see Larry and her from the stage? And if he had, so what? Nothing suspicious going on. In fact, that was what Ann was turning over in her mind as Joel's Volvo rode smoothly along the darkened streets of Spring Grove: What *did* happen in the back of the high school auditorium?

She was glad Joel wasn't in a chatty mood. He was likely fixated on his performance and replaying every move. Ann was doing the same. She touched her arm, trying to recapture the feel of Larry's flesh against hers. Even the leftover tactile impression made her heart quicken. She replayed his last words, "See you tomorrow night." She memorized them as if she were an actress in the show. It didn't matter that she knew nothing about him except for the short bio Leah had delivered.

It only added to his appealing mystery.

Ann rolled down her side window and inhaled the fresh country air, welcoming the breeze that helped reset her thermometer. Headlights lit the path a few feet ahead and picked up the occasional NEW HOMES, LOW DOWNPAYMENT signs planted on empty acreages. Stars dotted the blue-black sky.

An occasional train whistle alternated with birdsongs to compose a suburban melody. Basketball hoops above garage doors stood empty except for a lone player pinging the ball against the rim.

Once home, Joel went straight to bed while Ann slipped into the den to turn off the still-talking television set. As she approached their babysitter Susie, who was dead to the world on the couch, Ann could feel her anger rising. How could this girl fall asleep when her daughters were in the house in need of protection? Then she remembered: she had promised to call Susie from the theater, but it slipped her mind. She was the one who had messed up, who jeopardized the welfare of her precious daughters. These very girls who Ann professed worrying about the minute they were out of her sight.

Wasn't she the Jewish mother who nearly cried each morning as she guided four-year-old Audrey up the steps of the yellow nursery school bus? And didn't she feel as elated as if she was welcoming a soldier home from war when the same bus delivered her little daughter safely home each afternoon? And Jessie, who tagged after her mother, either following in Ann's footsteps or actually grabbing a fold of her slacks to keep her close. What happened to Ann's motherly love that evening?

This schoolgirl silliness with Larry Bennett has to stop. Besides, she was likely imagining anything extracurricular had occurred. But her reverie refused to turn off as easily as the den's 15" Sony. In bed, opposite a snoring Joel, Ann tried to sleep. But all she could think about was Larry, his voice (a baritone?) as he repeated lyrics for one of the singers, or his movements on stage as he showed Curly how to take the hand of his beloved. "Hold it like this, between your two hands," Larry had said. Ann could recite it by heart: "Gentle, but don't let it escape."

Ten

It was Friday. Opening night. Joel and Ann entered the auditorium and were going their separate ways when she heard Larry Bennett call out to her from the back rows, "I saved you a seat."

Ann looked at her watch. One hour to curtain. The hall was mostly empty, except for a few spouses like Ann who accompanied their jittery cast members to the theater.

"Why way back here?" she asked, after reaching Larry in Row X. She felt a bit odd to be talking to him because on the previous night, at the dress rehearsal, with a nearly combustible armrest between them, they had barely exchanged a word.

"Don't you want to be closer to the stage so you can see and hear your actors better?" she asked.

Instead of answering, Larry patted the empty seat next to him and left his paw on the cushion. She looked at the spot his hand had warmed. Then she turned around to be certain her husband, and Leah, were backstage. At this point, she wondered if Joel would even care if her attention swayed to some other adult. Between his job morass and his involvement in this production, Ann felt as if she had slid way down Joel's list of concerns.

As for Leah, Ann remembered her lecture on adultery, and although this thing with Larry Bennett was merely a flirtation, she didn't want to give Leah any additional cause for criticism. Best to leave her pious friend completely out of the picture.

"I'm happy to see you," Larry said, focusing on Ann, oblivious to the people starting to fill up the rows, to the students who shouted "Hey, Mr. Bennett."

"Me, too," she said. She dropped into the seat next to him. She was glad she had taken time to primp for the evening: black dress to disguise any lumpy flesh, hose a dark grey shade to complement her slim legs, high heels for elevation. Her hair was also high and solid (she had visited the beauty shop that morning and it hadn't wavered since).

Her clip-on earrings were black disks, and her makeup (Sylvia would've been proud.) was applied according to a blueprint from Self magazine. The final touch, L'Air Du Temps (toilet water, not the costlier perfume) had been a long-ago birthday gift from Joel. She justified its use, as it was her husband's opening night after all.

As for Larry Bennett's attire, he was all in black, too; long-sleeved shirt open at the collar and two buttons left undone. His cotton pants sported a leather belt with a large silver Indian buckle. Artsy, earthy, and, well, sexy.

Somehow, Ann managed to sit through the overture and the first act, moving only to clap when prompted by the audience. Her arm took its position pasted to Larry's, but as the curtain lowered signaling intermission, he grabbed her wrist and said, "Let's go."

While the audience herded out into the lobby, Larry pulled her to a side exit. Ann didn't ask Larry where he was taking her; she simply left the auditorium with the show's director.

If any conflicting thoughts arose—like her husband who was madly changing his costume and refreshing his makeup backstage, or her precious daughters who were eating popsicles on the den couch while their babysitter gabbed on the phone—she pushed them aside. Wait, that's not entirely true; her beloved family never entered her mind.

The parking lot where they wound up was deadly quiet. Larry unlocked the passenger door of a black Buick and put his hand in the small of her back to guide her into the seat. Then he entered his side, switched on the motor, turned on the headlights and crept out of the lot, the only vehicle in motion.

Ann watched his movements—no shakiness, no nervousness—while her own heartbeats were fast and frequent. "Tell me about yourself," Larry said, as he maneuvered the steering wheel with his left hand while his right arm drew Ann closer to him.

Without question or objection, she nestled in next to his body, enjoying the men's cologne she could almost smell the night before, but now was easily inhaling.

As they drove slowly for several blocks, Ann told him about her life in the city before Spring Grove, her unhappiness in the suburbs, and Joel's grousing about his job. She knew she was doing more than making conversation; she was listing grievances to justify her front seat appearance. As if he cared.

Larry listened without comment; smoking a Lucky Strike he had somehow drawn from a pack on the dashboard and lit without interrupting his embrace. He offered a few "uh huhs." He sounded like a therapist indulging yet another disgruntled housewife.

"Your turn," Ann said when she completed her biography.

"Let's see, I've been teaching here for five years, on my third marriage [why wasn't that a surprise?], all my kids live with their mothers, and I hate the city. Can't understand why you'd want to live in such a noisy, crowded place with all the crime and dirt. And blacks." He paused to blow smoke rings.

Despite his sour description of her beloved, abandoned city, and his, um, prejudice, Ann did not move from her spot, or debate him. Everyone's entitled to his opinion, after all.

He pulled the car to the curb of a darkened street, turned off the motor and headlights, took her face into his two hands and kissed her. A movie kiss, with tongue, the sordid taste of cigarettes. She responded, remembering this kind of lust from early romances, from the first years of her marriage. The technique and reaction came back to her, like a foreign language unused for years, but easily returned when inspired by a fluent speaker.

After a few more kisses, more heavy breathing, Larry looked at his wristwatch and said, “Damn, we gotta get back.”

On the short ride back to the high school, Ann straightened her clothing, touched her hands to her bouffant hairdo (still high and firm), and reapplied her lipstick.

As they pulled into the lot, Larry said, “Meet me back here tomorrow morning, 9:30, I’ll have backstage all to myself.”

“Okay,” she said, and at the same time concocting an excuse she could offer Joel.

“Hey, Larry, great first act!” someone shouted as they entered the lobby via the same door they had exited twenty minutes earlier.

“Thanks, needed some air,” he said, turning away from her.

The audience was just starting to fill the auditorium; Ann blended in with the crowd as she and Larry returned to their seats. And as the rest of the Spring Grove townsfolk were unwrapping packages of candy (proceeds to the high school athletic fund) and humming songs from Act One, Ann was nervously awaiting her own Act Two to take place the very next day.

“Follow me,” Larry said. He had just emerged from his Buick, slammed and locked the car door, and reached out a hand to Ann. She had arrived 15 minutes earlier than the appointed hour, and was waiting for him in the parking lot of Spring Grove High School.

She had fibbed to Joel that she was called to an emergency meeting of the ticket sales committee, so if her Honda should be spotted in the lot, she was on safe ground. Well, perhaps "safe" wasn't an apt description, for her heart was beating wildly and she felt as nervous as if she were Bonnie, about to pull off a bank job with her cohort, Clyde.

I've come this far, no turning back, Ann told herself as she stood behind Larry. He was digging into the pocket of his jeans and fishing out a jumble of keys. When he finally identified the correct one, he unlocked the heavy school door, and gave it a push with his shoulder. Ann silently followed him into the empty auditorium. Absent of patrons, actors, or music, with the sets looking obviously fake, the space seemed eerie, as if abandoned by a theatre troupe run out of town.

On tiptoes (although no one else was around) Ann trailed behind as Larry climbed a small flight of stairs to backstage. Flats of painted scenery suggesting a barn, and a meadow with tall stalks of corn stood at each side ready to be heaved into place at the exact cue. A metal hanging rack on wheels held assorted costumes, each well-worn outfit bearing the stains of numerous productions. A brown-and-yellow couch, likely donated by a student whose parents redecorated their living room, sat in a corner.

"Over here," Larry said, pulling Ann away from the prop table she was studying.

She joined him on the couch, horizontally. The tongue kissing restarted and was now accompanied by his hands unbuttoning her blouse.

"Hmmm," he murmured as his head lowered to her chest. "You've got great tits." For a drama teacher, he had a limited repertoire of romantic lines; but this was not a time for critique.

Just as Ann was about to unclasp her bra, to give him more room to roam, they heard a noise.

"I think I left it over here." It was the semi-high-pitched voice of a teenage boy.

"Hurry up, I've got to get the car home before my mom needs it for grocery shopping," said another voice.

"Button up, and stay down!" Larry whispered to her.

He raised his head from the couch and peered over its high back that was stained with various hair creams. (Thank you, God, for this country-style upholstery with its winged arms and three-foot back cushion, Ann thought, as she remained hidden and silent.)

"Oh, hi, Cory, I was just taking a snooze," Larry said to one of the two boys.

"Sorry, Mr. B., I was looking for my wallet. I think I left it somewhere here last night."

"I didn't see it," Larry said. "I'll keep an eye out and if I find it, I'll give it to you this evening."

"Great, thanks!"

When they heard the exit door slam, Larry turned to Ann, "Now, where were we?"

But she had already buttoned her blouse and her slacks, and stepped back into the wedged loafers she had shed before climbing aboard the ratty couch. "I'm going home," she said. "This was a little too close for comfort."

"They're gone. Relax. Come back."

She kissed him on the cheek, a safe distance from the mouth that contained that talented tongue. "No," she said, pulling her hand away from his. "I'm not ready for this."

❧

As she raced out of the auditorium to her car, keeping her eyes open for the lads, Ann wondered: What if they hadn't been interrupted? What then? Would she have gone all the way, as they used to say in high school? Would they have started an affair, or was this a one-night stand?

No matter. Nothing had really happened, merely some silly flirting and chancy experimenting. Once the production ended, she wouldn't see Bennett again. And she wouldn't share the adventure with Leah or confess to Joel. She'd find some other, less dangerous way, to find excitement, to repair her marriage. Curtain!

Eleven

"Who should we tell first?" Joel asked.

"I suppose your folks, since they were the ones who gave us the down payment for this place," Ann said.

"They're gonna be madder than a …"

Ann smiled as she watched her husband struggle to remember the ending of one of his favorite Southern sayings. As usual, when stressed or happy, he switched to a drawl. This occasion definitely fell into the latter category.

"They'll get over it," Ann said. She left her seat on the den's couch and draped herself across her husband's lap as he reclined in his favorite brown leather chair. They were lovey-dovey, partners again, almost like newlyweds, rather than a pair in their ninth year of marriage who spent many a night on opposing sides of the bed. "It's my mother who'll have a fit. Leah, too. Neither of them will understand."

Then Joel shouted out, in a voice imitating his father, "Leave all this, Joel Leonard? How could y'all leave this?"

They both laughed as Joel's hand swept across the room like a game show host unveiling a winner's haul. There was the green shag carpeting, books spilling off shelves of wood and glass bricks, toy chests overflowing with board games, dolls, and picture books.

"And don't forget all this," Ann said. She jumped from her husband's lap to race to the living room. Copying Joel's gesture, she swept her hand across the space and recited, "Twelve-by-fifteen wall-to-wall stain-resistant nylon carpeting without a stick of furniture to mar its surface."

"That should've been a clue to all of them, to us," Joel said, "that our hearts were never in this place. Never even furnished the goddam living or dining room."

He was right. When they first moved into the bi-level, they planned to decorate both rooms once Joel's salary provided the funds. The three-cushion couch that accompanied them from Rogers Park to Fort Maxwell to City Shores was now well worn and wouldn't suit the new house, but it worked in the den.

Their bedroom set—Danish Modern, teak wood, slim lines, cool in appearance—had also made those trips, but suffered less wear and tear, so that didn't need to be replaced.

Audrey and Jessie preferred to share a bedroom again, so they planned to turn the third bedroom into a playroom. But that space had been mostly bare, too. The girls typically hauled their toys to the den so they could be closer to their parents and the television set.

Yes, their postponement of furnishing their suburban house should've been a clue. It never really was home, was it?

"I can't believe it," Ann said, returning to her spot on Joel's lap. "We're moving! We're really doing it. Finally, we're moving back to Chicago! Glory be!"

❧

Ever since the day Joel returned home from work to fling his briefcase to the floor and declare he had had it with his job at the hospital, that he had made a mistake casting his fortune in the suburbs, Ann's emotions rose and fell like a roller coaster ride at Riverview, the amusement park of her childhood. Up one day, down the next, and finally, way, way up.

Before his arrival that evening, she had been reading a book borrowed from the Chicago Public Library on her last foray into the city. It was Betty Friedan's "The Feminine Mystique," recommended by her former City Shores' neighbor, Merle Brody. "We're reading it in our Women's Group," Merle had said. Earlier, she told Ann their old mom-and-tot group was converted into a feminine conscious-raising group. "See what you're missing," Merle teased.

"You've got to read it," Merle urged. She sounded as if she were passing on plans for an underground railroad, or some other secret mission. "Friedan really comes down hard on your suburbs. 'Those ugly and endless sprawls which are becoming a national problem.' That's what she's says. I'm quoting exactly."

As Ann read the book, waiting for Joel's return from his workday, she found herself mentally underlining sentences and nodding her head in agreement, especially with "the endless, thankless cycle of dishes and vacuuming and meals and her husband's ironing and her children's laundry." Of course, in Ann's suburban life, it was Betty, the housekeeper, who handled most of those chores. But still.

The line that really got to Ann was that "women had been coaxed into selling out their intellect and their ambitions for the paltry price of a new washing machine." Whew. This was where Ann got stuck. What *were* her ambitions beyond wife and mother? Once, she had been a schoolteacher. She didn't recall much thought or ambition going into that job choice. In the 1950s, Jewish girls became teachers, Gentile, nurses. And both would drop their careers just as soon as their husbands' paychecks permitted it.

If she had to choose a new profession, Ann was at a loss. Perhaps once her daughters were in school fulltime, she could go back to work. Not teaching, though, as those traumas were still fresh. Perhaps she'd work in a bookstore. That sounded nice.

"I have to talk to you about something," were Joel's first words on the evening she was engrossed in Friedan.

She couldn't tell from his expression if this was going to be another kvetch about his job, or maybe something more serious. A divorce! Was Joel as unhappy with their relationship as she? Had he learned about Larry Bennett?

"I want to quit my job," he said. He had a pleading look on his face. "I'm sorry."

She was relieved she wasn't the culprit, but distressed this was the second job in as many years he'd be ditching. "What would you rather be doing?" she asked. (A question for herself as well, prompted by Friedan.)

"Well, sugar, [Her nickname had returned! This must be good news.] I know you've been unhappy here, so I thought I'd look at the job listings back in the city."

This was the down part of the roller coaster; she worried about their uncertain future. But on the very next day, when Joel declared he had "found the job of my dreams on LaSalle Street," Ann allowed herself to enjoy the rest of the ride.

And the best part of the amusement trip; the most thrilling? That came when she discovered a new home in the city that could fulfill her *own* heart's desire. That's where she paused her ride, at the very top, with possibilities as far as the eye could see.

❧

"Momma, Daddy, we've got something to tell y'all," Joel said to Manny and Pearl who were seated on the white sectional couch in their Winnetka living room.

"Y'all are having another child!" Pearl said, jumping up from her seat to hug Ann.

"No, Momma, no," Joel said. He removed his mother's arms from his wife's shoulders and gently pushed her back onto the couch.

"I've taken a new job in Chicago and we've put our house on the market." He crossed his arms in front of his chest.

"Now you've really gone and lost it Joel Leonard," Manny said. "How many jobs are you gonna run through before you're satisfied? In my day..."

"Dad," Ann said, interrupting her father-in-law. "It's not..."

But then Joel gave her a hard look that seemed to say, "I'll handle this." For a moment, she shifted to a pout. But when she realized Joel needed to be the one to stand up to his parents, she softened, and then she shut up.

"You'll be happy to hear I'll be on a partner's track at Stein, Bergman, and Greenberg," Joel said. "They're a fast-growing family law firm; and they've made me a great offer."

"How much?" Manny asked.

"Hush now," Pearl said. She turned her attention to her son. "What about my precious babies? You mean to tell us y'all are taking my precious babies to the city? Why can't you stay in Spring Grove and commute? Your friend, Ken Friedman, takes the train to his lawyering job. You told me so yourself when..."

"It's me, Mom," Ann said. This time, she rose and stood her ground. Friedan's counsel was reverberating in her head: Insist on equal opportunity, take responsibility for your life, demand to be heard. "*I* want to move back to the city. Joel is doing this for me." She was standing when she said this, face-to-face with her in-laws, rather than sunk down in the plush couch.

"Why in the world would y'all want to move back? Where will the children go to school? Surely you don't intend to put them in those horrible public schools I've read about?" Pearl said.

"Well, actually, that's exactly what we're planning to do. But the school they'll be going to won't be horrible, just experimental," Ann said.

"Experimental? What the hell does that mean?" Manny asked.

Joel took a seat on a section of the couch far removed from his parents. He relinquished the floor to Ann. "Here, read this," she said, handing to her in-laws a brochure she had stowed in her purse.

Manny started reading, curbing his Southern accent and intoning the words as if he were a newscaster, "Imagine. Living just five minutes from downtown. Growing up in an environment of trees and grass and playgrounds, in a total community where you can get to know your neighbors. That's what townhome living is all about at Berkeley Square."

Then he threw the pamphlet back to Joel (even though it had lived in Ann's purse) and added, "Doesn't say anywhere the place is a slum. I read about your Berkeley Square in the real estate section of the paper. Y'all sure that's where you want our grandkids to grow up?"

Pearl retrieved the brochure from Joel and started her own review.

"Former slum," Ann said to Manny. She was still standing. Now, her arms were crossed in front of her chest, like a sentry. "And it'll be good for the girls to have friends who aren't exactly like them."

"Here's something else," Pearl said. Then *she* read aloud, " 'an experimental new town, built to reverse urban decay that will embrace the city's racial, social, and economic diversity.' Oh dear."

But Ann's heart raced with the delicious sounding words: experimental, urban, diversity. That description may have brought terror to her mother-in-law's heart, but to Ann they were as sweet as the richest chocolate candy and as nourishing as a meal following a Yom Kippur fast.

She imagined her family ensconced in Berkeley Square. Instead of the suburban sod, infant trees, swing sets and barbeque grills, she saw the four of them intermingling with their new neighbors who were a rainbow of colors—just like City Shores, which was a mere three blocks east of their soon-to-be new home. She saw herself part of the women's group, where dialogue covered latest headlines, rather than domestic concerns.

Perhaps Joel would be in another group, protesting corruption or some other worthy cause. Her daughters would surely be playing happily with children of all shades. She could even see into the master bedroom (not as generous as Spring Grove's, but certainly adequate for their furnishings), where Mr. and Mrs. Joel Robins would finally dismantle all barriers in their Danish Modern bed and resume their former positions.

When it came time to break the news to Sylvia, the discussion in her apartment was similar, but the setting more depressing. She and Sam were living in a one-bedroom apartment on Chicago's north side that would've taken one sweep of her hand to show off. The walls were faux stucco, painted white, and bore several of Sylvia's needlepoint pictures. The Asian figurines of Ann's childhood were still standing on various surfaces, but now scraps of paper with words scribbled on them, also shared the space.

"He forgets things," Sylvia said, when Ann first spotted the pieces. "So he writes it down, the date, the month, the president."

"Oy," Ann said.

Sylvia listened as Ann described Joel's new job, the quick sale of their Spring Grove bi-level, and the purchase of the three-story townhouse in Berkeley Square.

"We'll be closer to you, Mom," Ann said. Then she handed her mother the Berkeley Square propaganda.

"But I love the house you have now," Sylvia said, without looking at the brochure. "So big, no climbing stairs, so quiet. All your nice Jewish neighbors. The yard, the garage. I don't get it."

"I know, I know," Ann said, taking a seat on the couch next to her mother. "I know you don't understand. I just want you to wish us luck, try to be happy for us."

Sylvia rose, dabbed her eyes with the Kleenex she had withdrawn from her pocket, and then replaced the mascara-dotted tissue back in her apron. She walked a few steps into the kitchen, removed a Corning Ware square dish from a cabinet and took it to the stove. "I made a brisket," she said. "You'll take some for him and the girls?"

Ann inhaled the cooking smells that laminated the kitchen walls, and then kissed her mother's forehead for a whiff of her familiar perfume. "Sure, Mom, sure. They love your cooking. We all do. Thanks."

"So, what's the big news?" Leah asked.

"Sit," Ann said, pointing to a ladder-backed chair in Leah's kitchen.

"Oh, oh. Am I going to be happy or sad?" Leah asked.

"I'm not sure."

Leah listened as Ann related the changes about to take place in the Robins' lives. She said "hmmm" as she read about Berkeley Square and studied the advertisement's photographs of white and black couples smiling as they watched their white and black children happily playing together on the swings, teeter totters, and slides.

"So?" Ann asked. "What do you think?"

Leah rose from her chair, hugged her friend, and then blurted her own surprise. "I was waiting to tell you until everything was settled. But now, with you leaving, I can't keep it a secret any longer. We're moving to Paris!"

"What!" Ann exclaimed, jumping out of her chair. Suddenly Berkeley Square sounded like the boondocks compared to the City of Light. "When? Why? How could you keep this from me?" She looked around the kitchen that was decorated in Spanish décor, and wondered at Leah's ease in switching allegiance from one European soil to another. But it was Paris!

"Ken made me promise to keep my mouth shut. He was afraid if we talked about it, it would jinx the deal. You know Jewish superstition. Sort of like not buying baby furniture until the kid arrives. God forbid you should be too happy."

"Paris. I can't get over it," Ann said. "I'm so jealous."

"We'll put our house on the market as soon as the contract for Ken's new job is signed," Leah said. "He's got people from his Paris office scouting apartments for us. And there's a strong Jewish community there, so we should feel at home."

"Paris," Ann said. She closed her eyes and tried to imagine strolling the boulevards, lunching at outdoor cafes, buying groceries from neighborhood stalls. But somehow, she couldn't pull it off. Berkeley Square, on the other hand, came in clear as a bell: their skinny house with an African-American family on one side and white on the other, the playground with children of every shade, Ann at the bus stop for an easy foray downtown, Joel, happy and confident in his new job. All that she could easily envision.

Twelve

If it were the 1800s instead of 1969, the Robins and their belongings would have been traveling west in a covered wagon. But since this family of four were *urban* pioneers, rather than Old West homesteaders, it was Joel's Volvo and a large moving truck that carried them to their new neighborhood on Chicago's near south side.

In Ann's quirky imagination, Berkeley Square had other similarities to the tales of those hardy settlers. While the original pioneers may have been escaping religious persecution, or seeking their fortune, the residents of this experimental community wanted to practice a new way of life. It was called: Integration.

The majority of people who moved to Berkeley Square in its early years—doctors, lawyers, businessmen, social workers, government employees -were lured because it promised a place where people of different races, ages, and incomes could live together; and prove it could be done. (Of course, there were those who came because it was just three miles from downtown, and more affordable than north side housing. But Ann, in her rosy view of Berkeley Square, rarely included this group in her parable.)

"It really is like pioneering," Ann exalted to Leah on one of their long distance phone calls between Chicago and Paris. "We have a one-room schoolhouse. Well, really, a one-building schoolhouse in the middle of the place. We have a newsletter, a nondenominational church, and Rev. Rowland is sort of the mayor because he's also director of the community center."

"What about a sheriff, a banker, a music hall?" Leah teased.

"We don't have a lawman," Ann answered seriously. "But we do have the Berkeley Square Security Guards. No badges, just embroidered emblems on their uniforms. I guess you could call Jack Blum, the guy who built the place, the banker. As for the music hall, perhaps that'll come one day. After all, the place is still kind of raw."

What Ann omitted from this conversation, and from any other glowing descriptions, were the dangers surrounding Berkeley Square's compound. Because it was in City Shores' territory, some of the hazards were familiar: the derelicts who hung out outside of liquor stores a few blocks away, and now, the occasional mugger who saw newcomers as fair game. Oh, and there was also a population that didn't want Berkeley Square there in the first place. Instead of praising city planners for slum clearance, these former residents of the 30 acres saw the Berkeley Square-ites as invaders, who confiscated land once belonging to them.

But Ann refused to let these negatives cloud her vision. Like her strong-willed and altruistic forbearers, she rolled up her sleeves and created a homestead. This time, the Robins wasted no time in furnishing it. They continued the Danish Modern theme started with their old bedroom set and selected living room furniture and an area rug in brown, beige, and oatmeal. Their new sofa was fat and striped, and two large chairs had padded sausage-shaped arms. The dining room table was teak wood, which looked perfect adjacent to the autumn color scheme of the living room.

The kitchen, which was actually on the second level of the house, overlooked a large courtyard. The Robins left behind the round table that fit the suburban bay window, and for their townhouse kitchen selected a butcher-block table and four Bentwood chairs. The chairs, with cane seats (they eventually would sink and get holey) and black scrolled backs were not the comfiest, but were popular at the time.

Because their daughters were no longer infants, the Robins figured they'd like to have their own bedrooms. But Audrey and Jessie once again thwarted efforts at separation, and took turns joining either sister at night. One or other room was always absent a sleeping child.

While their Spring Grove bi-level was low and wide, their Berkeley Square townhouse was tall and narrow. The entry hall led upstairs to the "living level" while downstairs were two rooms that could be turned into an office (as some of neighbors had showed Ann) or a playroom.

The Robins put a studio couch with a zebra-patterned cover (animals prints were also popular at the time) in one room and a trundle bed in the other. Ann wasn't sure why she wanted extra sleeping space, but felt it important to fill up every room in her new home. What could be better, she thought, than to have plenty of beds for out-of-town guests? (As it turned out, the downstairs mattresses served more as bouncing pads for the kids and their pals.)

❧

While Ann and Joel were partners in picking furniture, it was Ann who jumped into every committee and program that was created to fulfill Berkeley Square's noble mission. (Joel begged off in favor of making a good impression in his new job. Ann could find no fault with that excuse.)

Ann's gung-ho spirit was stoked on a Saturday tour she took of the community's multi-purpose center. The structure, which housed the local kindergarten to 3rd grade school, the church, and a gymnasium, was large, one story, and plain; and sat in the center of clusters of redbrick buildings that covered several city blocks.

While the exterior was ordinary, and in truth, the interior had an institutional look, the place was alive with activity. Perhaps it was the variety of people who were streaming into the center that day that made the building seem so vibrant. They were a mini-United Nations, just as the ads had promised: white, black, Asian, and Hispanic; and their ages went from babes in buggies to grey-haired and cane-assisted.

Music bellowed from one door. When Ann peered inside, she saw several rows of youngsters blowing gustily into trumpets as they followed scores that sat atop metal music stands. A young African-American man stood at the front of the room and used a baton to guide the junior musicians through their piece.

As she watched, Ann imagined her daughters clutching an instrument, or perhaps taking a different lesson in the building. Joy, passion, creativity; that was what Ann wanted her family to discover.

She stood outside the door of another room and saw a long rectangular table filled with fabric, buttons, yarn, scissors, and paste. Here mostly women, and mostly elderly (the sign, Senior Citizens Craft Shop, confirmed her assessment), chatted as they passed each other scraps of felt, which they pasted on dolls taking shape in their hands. One of the women spotted Ann and waved her in, but at 31, Ann merely smiled back, and shook her head.

The gymnasium was the loudest place, more raucous than the novice trumpeters. Men and teenage boys, in body shades from pale white to ebony, were dressed in sleeveless t-shirts (although some had shucked them and their bodies glistened in the overhead lights), shorts, and black-and-white high-top gym shoes. They shouted to one another, "here, here, over here," as they raced up and down the court flinging a basketball until a player lifted a wide hand to cup the ball and shoot it towards a basket. Ann stood there long enough to see a point (two points?)

scored, and catch the eye of one of the shimmering black males, who playfully waved her in. Again she smiled, again she turned away.

When she reached a door that held a hand-lettered sign, Berkeley Square Theatre Group; this time, she yielded. "Come in. Join us," said a young man who was reeling Ann in from the doorway. He was tall, likely in his 20's, with short brown curly hair; skin the color of coffee with two shots of cream, and sporting a mustache and short beard.

"Just looking," Ann said shyly as she inched into the room. "I've never acted before. I'm a behind-the-scenes kind of person."

"Not a problem, all you need is desire," said the young man. It turned out his name was Roger and he was the group's artistic director. He was dressed in khaki shorts, a faded t-shirt with a long-disappeared logo, and Birkenstock sandals. Holding a script in one hand, he used the other to begin introductions.

As Roger called out the names of the dozen or so people in the room, each rose from his or her black folding chair to shake Ann's hand.

"Hi, I'm Ann Robins," she said, smiling giddily with each offered palm as if she were a child allowed to roam free in the toy department of Marshall Field's.

It turned out the group was preparing a production of Edward Lee Masters' "Spoon River Anthology," which as Roger pointed out, was a breeze for actors because "you only have to memorize one piece and address the audience. You don't have to listen for cues from other actors, you're on stage for less than ten minutes, and once you've said your piece, you're off until curtain call."

Unlike the lothario and prima donna Larry Bennett, Roger was the social worker type, as eager to fulfill the "urban, integrated, diversity" motto, as he was to mount a good show. And the rest of the members of this group, keen as Broadway ingénues, matched Roger in his ambitions. So, Ann signed on.

❧

One week after that first meeting, Ann stood in front of her bedroom's full-length mirror repeating the first five lines of her part:

I was the milliner
Talked about, lied about
Mother of Dora
Whose strange disappearance
Was charged to her rearing.

When she felt confident enough, she added the next six:

My eye quick to beauty
Saw much beside ribbons
And buckles and feathers
And leghorns and felts,
To set off sweet faces,
And dark hair and gold.

She had a total of 25 lines to memorize for her role as Mrs. Williams and figured if she practiced a half hour a day, she'd be ready by opening night. This day, she was relieved Joel had already left for his office and her daughters were in the courtyard because she was embarrassed to be emoting to her mirror, in her bathrobe. The robe did seem to be a good stand-in for the costume she'd be wearing in the play. All of her other outfits, like her polyester blouses with matching short skirts, and tall white boots, hardly evoked the period she was going for. She added high heels and tied a woolen scarf around her neck. Now, she could play-act to her image, and try not to laugh at this wacky get-up and her dramatic rendition.

❧

On opening night, when the applause ended, Ann finally gave herself permission to stare into the audience and pick out her family. With the bouquet of flowers someone had pressed into her hands, she waved to Joel and her daughters who were seated about a third of the way down in the rows of folding chairs. They were clapping wildly. "Yea! Mommy!" the girls yelled out. "Bravo," Joel shouted, a wide smile on his face. And because the audience in the community center's gym was comprised of friends and relatives of all the actors, each performer received a similar ovation.

Roger was stationed in the wings and was welcoming and praising each actor as they left the stage. "You were terrific!" he said to Ann.

"Perfect," Susan, the assistant director, agreed. Formerly Susan Wilson, she was now a Richardson, for between the time Ann was persuaded to audition, and this performance, this thin, black woman, with a short Afro, married Roger at a sunrise ceremony on the 57th Street beach, with Rev. Rowland performing the service.

"Thanks," Ann said, returning Susan's hugs, "but I still think I prefer behind-the-scenes."

"Okay, if the theatre isn't for you, what about The Berkeley Bulletin?" Susan asked. "We need typists, reporters, production people. How about that?"

"Sounds great," Ann said, and she meant every word.

❧

Ann didn't rejoin the City Shores' women's group because before long, she had enough on her hands at Berkeley Square. She became a member of the Berkeley Square Political Organization, The Committee to End Police Brutality, The Management-Tenant Association, The Arts Club, and The Community Center Planning Committee. At first, and she told Joel this, she joined each group just to get to know her neighbors. But as time went on, she unearthed talents she didn't know she had.

For example, at a CEPB meeting, some activist neighbors, who had been roughed up by cops during a citywide demonstration, demanded their local committee take action.

Ann jumped in with a suggestion. "Let's make a list of goals," she said, pulling from her tote bag the yellow legal pad and Flair pen she always carried. She started taking notes as members threw out, "Request a meeting with our local commander," "Suspend the cops who act like thugs," "Take pictures of those that got beat up, focusing on their wounds."

Then, after they had run out of ideas, they turned to Ann for the next step. She paused in her recording to say, "We should probably hold a press conference." She'd seen other left-wing groups do this and get attention in the newspapers and on television.

"Sounds great," said Don Barnett, who was the CEPB chairman. "Can you write a news release, my speech?"

"Sure," Ann said, enjoying her anointment. Maybe this was her calling? She loved to write; that was certain. In her childhood, she had filled diaries with crushes on neighborhood boys, plots of forbidden books ("The Amboy Dukes"), and lyrical swoons over crooners like Johnny Ray and Frank Sinatra. In high school and college, she'd won A's for her papers; and when her brother Danny was stationed in Hawaii during his Army stint, she'd happily write long letters to him every week. Now, she was being called upon to write for other readers. What could be better!

Before you knew it, Ann was assigned similar writing tasks with every other one of her organizations: the BSPO, the MTA, the AC, and the CCPC. Of all her volunteer posts, her favorite was on-staff at the Berkeley Bulletin, for it combined everything Ann treasured: pens, pencils, typewriters, words, lists, and deadlines.

Although she started at the bottom, typing other writers' contributions, she soon moved up to columnist (she wrote a humor piece fashioned after Erma Bombeck), then calendar editor (all those committee announcements and their guest speakers), and finally, after Susan moved with Roger to New York, Editor of the Berkeley Bulletin.

❧

"Sure it's a lot of work," Ann confessed to Leah. "But I get a charge from the attention that comes with the job."

"Like what?" Leah asked. She had already brought Ann up-to-date on her French lessons, Ken's latest travel assignments, and the boys' progress at the American school.

"Well, I sort of feel like a celebrity," Ann said. "Any place I go, people stop to tell me my column made them laugh, or suggest a story for the Bulletin, or just thank me for doing a good job."

Leah said nothing on the other end of the line. Ann wondered if her silence was due to jealousy. Did she think Ann was getting a swelled head; that she looked down on someone who was merely wife and a mother? That would be silly, of course. But instead of clearing it up, Ann acted as if there was nothing unusual in Leah's response. She just rolled on, continuing her rosy reporting over long distance wires.

❧

In Ann's view, she wasn't the only member of her family blossoming in the rich soil of Berkeley Square. Her daughters were thriving as well. All she had to do, to witness her children's burgeoning confidence and creativity, was to stand in her kitchen, look out the windows, and watch Audrey and Jessie at play in the courtyard. On any given day, her daughters could be seen dressed in costumes improvised from their parents' closets. High heels, beaded necklaces, scarves, and long-sleeved men's shirts adorned one or the other girl.

From her catbird seat, Ann could see the central courtyard that was surrounded by townhouses whose front doors opened onto the outdoor space. Along with grass, trees, and shrubs, the courtyard held playground equipment for the toddler set and benches for parents who wanted to oversee or chat. And, the amiable space also became the site for July 4th and Labor Day barbeques, birthday parties, and other festivities.

One afternoon when Ann was gazing at her daughters, she unlocked the large window to hear 7-year-old Audrey order one little boy, "Stand next to her, not behind her." Then she pulled him into place.

"But I..." he started to complain.

"Listen to my sister," Jessie, 5-1/2, said, taking another child by the hand to lead her into position.

Most of the kids who were obeying her daughters' directions were townhouse neighbors, but a few came from the apartments across the street, the ones subsidized for Berkeley Square's low-income tenants. The children were white and all shades of black, with the lightest beige the product of the many mixed marriages in the complex. No matter their family's financial status, their religious or ethnic background, or the color of their skin, the boys and girls of this new territory played together harmoniously—just as the planners had envisioned, and just as Ann and the other parents counted on.

Not everyone in the Robins household was as smitten with Berkeley Square as the womenfolk. "You're making too much noise, I can't sleep." It was Joel, 8:00 o'clock on a Saturday morning. He was halfway down the stairs from the bedroom to the dining room where Ann was typing on her red Selectric. The table was a foreign setting for the machine as she usually pounded its keys in the church office. But at the end of the day on Friday, she brought it home and placed it on the table, along with her notes and mimeograph paper.

On the stairs, Joel was dressed in his pajamas, and without his eyeglasses, which still stood upright and unfolded on the bedside table, blinked to make out the scene below.

"Sorry," she said, without looking up. "But I have to get my column finished so we can meet this week's deadline."

"Shit," he said, and turned to climb heavily back up the stairs.

❧

That evening at dinner, when their daughters were out of ear-shot, Joel said to Ann, "You've changed, sugar. Before we moved here, you'd welcome me home when I came in the door. Seemed happy as a clam to see me. Now, I get the short end of the stick. You're either at the community center, on the phone, or even if you *are* here, your mind is a million miles away. Is it too much to expect my wife to be happy to see me? I bust my tail at the office so you can volunteer for every cockamamie cause; and what do I get? Who do you think puts food on the table, pays the mortgage? Don't I deserve some gratitude, some attention?"

Ann remained silent, so Joel continued, "I see it every day at the office. A couple is married ten years, everything is honky dory, and then suddenly the wife becomes a woman's libber. 'I'm sick of housework,' she says. 'I want to get a job, do something meaningful,' she says. Now she's out the door more than she's home. Then the poor sucker of a husband decides he doesn't want to fight anymore, so he finds a girlfriend. And before you know it, the couple winds up in my office wanting a divorce. Is that what you want, sugar, is that what you want?"

"No, of course not," Ann said. "Of course I don't want that." She rose from her chair and re-tied the apron that had come loose. Then she went to the stove to dish an extra helping of mashed potatoes onto Joel's empty plate.

"I've gone overboard," she agreed. "I'll cut back; I promise." Then, she walked behind his chair and put her hands on her husband's shoulders.

Pressing down hard, she used her thumbs and fingers to massage away the day's aches. "How's this?" she asked.

"Great, sugar," Joel said, and closed his eyes to absorb the rub.

Ann closed her eyes, too.

Thirteen

Although it was early afternoon, the bar's darkness, plus the cigarette smoke clouding her view, made Ann feel as if she had slithered into a late night dive. A small crowd had already assembled and were scattered among a dozen or so round tables near the stage. The people were mostly African-American men and women—Ann was one of the few white women there—and they were stylishly dressed, as if they were seated in a downtown club rather than this Hyde Park lounge.

When her eyes became adjusted to the dark, and when the smoke cleared, Ann studied the couples—not staring, just peeking—to figure out which ones were married and which were sweethearts.

Here's what she decided: if their heads leaned in together, if they were holding hands or otherwise touching the other's arm, or if they were smiling at their partner's words, they were lovers. But, if they sat back in his or her chair and approached the table only to lift a drink and set it down, and if no communication could be seen or heard, they were married. Just like her.

She was grateful the room *was* dark because whenever she thought about her marriage, tears overtook her. Joel's suggestion, actually his preference, really his demand, that she scale back her community involvement, had hit her hard. She'd miss the sense of importance, accomplishment, and contribution she experienced in all those organizations. But also, she was saddened that her husband didn't see how much all of that meant to her.

If he really loved me, he'd be happy to see me enthusiastic and admired, she thought. If he knew me, really knew me, he'd see how I've grown since I was that girl on the park bench being wooed by a heartsick boy. And, it was that realization—that the man she had been married to for 11 years didn't know her at all. That was as painful to Ann as what she was forced to give up.

Oh, she supposed she could defy him; refuse to drop every one of her committees or programs. But what good would that do? Their marriage, only recently repaired with the move back to the city, might suffer. So she swallowed her anger; but more often, it was Ann who rolled over to the opposite side of the bed. They'd have sex occasionally, but it was more like a doctor's prescription (or advice from those stupid women's magazines). A temporary fix to heal the immediate pain; not a permanent remedy.

She wondered if their passionless sex satisfied Joel, but she never asked and he never volunteered an answer. Perhaps he was too weary at the end of the day to do the hard work on his marriage. Maybe he preferred a resumption of the cold war. It would at least let him get some sleep. As for Ann, nightly repose took longer; but eventually, she, too, would fall into a deep sleep.

In the Hyde Park lounge, a quintet, with her friend Collin Washington on tenor sax, was still setting up—drums towards the rear, piano on stage left, bass on the right, and horn players moistening their lips. The hushed voices of the audience as they wound up conversations (that would be the lovers, of course), plus the tentative sounds of each instrument, and the stage manager's "check, check" into the microphone, composed their own off-key jam.

Although she fully expected to enjoy the music, Ann was at the bar on business —for the Berkeley Bulletin. It was the one volunteer post she clung to after giving up all the others. With her yellow legal pad and Flair pen lined up before her, Ann was set for this assignment. But the JB and water that Collin sent to her was starting to affect her penmanship, and her imagination.

She had met Collin in the Landlord-Tenant meetings. He was a high-rise resident pressing for more security after his Buick LeSabre was broken into while parked in his building's garage. Management agreed to add another guard to the home-town squad and that mollified Collin. After Ann quit the committee, and Collin won more eyes on his beloved automobile, the two of them remained friends.

She sipped the drink slowly so she could still write a coherent review of Collin's group for the newsletter, as she had promised him. But with each taste of her scotch, her mind shifted from the scene playing out on stage, to one that occurred more than fifteen years earlier, when she first fell in love with jazz.

In that long ago vision, she saw the younger Ann lying in bed with Alex Jacobson, a boy she dated during her college years. They were in his parents' apartment on North Clarendon, fully clothed, when Alex said to her, "I'm going to introduce you to Daddy-O Daley. You know 'Daddio on the Raddio on WXFM.' He invited me to his midnight show and said I could bring a friend."

"Midnight?" Ann said. "That means we won't get home till morning. My mom will have a conniption fit."

"Don't tell her," Alex said, brushing Ann's hair back from her face. Although Alex was handsome, in a Paul Newman-sort of way, Ann knew she was one of several girls he took out. No way would this sexy guy tempt her to go all the way. After all, she was a good Jewish girl and chastity ruled. If Alex really wanted to get laid, he could turn to the *shiksas* at school, or to the rumored cathouses in Peoria.

"Just say we're going out on a date. She'll be asleep when you get home and won't know the difference," he had said.

❧

When Collin's quintet launched into its first tune, a mellow version of "Can't Get Started," Ann left her memories and turned her attention to the stage. Slightly off kilter thanks to her sips of scotch, she tried to refocus by studying the musicians and settled on a saxophonist who was alternating riffs with Collin.

Unlike Collin, who was very dark skinned and beefy, Neal Spencer—she caught his name and clung to it when the group was introduced—was a slim and light-skinned black man with freckles sprinkled across his face. While his horn's smooth sounds first drew Ann to his place in the spotlight, it was his eyes targeting hers that kept her locked in place.

As she listened, bobbing her head to the music and tapping her fingers on the table, she flashed back again to that long ago evening with Alex in Daddy-O Daley's studio.

"Hello sweetheart," Daddy-O had said when they were introduced. Flirty, and grinning widely, he added, "Is this guy corrupting you?"

"With my permission," Ann answered, smiling back. "Thanks for letting me sit in."

"Pretty ladies are always welcome here," Daddy-O said. He leaned over to kiss her cheek, and she could smell his hair's pomade and cologne.

After introductions, Daddy-O seated Ann and Alex in two chairs outside his glass-enclosed booth. As they watched, Daddy-O played his records and purred to his radio audience as if they were next to him instead of in their homes, cars, and workplaces. Ann imagined his listeners—couples making love in dim-lit bedrooms, sweethearts returning home from a date, and night cleaning crews carting their portables along with a mop bucket.

That night at Daddy-O's, Ann learned the names and popular tunes of jazz singers and became a fan of all of them. The women: Carmen McRae, Ella Fitzgerald, Dinah Washington, Nancy Wilson, and Sarah Vaughn. And the men: Joe Williams, Barry White, Johnny Hartman, Frank Sinatra, and Mel Torme.

As they listened to the recordings, Alex pulled Ann's chair next to his and put his arm around her shoulders. From inside his booth, Daddy-O winked, as if to say, "Enjoy."

"Hmm," Alex murmured, putting his free hand on Ann's knee.

"Hmm," she agreed, and put her own hand on top of his—to feel the connection, but also to impede its progress. She was grateful they were in a public place, rather than in Alex's bedroom, because the late-night hour, the low-pitched crooners, the syrupy songs, and Daddy-O's thumbs up might've been just enough to move Ann from her firm position to one horizontal and compliant. Or not.

At the end of the broadcast, Daddy-O removed his earphones and emerged from the booth to bid his guests adieu. Alex's fingers gave a final squeeze to Ann's thigh, and then they both rose to take the disk jockey's offered palm. Ignoring Alex, Daddy-O turned to Ann and asked, "So, sweetheart, how was your jazz immersion? Do we have a fan?"

Instead of stopping at the handshake, Ann stood on tiptoes to kiss Daddy O's cheek. She wasn't sure why she added the affectionate gesture; perhaps it was the jazz music that flowed through her body and was still playing on an endless loop. Or perhaps, it was because she just felt wonderful.

After she and Alex left the studio, they drove silently while he tried to find similar music on the car radio. When they pulled up at Ann's building, they capped the evening by making out in Alex's Chevy Impala. Of course, Ann's version of *making out* involved kissing, but no unbuttoning or unzipping. Although the music *had* affected her, the drive home with the windows open, and the dashboard clock that showed the late hour, quickly rescued her from the danger zone.

"Thank you," she told Alex when he switched off his motor. "I'll never forget this night. I loved every minute of it."

"I'm glad you enjoyed it," Alex said, and used the back of his hand to wipe away her lipstick. When he glimpsed his wrist-watch's time, he added, "Good luck with your mother." Then, he reached across to unlock the car door and watched as Ann rushed to her apartment building.

She was quiet as could be when she unlocked the deadbolt to the basement flat. After tiptoeing down the two steps to the living room, she spotted her mother. Sylvia was in her chenille robe curled up in a corner of the couch, twisting a Kleenex in her arthritic fingers.

"Where have you been?" Sylvia asked. She used the tissue to wipe away still-flowing tears. "I've been worried sick. Do you know what time it is? I thought you were dead somewhere in an alley. How could you do this to me? It's not enough your father drops dead and leaves me alone? You're going to kill me, too."

"Mommy, I'm sorry," Ann said. She dumped her purse and jacket on the steps and rushed to join Sylvia on the couch. "I went to a radio show with Alex. I was going to call you when I saw how late it was but I didn't want to wake you up."

"I don't deserve this," Sylvia said, "I don't deserve this."

When Neal finished his solo and relinquished his spot to Collin, he sat on a stool tapping his foot, but his eyes never left Ann's. By now, she had given up hope of writing anything—what with those memories that kept popping up and Neal's stare—so she tucked away her paper and pen in the tote bag at her feet. With more sips of the scotch, Ann could devote her full attention to

Neal and wasn't at all surprised when he approached her table at intermission.

"Hey," Neal said. "Collin told me the beautiful lady I've been keeping my eyes on is a friend of his." He pulled out a chair, sat down, and inched closer to her. "Did you enjoy the set?"

"It was wonderful," Ann said. "You were wonderful."

He ordered an iced tea for himself. Ann waved away a second scotch he offered, and then she launched into questions about his start in the music business, his experience on European tours, and his ambitions. She wasn't writing anything down as she had planned to do for the Bulletin, but instead recorded his answers in her head. Nice guy, not the ego-filled rakish musician she had typecast.

"If you liked today's show you might really appreciate the jazz collection I've got at home," Neal said. "Classics. I'll be in tomorrow. Maybe you can stop by around two?"

"Tomorrow? Thursday?" she asked. To herself she thought, our cleaning woman will be at the house. Betty could be there for Audrey and Jessie when they come home from school.

The next day, Ann sat in her car, matching the South Side address Neal had written on a cocktail napkin with the house number she was staring at. It was two in the afternoon, right on time, and now all she needed was the courage to open her driver's side door, walk up to the house, ring the bell, and be welcomed by Neal.

It helped the weather was lovely; warm, bright sun, not a threatening cloud in the sky. An ideal day for gardening Ann noted when she left her townhouse and spotted her neighbor, Diane Young, planting flowers outside her front door.

"Tulips," Diane said, without waiting for Ann's query. She nestled a bulb in the hole she had carefully carved out, and asked, "Where're you off to?"

"I'll tell you later," Ann said, moving quickly to her car. "Enjoy your gardening."

❧

The Hideaway Bar's napkin, with 6-7-2-8 written on it, fluttered in her nervous fingers. It wasn't too late; she could still turn back. What in the world was she doing? Why risk her marriage for a fling with a saxophone player? But what if Joel never found out? She certainly wasn't going to confess.

Minutes ticked by; she leaned back from the steering wheel and replayed the dark bar, the music, Neal's long-lashed eyes, his touch as he handed her the napkin. Then, she took one deep breath, exited the driver's seat, and rang the doorbell.

"Hey, pretty lady, you're here," Neal said, smiling as he opened his front door. He reached for her hand and guided her into the living room. "I'm so happy you came." Then he kissed her cheek, as innocent as if he was welcoming an elderly aunt for tea.

After closing the door behind them, Neal motioned to Ann to take a seat on the living room couch. He placed a record on a turntable, turned to her and said, "This is Carmen McRae, my favorite vocalist." And then, from a small wooden box on the coffee table, he removed a tiny cigarette and a box of matches. "Want a hit?" he asked. "It improves your listening pleasure."

In fact, she did want to try her first joint, another highlight of the '60s—like free love—that she had regrettably missed as a young wife and mother. She remembered flipping pages of magazines, watching television coverage, and feeling some envy at the hippies' cavorting without a care in the world. It wasn't that she regretted marriage and children, for she had wanted all of that desperately. But when she saw the free-spirited young women—with their long hair looking as if had gone weeks between washings, dressed in their colorful costumes, and the look of joy on their faces –she'd feel a stab of envy. That freedom and creativity likely extended to their sex lives where they must've been animate, experimental, and uninhibited. She wondered if she could ever be the same.

Between drags of the marijuana, the music of this lush singer (who would become Ann's favorite, too), Ann offered no resistance when Neal took her by the hand into his bedroom. She couldn't remember the last time a man had wanted her, the last time her heart beat so fast she worried about her survival, the last time she wanted the experience to last forever. Although Neal just walked into her life, she was confident he could return her to those long ago feelings.

Inside the bedroom, she studied the framed photograph of Martin Luther King, Jr., and autographed pictures of Neal with other musicians—Carmen, Miles, Duke—that decorated one wall. Shelves of sleeved albums, and a dresser where Neil placed the ashtray and cigarette shared another wall. She looked in the mirror that hung above the dresser, and saw her white face—bland among the wall's ebony line-up.

Her red hair was in place, thanks to the Aqua Net she had nearly emptied before leaving the house. As she started to unbutton her blouse, Neal—taller than the mirror—came up behind her. She turned around, and let him finish the task.

Neal turned out to be as virtuoso a lover as he was a saxophonist. Slow, smooth, one note at a time, tempo and timber building gradually until both musician and his enraptured audience of one, reached a crescendo. Actually several. Ann felt as if she had left this earth and landed some place where she felt adored, free, and sensuous.

When they finished their lovemaking, Ann sighed. "Thank you," she said. "I had a lovely time."

"My pleasure," Neal said. "Let's do this again sometime. Soon."

On the five-mile drive back to Berkeley Square, she was dreamy and relaxed, due to the pot and the replaying of her afternoon. Ann forced herself to concentrate, praying to God to forgive her and bring her safely home.

As she pulled into her parking space, she lifted her eyes skyward and said, "Thank you."

But as she approached her house and saw Diane sitting on the stoop in front of her house, the very spot where the two mothers watched their children at play—Ann's gratitude evaporated.

Diane was crying, and paused to yell, "Look! Look what your kids did!"

Audrey and Jessie were seated on their own stoop, heads bowed until they saw their mother approach. "We're sorry, Mommy," they wailed in unison, running to her side. "We didn't know they were supposed to stay in the ground."

Scattered around Diane's front lawn were all of the tulip bulbs she had spent the day planting. While Betty was busy cleaning Ann's house, she had sent the girls out to play. They spotted Diane's trowel and spade lying unused next door, and decided to do their own digging. In the hours their mother was gone, her two daughters had upturned her neighbor's front lawn.

"I'm so sorry," Ann said taking a seat next to her friend and putting her arms around Diane's sagging shoulders. Ann's head cleared almost immediately. "We'll replant the whole thing. Please don't cry. I'll punish the girls. I'll make sure it never happens again."

"Where were you?" Diane demanded.

Ann didn't answer, but continued to hug her neighbor as she stared at the ruined garden. How long would it take to replace each bulb where it was supposed to have been? To fill in the rich soil that would give the tulips another chance? Since she wasn't a gardener, Ann didn't have a clue as to the job ahead. Nonetheless, she picked up the tools, which felt heavy and unfamiliar in her hands, and started in.

Fourteen

That's it! Ann said—aloud, even though no one was in earshot. She was in the reception area of the church office typing on her red Selectric, and Rev. Rowland was tucked away in his inner office. While pausing on the keys to contemplate a word, her eyes traveled the walls, past the plants cuddled in macramé, and landed on a banner hung to brighten the institutional gray. Rainbows and musical notes were sprinkled across the background and "A Joyful Noise" was written in multicolored yarn.

Of course, that's the answer. She remembered the Spring Grove Players, and Joel's happy participation in "Oklahoma" back when they lived in the suburbs. Why hadn't she thought of it sooner? A Berkeley Square Music Theatre—the music hall Leah had jokingly inquired about when Ann first moved into the neighborhood. That could be just the ticket to shake up Joel's all-work-no-play routine. And because the idea sprang from the walls of a pastoral office, Ann considered it a sign from heaven—one that might absolve her of the unfortunate tulip incident and what came before it.

Ann considered herself lucky she emerged unscathed. Despite the pot, she hadn't gotten into an automobile accident on the way home from Neal's. And Joel was unsuspecting; nothing gave her away. He came in the door that evening, calling out "Sugar, I'm home," just like always.

Although she had felt wonderful being swept away by passion; it was too big a risk. She could've had a car crash, been killed! Now, guilt and potential danger outweighed the earlier highs. She vowed it would never happen again.

"Here it is. Cut it if it's too long." It was Rev. Rowland, emerging from his office holding his weekly contribution for the newsletter.

Ann quickly swerved from remorse to hope. She grabbed his handwritten column, tossed it on her desk, and said, "Let's start a music theater!" Ann knew, with his mandate to bring together his diverse flock, this clergyman-community director would be open to her proposal. And because he was so well liked, he'd be ideal to help lure a cast and crew.

Rev. Rowland, who was about the same age as Ann and Joel, didn't look the part of a cleric (or Ann's vision of a man of the cloth), more like the friendly guy at the local Home Depot. In his role as Unifier-In-Chief, he wore long-sleeved white shirts folded over at the wrists, and navy slacks.

"We've got enough people to form an orchestra and cast a show," Ann said, "and I bet there'd be plenty of others willing to build sets and sew costumes. It'd be a great way to encourage people from the whole neighborhood to work together." She added the last as a bonus for him.

"Great idea," he said, and pulled up a plastic molded chair to continue the plan. "Just like Mickey Rooney and Judy Garland."

"Only with a much more colorful cast," Ann joked.

"You'll take charge, right?"

"Take charge?" she repeated. She hesitated because she recalled her promise to Joel to cut back. But her husband didn't have to learn she was the instigator. Previously, she'd have welcomed the glory that accompanied her creative endeavors. Now, secrecy was more important.

"Of course," she said to Rev. Rowland. "I'll do it."

❧

Relying on the church Rolodex and the address book she kept in her tote bag, Ann quickly rounded up key personnel: Gerald Holt, an eccentric and talented professor from the nearby Illinois Institute of Technology volunteered to be musical director. Angeline and Carm Pontarelli, Ann's townhouse neighbors—who with their brownish hair starting to gray, short trim bodies, happy-go-luck personalities—were as alike as matching salt and peppershakers. They were newly retired from advertising jobs around the country and signed on, to sew costumes, build scenery, and even sing in the chorus.

Barbara Madden lived in one of the high-rise apartments and worked as a technical writer during the day and freelance choreographer nights and weekends. She was a beauty—waist-length blond hair, slim figure, and long legs—surely Barbara could easily persuade the most flat-footed of her ensemble to pay attention.

Marlene Watson had straight hair perfectly coiffed, and wore jewelry imported from Africa. Her earrings and necklaces were large, but she was a big woman and could pull it off. She was a social worker who lived in Berkeley Square's subsidized housing and had two children who were in Ann's daughters' classes. Marlene volunteered to visit neighborhood businesses and score donations and ads.

The committee's first task was to select a show. Several popular Rogers and Hammerstein and Gilbert and Sullivan musicals were suggested, with each member pressing for his or her choice.

"I vote for 'Pirates of Penzance,'" Gerald said. "Great music, zany story, lots of choruses." Then he began to hum a few bars of "With cat light tread."

"If we do Gilbert and Sullivan, I want 'Mikado,'" said Carm, "better score." Then he stood up and lurched into "A more humane Mikado," as if auditioning for the namesake role.

"How about 'Carousel?'" asked Barbara Madden. "There's some lovely dance segments to give the show variety, and everybody knows the music."

"Sounds a little rough to me," Marlene offered. "If I recall, there's burglary, domestic violence, jealousy, deception, stabbing..."

Angeline chimed in, "But also important issues for women, like abandonment, commitment, intimacy."

"True," Ann said. She attempted to add more weight to the "Carousel"pitch. "The show has a gorgeous score, and also social themes of class and hypocrisy. And the contrast between the carnival's gaiety with all of the dark stuff you two just mentioned, makes for great theatre." She was just getting warmed up. "And then there's redemption [key for Ann], when Billy gets a chance to make it up to his wife and daughter. Think of the chills, the tears when everyone sings, 'You'll never walk alone.' I can already hear the bravos and applause."

"Carousel" it would be.

Next, Ann had to convince her husband, as he was the primary reason for this undertaking. One evening at dinner (delayed because he said he had to work late at the office), Ann said, "The Berkeley Square Music Theatre is doing 'Carousel.' You should audition." She slipped the sentences out casually, as if she was spooning another dollop of potatoes.

He pushed his chair back and eyed her as if she were on the witness stand in one of his courtroom cases. "What do you have to do with that group, sugar?" He wiped his hands on his napkin and tossed it on the table. "I thought you were supposed to be scaling back."

"I did," she said. "I am. You know I dropped everything but the Bulletin." Then, grateful she hadn't placed her hand on a bible, continued, "I was writing about the group for the paper and thought you might get a kick out of it."

"We want to be in the show, too," Audrey said. She and her sister had been in the living room watching "Happy Days" on T.V. and raced into the kitchen when they heard their parents discussing the theatre group. "We do plays all the time in the courtyard and in school."

Ann studied her excited offspring and thought about the school productions where her girls could be easily spotted among the sea of African-American children. It seemed like more white families (and some of the middle-class black families) were leaving Berkeley Square every year.

Those that remained pulled their kids out of the community center school and enrolled them in private schools nearby. "More rigorous classes," some explained. "We want a Catholic education," others said. Whatever the reasons that her daughters became part of the minority at the school and in the courtyard, Audrey and Jessie were staying put. After all, neither of them commented about the ratio, and both were still winning high marks on their report cards.

"There's kids in the play, right?" Jessie said. "We could take those parts, easy. Debbie's in the show, Justin, Jamal," she counted. She used her fingers to list the friends already cast.

"There'll be late nights," Ann warned. "You'll have to do what you're told."

"Yea, yea!" the girls shouted, already in harmony.

"I don't have the energy to be in a play," Joel said. He lowered his face onto arms folded on the table. Then, he lifted his head and continued, "You have no idea how tiring it is, sugar, to listen to people bad mouth each other, day in day out."

"Daddy, please," Jessie said. "You never do anything with us." Her face was angry; he was spoiling the mood.

"Come on, Daddy, we want to sing with you." This from Audrey, who was trying a different tack. She had an endearing, hopeful expression.

"Just come to the audition," Ann said. She put a hand on his shoulder. "If you decide it's not for you, I promise not to bug you anymore."

Once again, as it happened in dullsville Spring Grove, Joel auditioned. This time, he moved out of the chorus into the role of Enoch Snow; and Audrey and Jessie easily slipped into the characters of his stage children. Soon, his tenor voice serenaded over the steam of his morning shower, and in the tunes repeated in his whistles as he left for work and his departures for rehearsals three evenings a week.

With Joel busy studying his lines and learning his songs; he didn't notice Ann compiling her To Do lists. Of course, she couldn't hide her duties for very long. Soon enough she was called to rehearsals, to do the bidding of whoever got to her first.

"What are you doing here?" he asked the first time she showed up. He was on stage, script in hand, practicing his lines before his on-stage sweetheart showed up.

"I'm sorry I kept it from you," Ann said. She took his free hand as if she were Carrie Pipperidge about to launch into their duet. She looked into his eyes, and imagining cues from an off-stage Gerald Holt, said in a contrite—but loving—voice, "Rev. Rowland couldn't get anyone else to take the job. I should've told you sooner. Everyone is counting on me; I can't let them down."

She was playing a syrupy role, but this musical theatre thing was important, not only to Ann, but also to everyone in the community who was depending on her. She liked that, too, feeling important, key.

"I guess it's okay," Joel said. "Just don't go overboard; remember your priorities." Then, he released Ann's hand to welcome 22-year-old, dark-haired, blue-eyed, Beverly Johnson to the stage. "This is where we are," he said, turning away from his wife to point to a line in his script.

"Bye, honey," Ann said as she exited stage left. After she reached the middle aisle, she looked back to see Joel take hold of Beverly's hand. The girl accepted it then reached to pick up his other one that held the script. Joel dropped the pages to the floor and let both his hands be clasped in hers. Beverly looked up into his eyes and together their blended voices, sang, "When the children are asleep, I'll dream with you." It was a song that brought tears to Ann's eyes. She stood in her place and listened for a few stanzas, then returned to her duties.

❧

What could she—or for that matter, anyone else who was there—say about the opening night performance of "Carousel" by the Berkeley Square Music Theatre?

A million dollar Broadway production, with big-name-actors, full orchestra, lavish costumes, scenery that dropped from the ceiling or rotated around the stage, couldn't have generated as much excitement or applause.

It all started two hours before curtain when Ann bid her nervous husband and daughters, "Break a leg." Before the audience filed in, Ann took her stack of mimeographed programs and placed each one on a seat. Residents of the senior citizen building were first to arrive. After handing over their $2 ticket fee (discounted from the regular $5), they claimed seats in the first three rows. Next, families of cast members rushed in, chirping excitedly as if a Hollywood scout was in the audience, ready to offer their spouse, son, or daughter, a movie role.

With every one of the 200 seats in the school auditorium filled, at exactly 7 p.m., Gerald Holt raised his baton, and the small orchestra, dressed in black, struck up the merry-go-round's opening notes of Roger and Hammerstein's perfect musical.

Everyone in the cast was wonderful. Voice students from nearby universities, church choir members, and shower serenaders like Joel, awed the audience. It took at least half a dozen curtain calls before they released the cast. Backstage, euphoria and bedlam took over. As people left the auditorium, re-reading their black-and-white souvenir programs to find the identity of Billy Bigelow, Julie Jordan, Jigger Craigin; and of course, Enoch Snow, exclamations of "beautiful," "wonderful," and "what a surprise," chorused in the emptying space.

With all of that hoopla, the evening certainly couldn't end there.

After the cast party, and once the kids in the production had been sent home under the care of babysitters, and Rev. Rowland had left the scene, Angeline came up with the idea to continue the celebration in the Berkeley Square outdoor pool. "A splash party!" she sang out. And fueled by relief and liquor, the cast and crew heartedly agreed.

All except Ann. "The gates are locked," she said. "There's no way to get in." This was an unusual role for Ann: killjoy. She wasn't sure why she played the sour puss holding the partygoers back instead of the one leading the charge. It may've been her "good Jewish girl" upbringing and respect for law and order, or that she had done quite enough risk-taking with Neal Spencer.

"We'll climb over," suggested Carm.

"By the time everyone gets their bathing suits on, the sun will be up. It'll be light out," Ann said. "We'd be caught." Now she was just trying to be practical, make clear the risks involved.

"Who needs suits?" Angeline said. She was already unbuttoning her blouse.

"I'm in," Joel said.

One by one everybody at the cast party—except for Ann who offered to act as lookout—abandoned their latest cocktail and raced to the swimming pool, unzipping and unbuttoning as they flew. When they reached the fence, one boosted up the other, until a few on the inside helped to cushion the jump for the last one over.

After all of the garments had been shed, the singers, dancers, scenery designers, costumers, and musicians leaped into the still waters of the Berkeley Square pool.

Splashing happily in the nude, not a one cared if any residents of the apartments overlooking the pool might be gazing out their living room windows for one last look at the evening sky. The giddy cast and crew (integrated in race, age, and income as the planners had intended, but probably not in this setting) continued their celebrations in this watery locale.

As Ann stood watch on the outside, she wondered: What was wrong with her that she could easily slip out of her clothing with Neal Spencer the saxophonist, a stranger, but unable to shed them in a group of friends that included her own husband? She wasn't a prude, that wasn't it. It was more that Ann preferred any activity that included nudity, fun, and freedom of expression to be done in private. Preferably with only two people in attendance.

There was only one sour note in the entire Berkeley Square Music Theatre experience: the robbery. Looking back, it was foolish of them to be so careless. For this production, instead of using the community center's stage like Tony's theatre troupe had done, the musical group voted to perform in the auditorium of Locke Grammar School, which was located within the next-door public housing complex. But that choice didn't come easy.

"I vote no," said Marlene. "I didn't move my family from the West Side to throw us back in with the projects."

"Public housing," Rev. Rowland corrected. "The people who live there hate the word 'projects.'"

"Let's have a show of hands," Ann said. She hoped there were still enough starry-eyed liberals on the committee to swing a vote for Locke.

Her side won, and truthfully, what happened there could've taken place anywhere. After the dress rehearsal, the cast exited the stage still singing lyrics from the final chorus. The male actors headed for the classroom designated for them and females to another.

"Where's my purse?" Angeline asked.

"I know I put my bag on this desk," said Barbara.

"Oh my God, all our stuff is gone," Angeline wailed as they raced between the rows of the classroom-turned-dressing room. Sure enough, during the evening, when everyone was on or near the stage and the room was left unattended, some unknown person, or persons, had absconded with all of the purses that had been casually tossed in the room.

This is my fault, Ann thought. She shouldn't have pushed Locke on everyone. "What did I tell you?" It was Marlene Watson. She heard the hubbub in the hallway and ran in to discover her own purse among those missing. She stared at Ann, who stood silently in the midst of the crime scene.

Angeline, likely sensing the finger of blame being pointed toward Ann, put a hand on her shoulder. "Why don't you go to the principal's office and call the police," she said. The principal's office, an appropriate punishment, Ann thought.

But that was the only disharmony, and the Berkeley Square Music Theatre was already gearing up for their next production. The location for that show was still being decided, but it wouldn't be Locke.

❧

Several months later, with Joel's ego still boosted from his "Carousel" immersion, it shouldn't have been a surprise to Ann, when on a Sunday morning—with lox, bagels, and cream cheese on the butcher block table—her husband turned to her and said, "I'm thinking of taking acting lessons."

She took a bite of her bagel and stared at him. At 39, he was handsomer than ever. He had added some pounds to the skinny frame of his youth, and the few wrinkles he acquired over the years only enhanced his good looks. "Pardon me?" she said. She had pushed the music theatre as a way to pump up Joel's fondness for Berkeley Square, but never imagined he would also find a new hobby.

"You know the theatre group is going to do another musical in a few months, sugar. Instead of a supporting role this time, I want to try out for the lead. And there are other amateur groups in the city I could check into. And dramatic lessons should help me be more persuasive in the courtroom."

Then, he leapt from his chair, lifted a cream cheese-lined knife from the table, and said to an imaginary judge, "See this dagger, your honor? My client, this pitiful woman you see slumped afore you, was threatened daily with bodily harm from this lethal weapon. Surely, this court will see fit to award her five million dollars."

Ann laughed and pushed away the knife that veered too close to her face. "I see what you mean," she said. She felt a mix of emotions as she absorbed his announcement: Happiness when she saw her husband's gleeful face.

Next, worry that he might neglect his law practice and jeopardize their income. Then, relief realizing his new pastime could loosen his demand of her attention. Finally, jealousy. She recalled Joel and his leading lady in rehearsal, the two of them staring into each other's eyes.

Fifteen

"How you doing, Ms. Robins?" It was Mr. Baldwin, smiling and removing his Panama hat as he entered the Berkeley Square management office. As always, he was polite as could be, just like all the elderly African-American men and women who used the handing over of their monthly rent check as a chance to leave their Senior Citizen apartment and chat with the friendly staff.

"Just fine, Mr. Baldwin," Ann answered. Although she knew his first name was Ned, she'd never overstep the propriety she had come to understand and respect in the black community. Adults were addressed by their last names, hats always removed upon entering, pleasantries before business, and private lives kept, well, private.

As Ann accepted the check from a wrinkled and freckled hand, she motioned to a chair in the reception area. "Have a seat, Mr. Baldwin," she said. "I'll write you out a receipt. Can I get you a cup of coffee?" She knew he'd enjoy a brief rest after his tiring walk, and an opportunity to use up even more minutes before returning to his widower apartment.

"Don't mind if I do," he answered. He sat slowly down, put his hat on his lap and his cane along side the metal chair. "Cream and two sugars," he said, "if it's no bother."

The year was 1976, seven years after they moved to Berkeley Square from Spring Grove.

Ann hadn't planned on going back to work, but when Jack Blum's offer for the secretarial job came, she couldn't resist. After all, her daughters were 10-1/2 and 12, and hardly in need of a hovering mother. And many days, they stayed after school with the Hyde Park friends they made since transferring to the Jewish day school.

In Ann's mind, the decision to move Audrey and Jessie to private school was forced on her. She had been at a meeting with other Berkeley Square parents who were pushing for a full eight grades in their local school when the principal quashed that idea.

"Sixth grade is it," Mr. Freeman said. He removed a large white handkerchief from his pocket and dramatically wiped his brow, as if to prove his exhaustion from the ongoing struggle. "I told the Board of Education your concerns, but they say they've done enough capitulating by going up to six grades. You know we were only supposed to be K through third grade, and then your children were to transfer to Locke. The Board feels its time to stop allocating funds for our small student population."

The thirty or so parents listened to Freeman's telling of the school's history, but were hardly appeased. "No way are my kids going over there," Marlene Watson said. "Those seventh and eighth graders are too tough, not the element I want my kids to associate with." Every head, male or female, black or white, nodded in agreement.

One of the fathers in the group chimed in, "It was enough for us adults to experiment with integration. We don't need to subject our children to that much social engineering with project kids."

Ann kept quiet. Her liberal conscience was pulling in one direction, and her Jewish mother anxiety the other. In truth, she, too, couldn't see her daughters being among a handful of white children in a school in the middle of public housing. In the end, the Berkeley Square parents had three options: send their 7th graders to Locke, transfer them to private schools, or move. All three were taken by various families, with the Robins choosing Door Number Two.

Although the Robins were separated by their days' activities—Ann with the Bulletin and household responsibilities, and Joel with his law career and acting classes—they were united in parenting decisions. Joel had supported Ann's original choice of keeping their daughters in the Berkeley Square school as long as possible. And he also was behind her in selecting private rather than project for the last years of elementary school.

For their part, Audrey and Jessie didn't protest. "It's okay," Audrey said, "no one in my class is going to Locke. We'll be fine at Jewish Day." And the change went smoothly, with the girls quickly making new friends and enjoying the challenge of a tougher curriculum that included Jewish studies.

Joel's busy life was another factor in Ann's decision to return to work. His law practice kept him occupied during the day. And with his acting lessons, frequent auditions, and occasional local theatre roles at night, she was left with plenty of time on her hands.

She did try to attend every one of Joel's opening nights (the girls, too, if the play's content was appropriate), and clapped wildly when he took his curtain calls. At first, she'd join him at the cast parties. But after watching members of the production act like one big happy (and exclusive) family, she felt an outsider and chose instead to stay home. When he'd return from those parties with no telltale lipstick on his collar, and only the leftover scents of booze and cigarettes, she was glad she had let him have his fun.

Sometimes she'd wonder how he could resist the actresses in his shows. She had felt old and frumpy the time she watched Joel and his latest leading lady in a local theatre company's production of "Picnic." Ann wished the bleached-blonde 20-something playing Madge Owens could've really broken a leg (instead of merely the traditional good luck wish to actors) so Ann could be in the wings ready to capture Hal Carter's heart.

She tried to curb any jealousy and be supportive of his theatre work. She often volunteered to rehearse with him, at home. She'd sit on the living room couch, script in hand, and feed him cues. One time, he was practicing for Arthur Miller's, "All My Sons."

"What the hell did I work for? That's only for you, Chris, the whole shootin' match is for you," Ann said. She had deepened her voice, pretending she was Joe Keller, who knowingly shipped out defective military parts, leading to the deaths of many American soldiers.

This was one of Ann's favorite plays, for it explored family relationships, unrequited love, guilt, and redemption. What more could an actor or playgoer ask for?

"Let me try this line again," Joel had said during their practice session. He was playing the part of Keller's surviving son.

"I want to be sure I get across Chris' love for his father, along with his disappointment." Then, turning to Ann as an imaginary Joe Keller, he emoted, "I know you're no worse than most men but I thought you were better. I never saw you as a man. I saw you as my father."

"Absolutely! You've nailed it," Ann said. She wasn't just stroking his ego, Joel was believable as the heartsick son— his shoulders sagged just enough to convey sadness, and his voice tender, but distraught. Then, they worked through the entire script until he was satisfied he'd have a shot at the part.

Ann thought "All My Sons" was an ironic choice, as Joel's own relationship with his father, Manny, had lately been strained. Because of his busy schedule, and the need to use weekends to catch up on his law practice or his latest show, Joel begged out of the obligatory Sunday night dinners and bridge games.

"You're sure you don't want to go?" she asked him at the first turn down.

"What do you think, sugar?" he said. He waved his hand around the dining room table that bore his worn leather briefcase stuffed with documents, a stack of law books—each too heavy to carry with one hand—and scraps of lined yellow paper that had been written on and balled up.

His parents didn't take his abandonment of them lightly. "Can't you talk to him?" Pearl had asked during one of her weekly phone calls. "We miss y'all so much. The girls are gonna grow up without knowing us."

"Why don't you come here, Mom? I could throw together something for dinner. You'd get to see the girls, and if Joel is available, you'd see your son."

"You know his daddy doesn't like coming into your neighborhood," Pearl said. "I think he's never gotten over your leaving the suburbs for that integrated place."

"I suppose I could take the girls and drive out to Winnetka ourselves," Ann said.

"That's sweet, darling, but if Joel can't make it, well, you understand."

Ann did understand, for she often felt the same longing for Joel; especially when she'd get a call from him at five in the afternoon. "Sugar, it's already too late to come home 'cause I've got a rehearsal at six," he'd say. "I'll grab a bite downtown and go straight to the theatre. Don't wait up for me."

So, with her daughters and husband experiencing new challenges that often kept them away from her, and with the Berkeley Bulletin her only outside activity, Ann was grateful Blum had offered her the job.

She and Jack Blum had become respectful opponents throughout her years in the community that included occasional protests against management. "If I hire you, will you stop rallying against me?" he joked. "No promises," Ann said. But she decided she could be an asset working from the inside.

She found she loved the repartee with Berkeley Square residents, like dear Mr. Baldwin. Even if the office visitor was belligerent—complaining that his kitchen sink was backing up and maintenance hadn't arrived when expected—Ann could use her skills to calm the guy and arrange a quick solution. Blum had made a smart move. As it turned out, Ann didn't become his patsy, but did help smooth over many a tenant-management scuffle.

The camaraderie with the Berkeley Square staff was a bonus, too. Ann was the only white person in the office; everyone had been kind to her from day one, especially Gloria Thomas, the full-time secretary. Gloria could've resented a Jack Blum-hire who never filled out an employment application, who lived in the townhouses rather than the rental buildings, who was white and not African American; but instead, she treated Ann like a pal.

One morning, several months into her job, Ann looked up from her desk to see a very tall, stocky, very dark black man, enter the office. She had noticed him before; how could you not, with his giant size and striking brown eyes that were partially veiled by heavy lids. Bedroom eyes they used to call them.

John Reeves was one of a dozen security guards and maintenance men who came in to pick up their weekly checks. When he entered the office this time, instead of heading towards Gloria, he chose Ann's desk. "Reeves," was the only thing he said to her.

This was odd, even a bit scary, because the other guys who worked for Berkeley Square typically engaged in friendly, teasing banter. But John's one word, plus his enormous frame, gave him a sense of peril, so she quickly sorted through the stack of pay envelopes until her fingers landed on his name that glared through the cellophane panel.

After she removed his check and placed it in his hand, "thanks," was his only response. Instead of grabbing his pay and rushing out, as Ann would've expected from his stoniness, John's large dark fingers curled over hers and held them for a split second. Then, he released her hand, saluted from his military-style cap, smiled, and strolled out the door. She sat motionless as she watched the door close behind him. Her view of him was changing. She wasn't frightened of him after all, but intrigued, and excited—the same sensations she felt when Neal Spencer walked up to her table at the jazz lounge.

Ann's weekly morning office routine started this way: she hung her jacket in the closet, put her tote bag in the empty bottom drawer of her desk, extracted the pen and pencils she would use for the day, and removed two pages from her One-A-Day desk calendar. On this Monday, as soon as Gloria saw the ritual completed, she wheeled her chair up to Ann's desk and said, "Hey, girl, I'm throwing myself a 30th birthday party Friday night. Everyone from the office, and from maintenance and security will be there. Want to come?"

"How sweet," Ann said.

She hesitated because although she fraternized easily with Berkeley Square employees during work hours, she had never partied with them. Perhaps now, she had proved herself black enough to be included in events that involved music, and liquids stronger than coffee.

"Come on," Gloria said, repeating her party invitation. "It'll be fun. Let loose, girl. We'll have music, dancing, liquor."

"Spouses, too?"

Gloria wrinkled her nose and said, "Not unless they're employees. They tend to put a damper on things, sitting around looking bored, 'cause they don't know anybody, opening their mouth only to ask 'when we going home?"

Ann laughed and studied Gloria, who was happily divorced; and with her honey-colored skin, very flat chin-length hair cut in bangs, and a body that rounded in the right places, she attracted flirtations from almost any man who entered the office. A party without Joel, who might fit Gloria's description of the out-of-place husband, would likely be fun. (She imagined Joel felt the same before cast parties when all the spouses left the building and the actors and crew could endlessly replay their performances and cavort without civilians spoiling their time.)

It *would* be fun, she thought, partying with this predominately African-American crowd, her workplace family. It sounded like a place she'd prefer being on her own.

"Friday?" Ann repeated. "Joel does have rehearsal that night, so he wouldn't be able to go in the first place. And I can get one of the neighbor kids to baby-sit. Sure, I'd love to come. Thanks for the invite."

Ann waited until the morning of the party to tell Joel her plans. As she kissed his cheek on his way out the door, she said, "Oh, honey, by the way, I'm going to Gloria's house tonight. She's having a small birthday party for her 30th. And I can get Renee, from across the street to baby-sit."

"Who's Gloria? Who's Renee?"

"The secretary in the office. The Conner girl who goes to DePaul."

"I probably won't be home till midnight."

"I know. So, is it okay? Do you mind if I go?"

"No, go, have fun, sugar. Be sure to get someone to walk you home."

❧

"You came! Atta girl," Gloria said, as she opened the door of her 10th floor Berkeley Square apartment. "I wasn't sure you were going to show." She took Ann's coat and pointed in the direction of the living room. "Make yourself at home. The bar's thataway."

Ann wove her way through the small crowd, greeting other guests with a hug or kiss on the cheek, until she reached the makeshift bar in a corner of the living room. Opposite, near the turntable, John Reeves stood.

He saluted Ann, just like he did in the office, his fingers tipping an imaginary cap. Instead of turning back to his stack of records, he slid a cigarette from a pack tucked in his shirt pocket, lit a match and held the flame until it nearly reached his fingers. He continued to stare at her, smiling like he did when he took his check, when his large fingers wrapped around hers.

She returned his smile, and then sang (softly, though, because she really couldn't carry a tune) with the record spinning on the turntable—it was the O'Jay's R&B hit, "Back Stabbers."

A few minutes after Ann had taken a seat next to the birthday girl, John strolled over. When Gloria saw John approach, she patted Ann's shoulder and stood up. "Gotta circulate," she said. Then, she waved to John and pointed to her empty chair. None of my business, Gloria's shift seemed to say, you two are grown.

"Hi," John said to Ann as he pulled out the chair and sat down. "Can I buy you a drink?"

Ann laughed; it was an open bar, drinks were free. "JB and water," she said. She recalled the liquor's warm rush when she first met Neal Spencer, the saxophonist, in the Hideaway Bar.

"Beautiful," John said, and left the table to fetch their drinks.

Ann watched as he swayed towards the bar snapping his fingers to the music. What was it about him that fascinated her so? His size? His sexiness? Or was it simply that he seemed taken with her—a reaction she found hard to resist.

When John returned with their drinks, he placed each on a paper napkin decorated with balloons and said, "You're quite the big shot lady around here, aren't you?"

She took a sip and sat straight up in her chair. So he speaks, not so menacing after all—more the gentle giant type. "Well, if you mean my job at the Bulletin," she said, "and the committees I used to be on, and now my office job, I guess people know who I am. But I'd hardly call myself a big shot."

"I meant that as a compliment," he said. He put his catcher's mitt hand on hers. "I see the way you are around here. You're not stuck-up like some of the other rich white folk who live in the townhouses."

"Thanks, I guess."

"How 'bout a dance?"

The top of her head barely reached John's chest, and when he pulled her close, her staccato heartbeats nearly drowned out the record.

"You move pretty good for a white gal," he said laughing.

Was she moving? Ann didn't believe any of her limbs were voluntarily going anywhere; they just seemed to be guided along by John's vibrations.

After they returned to their table, he questioned her as if *he* were the Bulletin reporter and she a fascinating subject. Over the loud music and chatter, she blabbed on, until he stopped her with, "It's noisy in here. Want to take a walk? Then I can tell you *my* life story."

"Okay," she answered. Perhaps she should've hesitated, for she knew John had his sights set on her. But she was sure she could handle a walk in the cool night air and a friendly conversation with this security guard. If more temptations arose, she'd figure out how to handle them.

"We're gonna catch some air," John said to Gloria as he helped Ann on with her coat. Gloria waved them good-bye and returned to her party. One or two of the other guests looked up to watch the pair leave; and then, without a word or obvious reaction, returned to their drinks, conversations, or dancing.

Sixteen

At first, Ann pinned the start of their affair to Gloria's party, and when they left to walk through the dusky and quiet grounds of Berkeley Square. But the more she thought about it, she realized its seeds were planted earlier, in the management office, when John first touched her hand and smiled at her.

But she preferred to recall the details of their evening stroll. "Now, isn't this better?" John had said as they exited Gloria's building, "just the two of us?" His voice was deep and smooth, and reminded Ann of the sexy soul singer Barry White, a comparison surely helping John's cause.

"Let's go past my house first," Ann said. "If all looks quiet, I can stay out for a few minutes longer." Not only was Ann's house dark and still, with only the porch light illuminating the front step, but the entire square of townhouses was closed up and pin-pointed with light in the same way. In the courtyard, the wrought iron lampposts were lit, and with their tall curved necks, appeared to be a flock of black flamingoes guarding the silent playground.

"Okay," Ann said. "Looks peaceful. Now, you promised to tell me your life story." They moved away from her house and headed out across the street towards the other end of the complex.

"Raised in Georgia, moved to Indiana so my daddy could get work, then my folks split and I came to Chicago with my momma. High school, two years in the Army, and a few odd jobs until I settled here. My lucky day," he said, smiling down at her. Ann noted he left out his marriage and two children, but she didn't correct him.

As they passed the swimming pool, where the water rippled slightly in the evening breeze, John reached into his pocket and pulled out a ring of keys. Alarmed, Ann said, "No, no midnight swims."

John laughed. "See those lounge chairs over there, with nary a soul sitting in them? Let's take two of them and continue our conversation seaside."

It was a nice touch. As Ann relaxed into the webbed chair, lulled by the sound of John's voice and the pool's soft babbling, she imagined she was on some tropical isle. Even the dark-skinned man in the next chair, who reached for her hand and held onto it while they talked, helped set the scene for an exotic vacation away from Ann's real life. (Just to be sure no one from nearby buildings could see; she lowered their clasped hands between the two chairs. Now they were submerged below the webs.)

She allowed John to keep her hand during the hour on the poolside lounges. Every so often, he'd squeeze it. Despite his size, she felt no pain from this gesture, just warmth that traveled throughout her body. As they rose from the chairs, she shook her hand loose from his. Then they walked, arms swinging from their sides, to Ann's house. There was no goodnight kiss that first evening at her front door, but no doubt the missed kiss would come later.

❧

After that first evening, they talked on the phone daily. She'd find a spot in the house where she was certain her daughters were out of earshot. John would call only during the day, never at night in case Joel was at home. And within two weeks, they had a schedule: On Thursdays, when Betty would be in the house to welcome the girls home from school, Ann would meet John in Gloria's apartment. (He had made the request, and if Gloria knew the identity of his playmate, she never let on. And despite the two women's friendship, neither one brought up the topic at the office.)

When Ann arrived at the apartment, John would be there to let her in. The first time she met him there; she took a closer look at the place, because at the party, guests and decorations had obscured much of it. The walls held family portraits and photographs of icons like Martin Luther King, Jr., and the Kennedy brothers. A small porcelain statue of the Virgin Mary, which Ann turned around to face the windows, sat on a coffee table.

In their rendezvous after that, the religious figure always faced that way, a gift from John.

When she asked about his placement of the icon, he explained, "I know you're Jewish and figured you'd rather not see her." Sweet, but the real reason was, she didn't want any religious symbol—Jewish or Catholic—to spy on the goings on between her and John.

They established a routine: he'd put a record on the turntable, and place a package of Kools next to an ashtray—for before and after. She'd find him humming, arms outstretched to seal her in the minute he locked the door behind her. Their lovemaking was passionate, tender, and different from her experiences with Larry Bennett or Neal Spencer. With those two, Ann knew she was one of several women they enticed. It was a game to them, no strings attached, just afternoon delights that each party could walk away from with no harm done.

In John, she had a lover who made her feel as if she was the smartest, most beautiful, sexiest woman in the world. "Hmm," he would murmur as his large, dark hands explored her body.

"Gorgeous, simply gorgeous." The padding around her stomach, the flesh that jiggled under her upper arms, the thighs that would meet and glide against each other on hot summer days? Every physical failing that might be criticized by white, Jewish husbands, turned out to be worshipped by John.

And although the sex was marvelous, it was his friendship Ann treasured. (Okay, maybe a draw.) Although seemingly opposites in every way, they talked easily about their childhoods, jobs, children (spouses were mentioned, but never vilified), and current events. He was never bored with their conversations, and she found his take on things perceptive for someone with only a high school education and who earned a modest wage. Street smarts, she decided, that's what John had, and that's what she admired in him.

As the affair continued into its third month, they became bolder. Sometimes, she'd catch up to him as he made his rounds and they'd stroll through Berkeley Square together—never holding hands—just talking and laughing at a shared joke.

Occasionally, he'd show up at one of the neighborhood events, take a seat next to her, and brush against her in a way that made Ann lose her train of thought. When she spoke at these meetings, she'd feel his eyes on her; and when she turned to face him, he'd be grinning, like a proud parent whose kid just won the spelling bee.

If anyone suspected anything, it never made its way to Ann's ears. In a community like Berkeley Square—tightly knit and isolated—Ann knew of other unorthodox pairs. A townhouse couple had an open marriage, where each partner had a special friend unhidden from one another, or their neighbors. When one of the married women in another townhouse brought her young boyfriend to a 4th of July picnic on an afternoon her older husband was at work, eyebrows were raised but not a word spoken. And of course, there were the flings that started on the music theatre's stage and continued after the curtain had fallen. In all of these examples, and likely more that were part of Berkeley Square's version of the swinging '70s, discretion and tolerance were watchwords.

*

Who knows how long it would have lasted if John hadn't stepped over the line? One night, as Ann's family was finishing dinner (Joel happened to be on time for this meal), the telephone rang. She picked up the receiver and heard, "Hey, baby, I've been thinking about you." It was John, obviously drunk. She was aware he liked his scotch, for he had told her of nights out with his pals when one of them had snatched away his car keys and ordered him to the passenger seat.

"You don't drive drunk?" Ann had asked alarmed, after hearing this story. They had never driven together, but she worried about his being pulled over by police, losing his job, and the resulting mess somehow spilling over into her life.

And then there was the time he had been at a bar and nearly gotten into a fight with a guy two stools over. He had told her the whole incident, with John taking the parts of the three people involved: "'So, you going home with me or not?'" John said. He was deepening his voice to imitate the tough guy speaking to the woman seated between them.

"'Don't think I will,'" John said. This in a higher voice, now the gal in the tale.

Then he returned to the villain, "'Listen you bitch, I've been buying you drinks all night, and now you're playing games.'"

"That's when I stepped in," John said. He was himself again, "Sir, you don't want to be speaking to a lady in that tone of voice."

Then he laughed and sheepishly said to Ann, "Course at the time, I had had a few and didn't notice his police revolver sitting in a side holster." Ann didn't join in his merriment. It was hard to picture this different side of John, one who grew emboldened by liquor.

"Then the guy pivots, turns just enough to show me his piece. 'Cool man, cool,' I tell him, and then I sat my black ass down." He smiled at Ann, likely expecting a laugh from her; but none came.

Those incidents happened in John's world and not Ann's; the boozy phone call to her house in the evening was the first time their worlds collided. "Oh, hi," she said to him. She was pretending it was someone innocuous. "Sorry I didn't get around to that. Can I talk to you about it tomorrow?" Then she quickly hung up before Joel could ask about the person on the other end of the line.

The next day when she saw John patrolling the grounds, before she could protest his behavior, he jumped in, "Oh, baby, I'm so sorry. It'll never happen again. I had a few too many..."

"You scared me, John, you scared me," she said, tears filling her eyes. "I couldn't sleep all night. I can't do this anymore. It's too dangerous." And she meant it. John's drunken call had startled her. What in the world had she been thinking? How did she allow lust to trash her judgment? What if Joel or her daughters found out? It was likely they wouldn't have the same live-and-let-live attitude of others in the community.

She felt as if someone had thrown a bucket of water in her face and splashed her awake. She tried to understand how she had let the affair go so far. Was she acting out of loneliness? Or anger at a husband who had lately abandoned her for other pursuits? Maybe she was trying to loosen the binds of motherhood and its responsibilities.

True, John had stirred up a desired side of Ann—the uninhibited, sensuous Ann; the one she found difficult to rouse in her marriage. No matter, the affair was finished.

For a few days after she ended it, John would approach her outside the office and beg her to change her mind. But she'd put a hand up to stop him. When the telephone rang at home, Ann would let the answering machine pick up. If there were a few minutes of dead tape, she knew it was John leaving his pathetic silent message. She never returned his calls. She stood firm, for she could no longer trust him. No matter what they had had together, it was no longer worth the risk.

Finally, he stopped trying. Now, whenever they saw each other in the complex, she'd only wave. John's wide hand would stay in the air an extra beat and it would take a few seconds for his eyes to leave her face. Then, they'd both walk away, in opposite directions.

Seventeen

Ann rose from the living room couch and walked behind it to reach the sliding glass doors at the back of the house. She tugged on the handles, pulled the door to the right, and stepped out onto the small balcony. Now she could look below to their compact, fenced-in yard. Absent of flowers, the rectangle looked barren, while on the other side of the fence, where Diane Young once lived, the new neighbor's garden was alive and thriving.

A burst of wildflowers: Black-eyed Susans, Purple Coneflowers, Columbines, Blue Chicories, and Blanket Flowers leaped from the yard's corners. Cassandra Moore had named each and every flower for Ann. Like a proud parent showing off her offspring, she had lightly tapped a petal, and then stepped back to receive Ann's admiration.

Ann, anxious to be a good neighbor but a dunce when to came to flora, was determined to commit each label to memory, so she repeated them back to Cassandra. She won a nod with each correct answer. But now, up on the balcony, Ann wasn't sure she hadn't gotten them mixed up.

Cassandra was on her knees, digging in the earth, and she waved back when Ann called out, "Hi, Cassandra. Garden looks gorgeous."

"Thanks." Cassandra stood up from her kneeling position and glanced over the fence into Ann's yard. Her expression was glum. "If you ever need a hand, just let me know. I'd be happy to help."

Ann looked once again at her fallow ground. She shook her head. "Thanks, but I think we'll just leave it as it is."

"Suit yourself," Cassandra said. Then she knelt down and returned to tending her own space.

Cassandra was nice enough, but she wasn't Diane, who left Berkeley Square a year earlier to move to a western suburb.

On the day Diane's moving truck had idled on the street, she and Ann stood on the sidewalk between their two houses. With tears in their eyes, they hugged and promised to keep in touch.

And at the same time in the courtyard, likely without tears but with similar sincerity, Audrey and Jessie and Diane's daughters played out a miniature version of their mothers' farewells.

Diane would be terribly missed, as she was the one person to whom Ann had confided her affairs. (She left out the juicy details of actual lovemaking, as Ann preferred those to remain private.) She knew her secrets would be safe with Diane, and best of all, there'd be no judgment.

All she got after revealing the tryst and tulip incident was, "So that's where you were. Interesting. Glad you got back okay." And when Ann told her about John's phone call to her house, Diane merely said, "That was a close call." No attempt to lay guilt feelings on Ann's already battered conscience.

Perhaps Diane was uncritical because she had also been privy to Ann's confession of loneliness. At first, during their front stoop conversations, Diane tried to offer Joel's side, "He's just building his career. Once he thinks he's in solid, you'll get to see more of him. I'm sure of it." She wrapped her arm around Ann, which encouraged her to lower her head on Diane's shoulder and wipe tears away with her sleeve.

But later, when Ann grumbled about Joel's absences growing more frequent and lengthier, Diane became less sympathetic to him. "That's a kicker, with him doing all that complaining about your volunteer stuff. Now he's doing you one better. Men." Diane's view of the opposite sex may have emanated from her own marriage, which had ended in divorce before she moved to Berkeley Square. Although she dated occasionally, it seemed she preferred the single life.

With Leah in Paris, and with her oft-spoken disdain for anything improper, Ann was grateful she had Diane as a sympathetic listener. In appearance, she was almost the opposite of Ann. Diane was tall, her skin tanned from the hours spent outdoors gardening, and her hair was jet black and curly—which she kept cut short so she could knit a hand through it to serve as touch-up. Her only makeup was a pale lipstick, a hint of rouge, and a quick sweep of mascara, mostly reserved for special occasions.

Ann, on the other hand, at 39, was insecure about her appearance. She continued to use henna to cover any encroaching gray; never left the house without full makeup (as preached by Sylvia), wore a girdle to restrain her tummy, and never ever wore shoes without some sort of a heel. She often wished she could be more like her neighbor.

Many others, besides Diane, had already left Berkeley Square and Ann felt their loss as well. Rev. Rowland and the Pontarellis moved out of state about the same year. Barbara Madden went to an apartment downtown and Marlene Watson moved to a southern suburb. They all made vows to keep in touch, and Ann was doing her best to comply.

From her spot on the balcony, Ann looked across the street and studied the shopping center. The space that once housed a Jewel grocery store held a large "For Rent" sign on its front window. The door was padlocked. The drycleaner was still there. A store that sold home furnishings and African Art had taken over a long-vacant space. Security screens covered the other store windows in the center, or held signs similar to the one pasted on the Jewel.

Deserted real estate wasn't the only change. Ann's feelings about Berkeley Square had shifted as well. When Rev. Rowland left, she lost her taste for the Berkeley Bulletin so she relinquished her post to the clergyman who took over church and community center responsibilities.

With the end of the Viet Nam war in 1973, and Michael Bilandic filling Mayor Daley shoes in 1977 (the longtime mayor had been felled by a heart attack in 1976), there seemed to be less reason for neighborhood activists to get riled up. Organizations and committee meetings dried up, too.

Security issues remained: several cars had been broken into, a few apartments burglarized, and worse of all, a nurse returning home late from nearby Beth Israel had been murdered on the steps of the community center. That horrific crime (front page of the Berkeley Bulletin with a headline in bold caps) brought out an angry crowd and a confrontation with Blum. With Ann's urging—working from the inside—management added extra patrols, installed more lighting, and trimmed landscaping to prevent lurking.

Although Ann didn't know the victim, the killing had devastated her (and most of the community). She made sure front and back doors and windows were locked at bedtime and forbade her daughters to be out after dark. Her old childhood fears resurfaced, and Ann found herself looking over her shoulder whenever she walked alone.

One evening, not long after the security meeting, Joel stood in the kitchen and peered out the windows that overlooked the courtyard. "I think it's time we looked for someplace else to live," he said. Ann joined him and linked one arm through his, to gain partnership and comfort.

The playground was empty of children and the benches free of adults. Every so often, a lone figure would appear out of the darkness and walk a diagonal line from one end of the courtyard to the other. Sometimes, it was a pair, or trio of men. When the lamplights illuminated their faces, they learned the people walking by weren't neighbors, but strangers trespassing through the property.

"If we wait much longer, we might have a tough time selling," Joel said. He drew Ann's arm closer to him, perhaps trying to soothe and convince her. "Now, while there's still a good market for the houses, we should start looking around."

"So much has changed," she said. She returned her husband's squeeze, thinking: Me.

If they could sell their Berkeley Square townhouse at its market value of $75,000, and with savings accumulated by Joel's high wages and Ann's small salary, they would have enough funds to purchase a place in a good, safe neighborhood somewhere on the north side.

There'd been some discussion over where exactly to live next. It would be the city, of course; a return to the suburbs had never been considered. Ann and Joel agreed it had to be near a top quality Chicago Public School. This was especially important to Ann; for although Audrey and Jessie had spent a year in the private Jewish school, she was determined they would return to public education as soon as possible.

Money was another issue for choosing public over private. Although Joel was doing well at his firm, Ann wondered how long her husband could continue to keep up his workload and his extra curricular activities. Every time she saw him burning the midnight oil to prepare for a case, or rise before dawn to rehearse his lines, she worried one of those pursuits would come to an end. For her family's sake, she hoped he would keep his job.

A more important reason for steering their daughters to public school was gleaned from their Berkeley Square experience. The last thing Ann wanted was to return Audrey and

Jessie to a privileged world where every child was similar in religion, income, or race—like Spring Grove. She knew a north side public school couldn't hold a match to Berkeley Square's diversity, but it certainly would be closer to it than a private school.

Her daughters were skeptical. "We won't know anyone in a new school," Audrey said when she first learned of the decision to move. "Why can't we stay until I graduate eighth grade?"

"What about me?" Jessie asked. "Why not stay here two more years so I get a chance to graduate with *my* class?"

Ann and Joel looked at each other, and for a moment considered their daughters' reasoned appeals. But then she remembered the crimes, the murder. "I'm sorry girls," she said. "We know this won't be easy for you, but it's time to go. But, the way you two make friends, you'll feel at home in your new school before you know it." Her daughters remained slumped on the sofa cushions, their arms crossed in front of them, turned down mouths on each beautiful, heart-shaped face.

As to the house itself, Joel fixed on a condominium with a Gold Coast address. "Let's live it up," he said to Ann. They were trailing a fur coated real estate broker as she pointed out an apartment's marble bathrooms; and Joel was using his persuasive litigator technique to win his point with Ann.

"Look at this, sugar," he said as his arm swept past the built-in shower with its pebbled glass door. The stall, with its protective glass booth, was in the His master bath. "What's money for, if we can't enjoy it?"

In the Hers bathroom, a whirlpool tub sat wedged into one corner of the white ceramic-tiled room. She imagined soaking in lavender-scented water, being drummed by ferocious jets, and then cleansed.

Once they decided on the fancy condo (Ann figured she could get used to the luxury), she took care of Berkeley Square business. She gave notice to Jack Blum. "Why not keep your job and commute?" he asked.

"I'd rather find work closer to home and be available for my kids," she lied. An important reason was she wanted distance from John Reeves. Although a whole year had passed without any contact, she wanted to put behind her that whole episode. Then, Blum offered to hire her as a freelance writer who would compile newsletters for six of his other properties.

"You can do the job from home," he said.

"Perfect," she agreed.

Gloria Thomas took the news stoically, as if she knew Ann would eventually join the exodus of Berkeley Square's white population. "Keep in touch," Gloria ordered.

"Of course," Ann said. But she knew this friendship, spawned on the job and muddied with the secret affair, would likely not survive the move.

Eighteen

Ann had a nightmare, one that reappeared several times a year, ever since her two daughters were born. She woke and threw off the covers; anxious to convince herself none of it was true. Audrey and Jessie had not been lost in a forest, she needn't search for them, nor wail out their names with her heart pounding louder with each futile step.

It was one of those nightmares where she had to be persuaded all the terrifying goings-on were real. "Please let me be asleep," she prayed. As if to taunt, a smarmy voiceover told her, "Sorry, this is really happening. Deal with it."

But it hadn't been real after all. Perhaps her confusion was tied to her surroundings.

She looked around and confirmed, yes, she was still in her high-rise condominium, not Berkeley Square, which they had left four years ago. She was in the spacious bedroom in a king-size bed with Joel's sleeping body next to her. There was the double row of drapes blocking out morning light. (She wished the window could've been left bare to grab the stunning lake view, but Joel insisted he needed his sleep and demanded absolute darkness.)

In her real world, Audrey and Jessie should be tucked into bunk beds just down the hall. To be certain, Ann hopped off the deep mattress, and padded over carpeted and parquet floors to the other end of the apartment. She quietly pushed open the door to the girls' bedroom and nearly sobbed at the happy sight of her children fast asleep under down comforters.

Wide-awake now, she went to the kitchen whose windows looked down 34 floors. She took a seat and let her gaze stretch towards the placid waters of Lake Michigan. As she sipped the milk that might lull her back to sleep, Ann tried to figure out what had triggered the nightmare. This was the one part of the experience she actually enjoyed. She'd review the previous day and could usually find something innocuous that had set off the dream.

Perhaps a stranger's name, that was the same as a long unheard-from friend, would appear in the newspaper. Then that very night, the real person would emerge in the dream to engage her once again. Sometimes, it only took a glance at someone on the street with the same features of a person known to her. Then bingo, up would pop the acquaintance the moment Ann's head hit the pillow.

This nightmare's impetus was a snap to figure out. The girls in danger? Of course, it was yesterday's phone call from the high school principal. "Mrs. Robins?" he had said. "This is Marshall Stein. I'd like you and your husband to come to school this week to discuss some trouble your daughters have gotten themselves into."

When the call came, she had been in her office—actually a third bedroom where Ann could work on Blum's newsletters without having to clear off a day's work from the dining room table. The room was small, it's doubtful a bedroom set could've squeezed into the narrow space. It was perfect, though, as it allowed Ann to close the door and be left undisturbed to write, polish, and produce her pages. She knew she wasn't creating great literary works, for the subject matter was management's latest directive or improvement. But she persuaded Blum to allow her to write features on residents and stories of neighborhood history; and it was these pieces that helped feed Ann's creative juices. Audrey and Jessie had been game to give her that third bedroom and share one that held a bunk bed, with each girl taking turns on the safer bottom, or more exciting top.

In fact, her daughters seemed to prefer the enforced togetherness, because since the move, they appeared closer than ever. If she left her office door ajar, she could hear them tossing dialogue or song lyrics back and forth. When the sounds were too intriguing to ignore, Ann would stand outside their door to watch. She could stare at her daughters forever: Audrey with her red hair similar to her own, brown eyes as large as the buttons on her pea coat topped by thick brows, and a perfect nose and mouth. Audrey was on the short side, similar to her mother, but with a small waist and no body fat to speak of.

Jessie favored her father. She had his brown hair, and with her long, slim legs, was taller than her older sister. Her hazel eyes were big, too, but her brows were tamed—perfect crescents. And in Ann's view, her nose and mouth were just like Audrey's, perfect. Whenever she watched her talented daughters, she'd feel guilty for removing them from the fertile soil of Berkeley Square. Perhaps she could find a theatre school for teens? Until then, the Robins girls would have to confine their creativity to the walls of their room.

Thankfully, Audrey and Jessie were not the type to complain and they had adjusted to their new grammar school as well as to their sleeping arrangements. She recalled their first day at Sandburg Elementary when Ann had escorted the girls to school, holding each one's hand (more for her anxiety than theirs) until they reached the wrought iron fence surrounding the playground. Then, Audrey first, followed by Jessie, released their mother's hands, looked straight ahead and marched through the gate in between clusters of girls and boys, until they reached the school's double doors.

Ann envied her daughters' courage and willingness to jump in. She remembered her own fish-out-of-water feelings; that is until she found Berkeley Square. She hoped the girls wouldn't have to wait until adulthood to feel at home in the world.

❧

As she sipped her milk in her high-rise kitchen, Ann replayed a long-distance conversation with Leah soon after they settled in. "How are the girls doing in their new school?" Leah had asked.

"Okay, I guess," Ann said. "It was a little intimidating at first; big school, most of the kids from well-off families. Some even dropped off by chauffeurs. Almost all white; the only African-American students are children of diplomats who live in the area. And they're about as similar to the black kids at Berkeley Square as, as…"

Before Ann could come up with an apt comparison, Leah interrupted, "Listen Ann, not every place can match your Berkeley Square paradise." Her voice sounded annoyed. Even over the oceans apart, Ann could pick up the tone.

"You know you're a snob in your own way," Leah said. "What would be so terrible if your daughters wound up with Jewish friends whose fathers happened to be lawyers?"

"I suppose you're right." Ann was trying not to antagonize her old friend whose husband was a lawyer, and who herself was president of her synagogue in Paris.

"You talk all tolerant and progressive now," Leah said, "wanting your daughters to mingle with the downtrodden. But how would you feel if Audrey or Jessie announced they were dating a Gentile or a black? I don't think you'd be so open-minded."

Ann paused for a moment before answering. "I'd like to think I'd be perfectly fine with whomever they bring home."

"We'll see, we'll see," Leah said. Then she hung up.

❧

Despite its size and lack of true diversity, Ann's daughters' years at Sandburg Elementary went smoothly, and their grades were good enough to win them both spots at Rhode Tech. While their parents were pleased—the high school was as well regarded as any of the city's private institutions, but without their eye-popping tuition—Audrey and Jessie were hesitant.

"You know it used to be all boys," Audrey had said.

"Slide rules, calculators, engineering," Jessie said. "Yuk."

"And it's gigantic!" they chorused.

"It's been coed for years, Ann countered. "I'm sure they have courses you'd enjoy."

Joel was flipping through the school's brochure and said, "See, they've got an orchestra." He was looking at Audrey who had been taking piano lessons since she was six with Mr. Clifton, a young African-American man who came to their house weekly. Audrey never had to be pressured to practice. It was more like, "Enough already," and then either Ann or Joel would threaten to close the cover over Audrey's small fingers poised on the keys. (Jessie had been offered lessons, too, but after a few, opted to leave that talent to her sister.)

"And look, Jessie," Joel had said, "They've got an impressive art department."

"Let's see," Jessie said. In the way her eyes brightened, and her down-turned mouth changed to a smile, you could see she had been won over.

And once they enrolled, both girls quickly made friends and did indeed flourish in the orchestra and art studies. Ann was pleased to see that the variety of friends visiting their apartment were from blue-collar families.

Audrey was first to get a boyfriend, an adorable tawny-skinned kid (Latino? Ann didn't ask.). Jessie chose the Jewish star of the football team. Tall, good-looking, a pick that would've pleased Leah, but surprised Ann. Perhaps she shouldn't have been surprised, because Jessie seemed to understand her date could elevate her in schoolmates' eyes. Ann decided her younger daughter was the practical one, while her older one, the musician, marched to her own drummer.

Her daughters' success at Rhode made the principal's phone call especially puzzling. When she asked them why she and Joel were being called to the school, the girls looked at each other, shrugged their shoulders and said in harmony, "no clue." Instead of pressing them further, she decided to wait for the meeting, which was scheduled for the very next day.

As if to prove their daughters were part of a loving family, Ann and Joel held hands as they sat in chairs facing the principal's desk. Audrey and Jessie were seated against one wall, under a row of paintings depicting Rhode High School principals over past decades. Male, white, plain-faced, all looking somberly down at the pair of teenage rebels staring at their loafers.

"I'm sure you are aware of our time-honored traditions here at Rhode," Principal Stein said. Ann and Joel weren't, but they nodded in unison. "Well, your daughters [he tilted his head in their direction] have managed to taint those traditions with their unfortunate production."

Production? What production? Audrey played the cello in the school orchestra and Jessie took drawing classes, but as far as Ann knew, those were their only creative endeavors at this academically tough school.

"Production? You mean like a play?" Joel asked. He looked first at the principal and then his daughters.

Stein placed his palms on his desk, giving himself a small boost to exit his chair. He moved to the front of the desk, halfway sitting on it, which brought him closer to the puzzled couple. This seemed to be a well-practiced gesture meant to relax and disarm.

"Well, yes, like a play," Stein said. "But instead of getting involved with the school's drama club, which would've been the natural thing to do, wouldn't you agree?" He paused here, likely waiting for the parents to take his side. Once he saw those two well-coiffed heads nodding in agreement, he continued, "Your children started their own theatre group. The Off-Addison Players I believe they called it. Is that right, girls?" he asked, arms folded, turning to the defendants.

Without looking up, two heads of hair nodded simultaneously. Ann hid her smile with a Kleenex she held in her fist supposedly poised to catch tears of distress. So her daughters had decided to move from the back of the line behind Mr. Snow to the front of their new production company? Well, bully for them!

Joel, too, was silenced, likely by admiration rather than anger—praising his girls for taking after their daddy. Theatre must be in the blood.

"Your children are very persuasive Mr. and Mrs. Robins. Are you aware of that?" Stein asked. Then, he picked up a sheet of paper that lay on his desk and flashed it in front of the parents. "This is a list of students they recruited. Let's see." He used one finger to hold the paper and the other to track the names. "Bernstein, McCarthy, Washington, Yee." He continued until he came to the end. (Multicultural, Ann noted.) "Twelve, an even dozen."

Stein replaced the paper on his desk and tossed a look at the creative team who had raised their heads. Now, he looked hard at Ann and Joel. "Have you heard of our Spirit Boosters, Pom-pom girls, majorettes? All outstanding examples of wholesome, enthusiastic, athletic young women who support our football and basketball teams with their energetic routines."

Now Audrey and Jessie were sitting fully upright in their chairs, beaming as if they expected a Tony rather than suspensions.

"Their production?" Ann prompted. "What was it?"

"Audrey, Jessie, why don't you tell your parents about the first, and final, performance of the Off-Addison Players?"

That was the only cue they needed. They leapt up and pushed their chairs out of the way. Audrey opened, "You know the play 'West Side Story?'" She was keyed up, as if she was presenting to a pair of angels considering backing her play.

Jessie jumped in, "Well in our show, instead of Sharks and Jets, we had Spirit Boozers and Pom-pom Punks."

"Did you write that?" Joel asked, appearing to be a fan trying to score tickets.

"With original book and music!" Audrey added.

"Don't forget the costumes," Stein prompted. He sounded more like a critic than admirer. "Or the orgy scene."

Both parents were on their feet. "Orgy!" they chorused.

"Not a real one," Jessie said. She used a downward stroke of her hand to signal her parents' return to their seats. "Simulated."

Ann and Joel obeyed and settled back down. "And it was more of a love fest than an orgy," Audrey explained. She glared at Stein. "By the final act, all the actors had stripped off their gang clothing, which had been ripped to shreds in the earlier fight scene…"

"Simulated." Jessie said. "Ketchup, not real blood."

"And then, in flesh-colored leotards, engaged in a chorus line of…"

"Do you get the picture?" Stein interrupted. He folded his arms across his chest, probably disgusted at these parents who were acting like groupies rather than punishers.

"And the songs?" Joel asked. Was he still hoping for front row center?

"Perhaps your daughters can give you a private performance back at home, during the two weeks they'll be barred from school," Stein said.

Ann raised her hand. "One question. Who was the audience?"

"Several hundred students who gathered in the lunchroom to witness the show," Stein said.

"We got a standing ovation and several curtain calls," Jessie said. She was beaming as if she could still hear the applause echoing off the institutional walls.

Ann and Joel each took a daughter by the hand. "We'll handle this," Joel said. "Girls, apologize to Principal Stein."

"We're sorry," they said, "we were only trying to.." But their parents pulled them out of the office, escorted them out of the building, and stuffed them into their father's Saab.

On the way home, both Ann and Joel laughed until tears ran down their cheeks as both girls sang for them the entire hysterical score.

"That was something else," Joel said to Ann that night in bed.

"Something else," Ann agreed. This was a good feeling, the two of them united as parents, parents of delightfully talented offspring who likely skimmed some of Joel's theatrical talent and Ann's organizational skills. Whatever ill feelings Ann had towards Joel were evaporating as she realized his genes were an essential part of their daughters' makeup. Without Joel, no Audrey, no Jessie.

"Our daughters' bravery, their talent, their audacity, they've given me the courage to finally make a decision," he said.

Ann bolted upright.

"I'm going to ask for a leave of absence and see if I can make it as an actor."

Was this another nightmare?

Joel related the scene that played out in his law office. "Without pay, of course," Mr. Greenberg had said when Joel made the request. "Take three months, get it out of your system." Then, Greenberg rose from his chair, clamped a hand on Joel's shoulder and escorted him to the door. "If it was any other lawyer, he'd be out on his ass. But you've been a valuable asset to the firm, Joel, so I'm giving you some leeway. But you realize we can't carry you when you're not giving us billable hours. Your salary stops the minute you turn off the clock."

Ann at first felt dizzy when she heard this dialogue, but chose to remain supportive of Joel's decision. Three months turned to six, though, and that's when Ann was really grateful to Jack Blum. The freelance work helped, but their daughters' college funds were in danger of being tapped to pay the hefty monthly mortgage, assessment, and parking fees.

"No, no, I'm not asking my parents," Joel said when Ann made the suggestion after showing him their checking account with its rows of declining figures. He hadn't yet told Manny and Pearl about drama school, or his investment of time and money into lessons, head shots, vocal coaches. (That Southern accent could be problematic. Most of the time, Joel successfully kept it hidden. But every so often, when his emotions soared or plunged, it crept back in.). So news about his leave of absence would surely send his parents 'round the bend.

They were seated at the dining room table with the checkbook, a calculator Ann had taken from her office, and a stack of credit card and utility bills that were teetering on overdue. "I'm sorry, sugar," he said, placing a hand on her arm. "But I feel so close to it. I need you to believe in me. To stand by me; give me a few more months. Trust me."

Then, his tone changed. "Besides, I've had all the responsibility for providing for this family, for this luxury." He used his right arm to sweep past the lake view, the living room/dining room combination that could fit fifty. "Maybe it's y'all's turn to help out. Get a regular job, instead of those piddling newsletters you write."

Rather than being jabbed by this speech, Ann could see his point of view. It must've been overwhelming at times, being responsible for a family of four, with children who were surely college bound. Always the breadwinner, never the spouse who was free to volunteer, or who believed a freelance job was sharing the load. (In fact, she had too much time on her hands for it once permitted her to get into trouble. Did he deserve that, too?)

And maybe Joel was right about his chances; he certainly looked handsome enough to be cast in something important. At 44, just a fine paintbrush of grey flattered his temples and his hazel eyes were prettier, now that they could be seen through contact lenses rather than eyeglasses; and his acting was pretty good, too.

Sometimes, in the middle of the night, when his footsteps in the living room carried through the walls to their bedroom, she'd awaken and creep to the entry hall where she could watch him unseen.

The bright stars in the evening sky, which could be viewed through the nearly floor-to-ceiling windows, illuminated the dark room. And Joel had switched on a floor lamp, twisting its shade towards him to serve as spotlight.

Method acting, he had explained. He was to reach back into his childhood, his adolescence, young adulthood, and find experiences that brought him pleasure, or pain, or fright, or whatever emotion the part called for. Once, when she was especially moved by his rendition, she stepped out from her hiding place, and applauded. "Where did that come from?" she asked. "You were marvelous. I was almost in tears."

He smiled, put his right hand across his waist, and bowed. "Thank you, thank you," he said. Then, out of the character and back to Joel, "We're doing 'Diary of Anne Frank.' I'm playing the father Otto. So I thought back to the time we had to leave Charleston, when I had to say goodbye to my friends, to some kin I used to play with, to the hound I had to leave behind."

"Why couldn't you have taken the dog?" Ann asked. She imagined a beanpole Joel, on bended knee, petting the head of a sad-eyed animal. Now, tears really did flow.

She wouldn't be surprised if that very night, a boy would enter her dreams. He would have the same features of Audrey and Jessie, but it would no doubt be a boy. He'd be right beside her at one point in the dream, and then suddenly, gone! She'd search for the boy, but because she didn't know his name, would find the quest impossible. But maybe, because she thought out the plot ahead of time, the nightmare wouldn't happen after all.

Nineteen

She saw it the moment she entered the office. A piece of paper was lying on top of her red Selectric.

The desk where her typewriter stood faced a large window that looked west to the city, rather than east to the lake. Beyond the glitz of Michigan Avenue's boutiques, the scene turned grittier as it stretched farther and farther away. Highrises first, a few green spaces mixed in, some retail, like 24-hour currency exchanges and liquor stores, and then in the distance, the hodge-podge of dull brown buildings that made up the Cabrini Green public housing complex.

The paper lying on Ann's typewriter must've come from one of the open reams of 8-1/2-x-11 Letter White that were stacked on shelves to one side of her desk. Her office was so narrow, that all it took was a roll of her chair to the right to pluck paper, pen, or pencil from the supplies she had neatly arranged according to frequency of use.

A black, fine point, Papermate pen was on the typewriter, too, which irritated Ann because a careless move could've plunged it into the carriage and damaged her precious machine. The typewriter was essential; now that her family needed any extra income she could provide.

I'll have to talk to Audrey, or Jessie, or Joel, whichever one left the paper there for my attention, she thought, as she tightened the pen's top. Then, after she had given it a hard twist, she returned the capped pen to its home in the coffee mug she used for storing her writing tools.

Welcome to 100 East, the logo read. The Robins had received the mug the same day they were handed keys to their condo. But instead of stacking it in a kitchen cabinet, where it would be out of place amid the Crate and Barrel white everyday china, Ann took it to her office. Here, it found a more welcome home.

She took a seat in the faux leather chair that was too large for the office, but its name, Executive, and its affordable price, $69.95, persuaded her to order it from the Quill catalogue. Despite it overpowering the room, Ann loved the chair's protective high back and firm arms.

She studied the paper, expecting to see the familiar scrawls of Audrey or Jessie reminding Ann they'd be late for dinner, or the neater handwriting of Joel with the same message. But instead, she was puzzled by the unfamiliar slash of letters.

Hello Mrs. Robins. Do you remember me? I'm having some money problems and need $500. Leave the cash in an envelope and put it on top of the refrigerator. I'll pick it up tomorrow when I use my key to come in for a maintenance call. This will be between us—not my employer, or your husband, or your daughters. Thank you, An Old Friend.

Old friend! She knew exactly who the author was: Clarence Watson, formerly on the janitorial staff of Berkeley Square. She remembered seeing Watson at 100 East and immediately placing him. When he spotted her in the marble and gilt lobby of her new condominium building, Watson smiled and waved. She returned both gestures, weakly, for she had a sick feeling. She wondered: what does he know? But she often saw him around the building since then and nothing had come of it. She was safe, so she thought.

The paper shook in Ann's hand as she read, re-read, and reread its message. Then she jumped out of her chair and turned around to stare at its seat. Had Watson sat there to compose his demand? She pushed the chair away until it nearly banged the door. The pen—which *his* fingers used to write those frightening words—which one was it? Now, it was hidden among a dozen similar ones in the mug. It was impossible to figure out which pen he had used, which one she had handled, tightened its cap, and put securely away.

A blackmail note, in her office, in her home! Watson had a master key that allowed him to creep into her apartment, into her life, whenever he wanted. What would happen if she ignored him, if she didn't leave the money? Would he tell Joel, or her daughters about John Reeves? For surely that was what he was hinting. Why else would he believe he had ammunition that would force her to fork over $500.

Ann sat down, did some deep breathing and composed herself. Then, she laughed. Bad timing, fella, she said to the paper. Yes, the Robins still lived at the hoity-toity 100 East, which to Watson must've meant she could part with $500 as easily as the garbage she dumped down the hallway incinerator chute. But she watched enough T.V. crime shows to understand the $500 was just the beginning. If she folded, what would stop puny little Watson, the snake, the traitor-to-the black-code-of-silence, from demanding more?

What a poor excuse for a blackmailer.

A professional would've surely kept up with the news that Joel Robins, master of the household, primary breadwinner, had taken an extended leave of absence from his law career and was now following his dream of becoming a full-time actor. If it was money Watson was after, he'd have to stand in line with the other creditors who were making their persistent phone calls.

Ann saw herself as having several options with the blackmailer, none of which included paying him $500. She could go to the 100 East management office, thrust the offensive paper before the eyes of the manager, Linda Sherman, and demand Watson's firing. But then, Ms. Sherman, in defense of her employee, might ask: "Why in the world would Clarence believe he possessed any information that would persuade you to give him $500?" That was a question Ann preferred not to answer.

The police, FBI? Again, Ann could hear the same question. To prove her case to the authorities, she'd likely have to fess up to the goods Watson had on her. There was only one road left, the high one. She'd break the news to Joel first; then tell Clarence Watson what he could do with his information, his piece of paper, his stupid warning. As for Audrey and Jessie, she'd fib to Watson that they, too, had been informed; but truthfully, she'd postpone that confession for a few years.

"Please sit down, I've got something to tell you," Ann said to Joel when he returned from rehearsal that evening. She figured this block of time, when his ego had been stroked by leading ladies, and also when he'd be exhausted from emoting on stage for hours, would be perfect for her confession.

Well, not perfect exactly, she supposed there was no ideal time to tell your husband you had cheated on him with a brawny security guard, under his nose, for at least three months. She'd omit the details: the daily phone calls, the afternoons at Gloria Thomas' apartment, the JB and water, the music; and of course, the details of the lovemaking. (And there was certainly no need to bring up Neal Spencer.)

Joel was drinking a Coca Cola with ice that Ann brought to him as he read the blackmail letter. "What's this about?" he asked. He sounded as frightened as Ann when she first read Watson' note. Then, she blurted it out: how lonely she was at the time, how she knew it was a mistake, how she regretted her adultery (*Regretted*—but truthfully, for getting caught, rather than the amorous acts.), and then added a promise to never stray again.

"You're telling me this to get back at me, aren't you?" Joel said. He put the Coke on the nearby coffee table, without a coaster, sure to leave a ring.

"No, of course not, why would you think that? I'm telling you this so I can laugh in Watson' face."

"You couldn't keep it to yourself, could you? You had to wound me this way. Just because I'm no longer bringing in the big bucks, you're out to get me."

"No, no, you're getting this all wrong."

"What do you expect me to say now? That I forgive you? That it doesn't hurt to learn my wife, Miss Big Shot Community Leader, was fucking a security guard while I was working my ass off?"

"I thought you'd understand," she said. This was not going well. "You were so caught up in your work, in your acting classes, I didn't think you cared about what I did, other than getting your dinner on the table every night."

Not surprisingly, the discussion went further downhill from there, until Ann's high road took a wrong turn leading straight to a dead end.

"I've heard enough," Joel said. He rose from his chair, stomped off to the master bedroom, retrieved the gym bag he used for costumes and stage makeup, then headed for the exit.

"I'll call you when I figure out what I want to do," he said. He walked out and slammed the paneled, hardwood door behind him.

❧

FUCK YOU. She printed the two words, using a full sheet of paper, and a black Magic Marker for emphasis. She folded her message, tucked it inside a #10 envelope, and then went to the hall closet to retrieve a stepstool. She lugged the stool to the kitchen where she positioned it in front of the SubZero refrigerator.

She climbed three stairs, and then pushed the envelope back several inches from the brushed-steel appliance's ledge. When Ann retrieved her hand, she saw it had gotten blackened from dust that gathered atop the refrigerator. Betty should clean here more often, Ann thought. Imagine the *schmutz* behind or underneath where the cleaning woman's rag or mop never ventured.

For several days after that, Ann would get the stepstool and climb up, expecting to find an empty spot where she had placed the envelope. But each time her fingers felt their way around the refrigerator's top, the envelope met her touch.

When she exited the building's elevator, she'd look to the right and left, anxious to avoid Watson if he happened to be in the lobby. She was desperate to avoid a face-to-face confrontation, just as she dreaded it with her estranged husband. (They had told their daughters Joel was called out of town to fill in for an actor who took ill. Whether or not they bought it, the girls went along with their parents' deception.)

And just as Joel disappeared (actually, he claimed to be staying at the nearby Ambassador East hotel), Watson was nowhere to be found. Then Ann learned why Watson hadn't picked up the note and why he hadn't been spotted in the building: The day after he made his threat to Ann, he was arrested on other charges.

Ann was foolish to believe she was Watson' only victim. It seemed the scumbag had a habit of lifting various pieces of jewelry, which were left behind by vacationing residents.

The thefts weren't immediately discovered because Watson had cleverly waited until the baubles' owners fled Chicago for their chalet in Zurich or villa in southern France. He knew it would be months before the diamond ring, broach, or earrings would be missed. And when the returning homeowners did make the discoveries, they'd likely pin the burglaries on other suspects.

It might've been the maid who was instructed to use their absence to clean out the china cabinet. Or perhaps the nephew, the college kid who promised to retrieve mail and water plants? Did the kid's drug habit inspire visits to the local pawnshop?

Oh, there was no end of scenarios Watson likely dreamed up to keep him on the 100 East gravy train. But when the Winston's returned home early to attend their grandson's bar mitzvah; and the same week, the Smiths abandoned lousy ski conditions, they stormed into Linda Sherman's office demanding an investigation. Then, Ms. Sherman matched the maintenance schedule with the staff roster and put two and two together. Ann wished she could have witnessed the handcuffing, the whole perp walk, but it occurred late at night when Ms. Sherman was certain no residents would catch the building's embarrassment.

At first, Ann thought her confession had been for naught. But then she saw it differently, as an opportunity to repair and perhaps strengthen her marriage. Joel had spent only four evenings away from home. Then he returned, gym bag in hand, and complied with Ann's request to go to couples counseling.

Twenty

"Take a seat," Maria Palmero said, motioning them to a grey, three-cushioned couch that sat on one wall of the office. Ann and Joel obeyed, each claiming a far end and an upholstered arm. Ann watched Maria jot something on the pad of yellow lined paper that sat on her lap. As a writer, Ann was imagining Maria's notes and her choice of words to describe the sour-faced couple and the unused middle cushion. Would they be patients or clients? Seated at far ends of the couch. Sofa?

While Maria scribbled, Ann studied the room's décor. A potted palm stood in a corner near the window. On the coffee table that separated patient (that tag sounded right) from therapist, sat a small box of Kleenex and a miniature cactus plant in a pebble-filled tray. The walls were painted a soft, inoffensive beige, and here and there hung framed paintings: a lighthouse on a rocky shore, a sun-bonneted miss and a straw-hatted lad sharing a small wooden boat—fishing pole in his hand, open book in hers. Perhaps the pictures weren't benign, but instead starting points for silent patients. She imagined Maria's gentle prod, "What does the lighthouse symbolize to you?"

Maria was quite pretty, with olive skin, dark Italian eyes, and long black hair; but wore an unflattering loose-fitting tunic top and matching long skirt. Shrink wear, Ann thought. Flowing, unrestricted, the better to encourage open and honest dialogue.

"So, what has brought the two of you here today?"

Joel remained silent, so Ann jumped in and explained the blackmail threat, her confession (again omitting salacious details), Joel's reaction, her plea for couples' therapy, and his agreement to give it at least one session.

Then, Ann sank back into the couch. (Definitely a couch.)

Maria waited a few seconds, and then asked, "How long have you two been married?" She looked at Joel. She had a sly smile on her face, as if she knew the husband rarely had the count.

When Joel hesitated, Ann jumped in once more, "Twenty-three years."

"Joel, don't you think your reaction was rather harsh—walking out? I understand your anger, your sense of betrayal, but where is your love for your wife of twenty-three years?" Maria asked.

Still silent, but in motion at last, Joel rose from his corner of the couch, walked slowly to the window, placed two hands on the sill, and looked out. "There's someone else," he finally said. He directed *his* confession to the window, not to the open-mouthed women behind him.

Maria looked as if she was trying to stifle a laugh. Of course, there's always someone else her smirk seemed to say.

"What!" Ann said. This time her jump was off the couch. "Someone else? Who? When?"

Joel took a seat, put his brow in his two hands, and then lowered his head. "Lois Golden." He was barely audible.

"Lois Golden, from Chicago Teachers College? Lois Golden, who you were nearly engaged to, then dumped to marry me?"

Now he had sunk deep into the couch and sent his answer to Maria, the woman still calm and rational. Perhaps an ally even, in a room suddenly as prickly as the cactus. "She came into our office when I was still at Stein, Bergman, and Greenberg," he said. His face had a plaintive look, perhaps borrowed from a defendant attempting innocence. "She was getting a divorce from her husband."

"She was a client?" both Ann and Maria asked.

"No, no, not mine, Stein's. But when I saw her in the hallway, we got to talking, and I invited her for coffee. Just to be friendly, you know, apologize for my behavior back then. Well, we really had a nice conversation. Seems like she had forgiven me, married a CEO of some big company, three kids, monster house in Highland Park on the lake, another in..."

"I think we get the picture," Maria said. "You were relieved Lois was doing well, that you didn't ruin her life. Is that right?"

"Ruin her life!" Joel said. "She was coming out of the divorce with a multi-million dollar settlement. I actually think she was grateful to me. Well, anyway, we gave each other a friendly kiss when we left the coffee shop, and then, you know, one thing led to another."

"How does she look?" Ann asked.

She was hoping to learn Lois' once polished black hair was now lost in grey, that her stunning blue eyes were covered by bifocals, that she had layered her younger Miss America frame in more fat than Ashkenaz' corned beef.

Maria put out a hand to stop Ann, as if to say, we have more important questions.

"Joel," Maria said kindly, (She was probably aware the husband was simple-minded, a midlife crisis cliché.) "You say you met her a year ago? Has your affair been going on that long?"

Ann remained silent, feeling dumber than that idiot girl in the painting's boat. That fucker with the pole will likely stand up and toss you into the drink. Look at you, reading a book, thinking all is tranquil when you're about to capsize. She turned to Joel, and said, "So that whole indignant tirade when you learned about John Reeves, what was that, an act?"

This time, it was Joel who was trying to curb a smile. Did he believe his method acting had finally paid off?

"Joel," Maria said, leaning forward so her elbows were on her knees, as if she were talking to a kindergartner. "If your affair has been going on for a year, and you've kept it successfully hidden for so long, why are you telling Ann about it today?"

"Lois' divorce is finally settled. She wants me to leave Ann."

Maria's office was silent, save for the ticking clock that showed its large hand closing in on the 50-minute hour. Then, Ann erupted, "Go, go. Who needs you?

"But first, I have one question. All those nights you were supposedly staying late in the office working on a case, or in drama school, was all that true, or were you really with her?"

"No, that was true. Most of it. Sometimes, maybe once or twice a week, I'd be with her," he said. His expression was no longer apologetic, more prideful of his past convincing performances.

"I have a question, too," Maria said. She was using a tempered therapist tone. "When Ann made her confession about [she had to look down at her notes for this] John Reeves, how did it make you feel?"

"Truthfully? I wanted to tell her to keep her big mouth shut. Keep it to yourself, like me. Why knife each other like that? I was still trying to hold our marriage together. But when I told Lois about Ann's affair..."

"You told Lois?" Ann said. She felt as exposed and violated as she had been by Clarence Watkins' blackmail threat. Joel shrugged his shoulders and smiled, as if to say: You know how it is: after sex, a cigarette, talk.

"How do you feel about Lois' demand?" Maria asked Joel. "Do you want to leave your wife of twenty-three years [it seems she felt the number worth repeating; maybe now he'd remember it] to perhaps recapture something you think you threw away that many years ago?"

Joel looked at her with eyebrows raised; as if wondering, how did Maria know that was exactly the question keeping him up nights? Now he smiled, probably thinking, she's a damn good therapist, after all.

"I don't know," he said. He was serious now, sounding truthful. "It depends what time of day you ask me. Sometimes, when I'm at home with Ann, when we're sitting together on the couch, I look around and think, am I nuts? Why throw this away? Ann has stuck by me through my acting thing, my leave of absence, doesn't she deserve loyalty? And there's the kids; what will they think of me if I walk out? But then, there's the sex, which is almost nonexistent in my marriage. I'm not sure whose fault that is, but it's spectacular with Lois."

Ann's back was turned to Joel now. "Hmmph," was all she said. She was worn out, fatigued as if she had been forced to swim from that boat in the painting to the craggy shore, with only the phony lighthouse to show her the way.

"Sorry, but our time is up," Maria said. She looked at the clock turned to face her. "I think we have much more to discuss. Shall we book another session?" She rose from her chair and walked to the desk where she picked up her appointment book. "I have an opening..."

Ann interrupted, "We'll call you. Thanks."

They exited the office and walked towards the elevator. Was it right or left? Neither Ann nor Joel remembered. So they wound up going off in opposite directions until one of them realized the error and returned to join the other.

Twenty-One

No lawyers, for it would only be a separation, not a divorce. Ann and Joel were attempting rationality, rather than dramatics. The first thing they agreed on was to live apart and that meant the condo had to go. Not only couldn't they afford that fancy place, but also, what was the point in maintaining an image that had streaked and faded, like an oil painting left in the rain.

They were relieved their daughters took the announcement of their separation stoically (no details other than "we've grown apart"). When Jessie said, "Big surprise, we knew you two weren't getting along," her parents looked at each other, silently blaming the other for not doing a better job of hiding his or her behavior.

Joel's eyes glanced from one daughter to the next. He was clearly disappointed. His frown seemed to criticize his own performances. How did they know we weren't getting along, it seemed to say. Was he was more upset by his daughters' declaration, or that he wasn't as great an actor as he had thought? With all of their teenage stuff, like boys and which college to attend, he must've figured the girls were oblivious to their spats. Oh well.

As for Ann, she replayed their years in Berkeley Square, hoping to find scenes where the four of them enjoyed each other's company. Surely there were outings when they appeared as content as any TV sitcom family.

But she painfully realized their arguments, silences, or absences would loom larger for their daughters than any of the happy times. So all our Sunday dinners at the Hickory Pit, annual vacations at Sleepy Hollow, and colorful trips to places like Jamaica and Nova Scotia, get buried, while the other stupid stuff breaks through to the top of their memories—to the couches of their shrinks one day.

"No big deal, all our friends' parents are divorced," Audrey said. When their parents jumped in, insisting they were just separating, not divorcing, both girls rolled their eyes and looked at each other. "Whatever," they said.

This is what else Ann and Joel worked out: They'd split the profits from the sale of their 100 East condo. Joel would continue to support their daughters. Ann was on her own for living expenses. They would each move to their own place (leasing seemed more practical as neither one had a clue as to how temporary or permanent their new living arrangements would be).

Instead of choosing an apartment in the same Gold Coast neighborhood as their condo, or one further north in a safe, but less expensive neighborhood, Ann picked a loft west of the Loop on a street once considered Skid Row, but now up-and-coming. As for Joel, he chose an apartment-hotel, but was practically living in Lois' Highland Park home.

At the time, with Ann's self-image as wobbly as a first-time tight rope walker, the loft—with its wood beamed ceilings, brick walls, and exposed ducts—seemed ideal for the tough, independent woman she wanted to become.

"I'm recycled, just like this warehouse," she told her daughters on their first tour of the place. "The owner could've let the building decay, then tore it down, but instead transformed it into this great living space." She was admiring a massive timber column, which the architect left undisguised and sturdy in the open space. Her fingers brushed against the wood, carefully, to avoid any splinters that hadn't been smoothed over.

"You won't miss 100 East?" Audrey asked. She was checking out the bedroom she'd be sharing with her sister. She looked out and surveyed the industrial buildings and the occasional vagrant that could be seen from the giant windows. No lake, no Michigan Avenue shops, no fur-coated matrons or chauffeured cars.

She and Jessie had already figured out their route to school, and as city kids, prided themselves on their comfort and familiarity with public transportation.

But Audrey seemed to be wondering about her mother; was she loony or courageous? Her smile, when she caught Ann's attention, was evidence of the latter.

"Won't miss the Gold Coast a bit," Ann answered. She meant it, for Ann liked to think she was the sort of a person who looked forward rather than back. She didn't want to dwell on the past—what was done, was done—and she preferred to imagine a brighter future ahead. And in that spirit of optimism, she continued to study the large open space, trying to figure out where she'd place the pullout couch that would serve as her bed.

Joel was relieved he didn't have to share the news of their separation with his parents, for Manny and Pearl had embarked on a 'round the world cruise, and left instructions to reach them only in an emergency. Since neither Joel nor Ann knew the full extent of their rupture, he opted to postpone his announcement.

Ann made the same decision regarding Leah. She wasn't prepared to reveal to her old friend the whole prologue that lead to the separation, so she put it off for the time being.

As for Sylvia, Ann decided to get that phone call over with as quickly as possible. "Are you sitting down, Mom, I've got some news." She wondered how much she should share with Sylvia;

certainly not John Reeves and not even Lois Golden. She didn't want to give her mother any further ammunition to dislike her son-in-law. Before she had a chance to use *we've grown apart*, Sylvia jumped in.

"I've got my own headline," she said. "And from the sound of your voice, mine is happier than yours."

"Go ahead, tell me," Ann said. She was glad to delay Sylvia's likely, *I told you so*.

"I'm trading my Swirl housecoat for an island sarong! Can you believe it? Your brother Danny asked me to move to Maui. He misses me. He tells me it's paradise. 'Why put up with Chicago's lousy weather,' he says. 'I'll get you a place in my building. It's time you had some pleasure in your life,' he says. How could I argue with that?

"I've already buried two husbands, how do I know how many years I've got left?"

At first, Ann was too stunned to respond. Then she thought, of course she's right. It'd been six months since Sam Feldman died of Alzheimer's and other illnesses, and although Ann and the girls tried to see Sylvia more often, it certainly couldn't compare with Danny's promise of paradise. And Danny.

As for Danny, he'd never been happier. He and the sullen Julia had divorced after 18 years of marriage, and he eagerly returned to Hawaii where he was stationed during his Army days. With his sunny personality and his new bachelor vigor, Danny quickly built up a successful adventure guide business, as well as a little book of female names.

"Sounds terrific." Ann finally responded to her mother's news. "But won't Danny feel you're cramping his style? You know, with all the bathing beauties he's been dating."

"I'm his best girl," Sylvia sniffed.

Ann imagined her mother brushing her hair back with her hand, maybe walking to the bathroom mirror to confirm she was still a beauty; seventy, but still a looker.

"Besides, he's getting me my own place; same building, different apartment. So [she dragged out the *o* for an extra few beats], what's your big news?"

"Joel and I are separated."

"Big surprise," Sylvia said.

On her end of the line, Ann sat silent. She was starting to cry because although she expected this response, she would've preferred empathy. No matter how she felt about her son-in-law, ideally, Sylvia should've shifted her focus to her daughter's needs. Instead, she chose to emphasize her prescience. What else was new?

But then, Ann caught herself. She was nobody's victim after all. It would be foolish to pretend she was the grieving left-behind woman. Her marriage to Joel had been floundering for quite some time and Sylvia must've picked up on that. Perhaps Sylvia was really supporting her daughter. Intimating, *you can handle it; you'll be fine.* Although Ann may have initially wanted, *Poor baby,* Sylvia's response was what she needed. Once Ann figured all of this out, she was happy for her mother.

❧

And after Sylvia got settled, she sent Ann glowing descriptions of the Polo Beach Club where Danny had his two-bedroom unit and Sylvia her one. In airmail letters written in her mother's perfect Palmer script, she reported on the eight-story sun-bleached building, the outdoor swimming pool steps from the ocean, and "palm trees everywhere you look."

She sent photos, too: Danny and Sylvia looking pretend-scared as they peered into a volcano; then another on a helicopter tour, and one with the two of them enjoying a sunset cruise. The son was treating his mother like a sweetheart, the best of several real ones scattered on the island.

As Ann studied each photo, her emotions shifted. First, there was jealousy: here was Sylvia enjoying a new phase of her life in the company of her adored son. Why wasn't Ann the adored one? And why did Sylvia deserve such an upbeat future when Ann's could be headed downhill?

But soon enough, when she saw Sylvia's blue eyes sparking in the color photos and her red-lipstick mouth smiling, she recalled her mother's troubled marriage to a sickly Gene, then another unhappy union with an aged Sam. If anyone desired a shot at happiness, in a setting as luscious as Hawaii, it was certainly Sylvia.

There was no doubt she'd miss her mother, just as she missed Danny and Leah. At a time when people closest to her were leaving—Joel for another woman, soon her daughters for college—Ann could certainly need people around who could support and comfort her. Alas, it wouldn't be Sylvia.

Twenty-Two

The telephone's ring startled her alert. Ann was in her apartment, engrossed in writing a newsletter due by the end of the week.

"Robins Publishing," she answered. She hoped the caller might think they had reached a staffed Loop office instead of a dining room table with one employee.

An unfamiliar voice barked, "Hey, Robins, this is Dave Harris, from the Chicago Ledger." She recognized his name because she'd read his title, Metro Editor, every morning on the newspaper's masthead. And she knew of his name in another setting. She had been in the office of 6700 South Shore Drive, interviewing George Franklin, the building's manager for its quarterly bulletin when Franklin leaned back in his chair and boasted, "You know Dave Harris, of the Ledger? He's a tenant here."

Ann loved that about Chicagoans, our fascination with newspapermen, like Mike Royko, Harry Golden, Jr., and Dave Harris. Especially now, in 1981, with Jane Byrne as mayor, reporters who wrote about City Hall's mercurial chief executive, were as celebrated as any Hollywood film star.

Ann tried to catch her breath to respond to Harris on the other end of the line, but he barreled ahead. "I'm sitting here reading the newsletter you put together for my building. You're a damn good writer. How'd you like to come in for an interview? We've got a spot for a junior reporter and I'm sick of all the spoiled brat journalism grads they've been sending me. Just because they're the son of an advertiser, or a nephew of the publisher, they think..."

Ann was trying to pay attention to Harris' tirade, but her mind got stuck on, "You're a damn good writer." David Harris, Metro Editor of the Chicago Ledger said about Ann, "You're a damn good writer." For a moment, she wished she had let the answering machine pick up. Then she could've replayed those words over and over again.

"Anyway, never mind that bullshit," he continued. "Seems I've got to add a female to my staff. Goddam affirmative action assholes have been on my back. So, what do you say, sweetheart? Meet face-to-face? See if you've got the balls for a real paper?"

Without thinking, Ann blurted, "Yes, yes, of course I'd love to." Looking back, she probably should've thought more about the salary, which was likely minimal. But that wouldn't have made any difference; this was the opportunity of a lifetime. No way was she going to pass it up, or keep on reading the classifieds for a better-paying job.

After she and Harris had settled on a date and time for her interview, Ann hung up the phone and just stared. She couldn't believe her good fortune. She was in the running to be a reporter! A real writer, perhaps with a byline. Her work could be read by millions, instead of her small newsletter audience.

Of course, she'd have to leave the comfort of her home office, be forced to mingle with hard-boiled, experienced writers, likely dismissive of the new female without credentials. Could she handle it? She left her chair and walked to the windows.

As she looked out on the rugged view, she recalled how she survived the transition from Michigan Avenue to West Madison Street. From dependent wife to working woman. No holding back now. The future, where she would rub elbows with journalists, couldn't look any brighter.

❧

"You're hired," Harris had said after a 15-minute interview. Ann's first thought, when she saw Harris with a Tiparillo between his teeth, was that the tiny smoke didn't match his size or personality—both of which were big. He wasn't tall, but he was wide (actually, his frame reminded her of Gene, her long-dead dad). Harris' gray hair was mixed with black, and his brown eyes were the same warm color as Gene's. A small beard covered his chin, and as for his wardrobe, he was dressed in a rumpled white shirt with rolled up sleeves, suspenders, and a creased pair of slacks that suggested the absence of a wife.

"You can hang onto your freelance gig," he continued, "but don't list your name as editor. We can't have our readers see Ledger bylines on anything but our paper. So keep your mouth shut about it." Ann knew how to be discreet, didn't she?

"Here's your desk."

Were there any more beautiful words in the English language than those three?

Ann didn't think so as she looked down at the simple piece of furniture, topped by a computer, that David Harris was pointing to. Although they were standing in a corner of the Chicago Ledger's newsroom, far from the seasoned journalists who were closer to the action, Ann couldn't believe her good fortune. A reporter for the Chicago Ledger! To convince herself, she lifted the identification badge she wore 'round her neck and stared at her photo. Yep, that was her, Ann Robins, Staff.

She started to pull out drawers to determine their contents, and tried to find her computer's "On" button, when Harris interrupted her with, "Here's some press releases from PR firms." He dropped a stack of papers on her desk as if he was at the Laundromat unloading a week's worth of soiled clothing. "Rewrite this crap so they don't sound like commercials." He spit out the words, alternating with drags of a small cigar.

❧

This morning wasn't going well. It was several weeks into her new job and Ann had finished her assignment—a rewrite of a press release announcing a new daycare center that would be open 24 hours to accommodate parents on nighttime shifts. She was reading it one more time to check for spelling or grammatical errors. Ann was proud of this piece. In addition to the who, what, where, when, and why, she had interviewed the center's director, as well as one of the mothers—a nurse who intended to sign up for the facility. Ann was sure both women's views and emotions came through in her reporting.

But Harris took a quick glance at her copy and threw it back to her. She stood on the other side of his desk, too stunned to move. "Robins, what's this shit?" he growled.

"My assignment, the new daycare center." She stuttered out her answer.

"Who told you to embellish it?" He was already looking away from her, concentrating on his computer screen.

"But I thought..."

"No room for extra graphs. No room for thoughts." Then he waved her away as if she were a peasant who had just placed a cackling chicken at the feet of the king.

Holding back tears, she walked to her desk, dropped the pages on her chair, and headed straight to the woman's bathroom. She stared into the mirror above the sink examining her red puffy eyes. As she used one side of a tissue to blot mascara and the other to curb her sniffles she spotted a woman studying her.

The reflection, that wasn't Ann, had dark hair cut in a pageboy, eyes almost too big for her small face, earrings that overwhelmed her tiny lobes, and she wore a suit with shoulder pads that widened her slim figure.

"Bad day?" the woman asked.

"My editor just threw my copy at my head," Ann said.

"Asshole."

"I was so proud of it, too," Ann said. She turned away from the mirror to lean her back against the sink. "Walked into his office, dropped it on his desk, and as I was about to leave, to give him time to read it, he says, 'Robins, what's this shit?' He read through it in less than a minute, and I guess his opinion differed from mine."

"I'm Rita Diamond," the woman said, smiling and extending her hand. "Fashion desk, guess that's why we haven't run into each other.

"Ann Robins, nice to meet you. Sorry we had to meet under these circumstances."

"Isn't that what the women's john is for? Not just to pee, but also to shed tears we can't show in the newsroom?

"God forbid our shitty bosses or coworkers witness a woman acting like a human being."

Ann laughed, then wiped away her tears, stuffed the Kleenex into her pants' pocket, and asked, "Are you free for lunch?"

Twenty-Three

"Cheer me up," Ann said to Rita.

"No problem; it's happy hour."

They were seated at the bar of Riccardo's Restaurant on Rush Street. Ann had her JB and water, Rita her martini, and they were perched on the same stools they occupied almost every Friday night since the two women first met.

"What are you so glum about?" Rita said. Then she turned away from her best friend to wave at a man who just entered the restaurant.

"Well, that's one thing right there," Ann said. "All the guys who smile at you, falling over each other to catch your eye. What am I chopped liver?"

Ann didn't actually think of herself as chopped liver, more spring chicken. At 44, she was at more-or-less ideal weight, her hair was still red—thanks to that monthly application of henna—and contact lenses allowed for some, *you have such pretty eyes*. But Ann's choice of wardrobe: loose fitting tops, blue jeans, and wedge shoes, contrasted with Rita 's tight-waisted suits, short skirts, and high heels, were likely one reason male stares swiveled towards her good friend.

"Whoa, you're really spoiling the mood," Rita said. "It's Friday, end of the workweek. We're in Riccardo's; the closest thing to the Left Bank Chicago's got. Look at this place. The paintings, they should cheer you up." Rita said. She waved her left hand at the giant murals above the bar.

Ann obeyed and directed her eyes to the paintings that were created by Chicago artists who were part of the Depression-era's Work Progress Administration program. Each piece depicted one of the seven lively arts. As always, Ann's gaze went first to Rudolph Weisenborn's "Literature" since that was the art she was supposedly connected to. "Still can't figure out what all those cubes have to do with literature," she said of the brightly colored painting.

"Don't search for meaning," Rita said. She took a sip of her cocktail and followed Ann's stare. "Just enjoy the colors, the patterns, the feelings they invoke in you. You're trying too hard."

"Actually, Albright's 'Drama' is more representative of my mood tonight," Ann said. She nodded towards the character of Mephistopheles painted by Ivan Albright. "You know the devil is supposed to be Rick, the dad, the original owner of this place."

"That's what I've heard," Rita said. She leaned her head first to the right, then to the left to find a better viewing angle.

Ann stared at "Drama." "The ruination of man. Perfect."

"Okay, enough of this kvetching. What's up?"

"I'm a lousy reporter, that's what's up." Ann moved her drink back and forth watching the ice cubes swirl and knock into each other. "If I don't learn how to be more aggressive, I'll be stuck wading through city budgets, sitting in on late night community meetings, or being exiled to some obscure county bureau. Harris has been patient, so far, but I can almost hear the hoof beats of those Medill grads charging to my spot. Honest, Rita, I don't know how much longer I can fend them off."

"Bullshit," Rita said. Although she worked in the Ledger's Fashion section, and was as beautiful as the models she photographed, Rita was surprisingly hardboiled—certainly more than Ann. Rita's language could be salty, she preferred to watch boxing matches over runway shows, and dressed in leather bomber jackets rather than silk and lace.

To make her an even more enjoyable and fascinating companion for Ann, several times a year Rita fell in love with guys who were the He-Men type, not the intellectuals Ann usually favored. (Of course, there *was* John Reeves, hardly an intellectual but not a He-Man either.)

For Ann, though, Rita Diamond's very best feature was her openness and non-judgmental attitude. In that way, she was similar to Ann's former neighbor, Diane Young, but Rita did Diane one better; she supplied her own adventures—with African-American men, married men, or other questionable choices.

When Ann had revealed her close calls with Larry Bennett, Neal Spencer, and John Reeves, Rita said, "I can top those." And they both laughed at one story Rita told of the time she fled a guy's bedroom just minutes before his wife arrived home.

Ann loved that particular tale because it made her feel as if she wasn't alone in her escapades. Here was Rita Diamond, another "good Jewish girl," engaging in similar episodes, but with her self-esteem, reputation, and career intact. There was hope for Ann as well.

❧

The first time Ann and Rita shared their ribald stories, Rita raised her glass, "This calls for a toast." Holding her martini at eye level and turning to face Ann, she said, "To friendship." Then, after taking a sip, "To us, two gorgeous scarlet women."

On this Friday night, when Ann's sour mood threatened their fun time at Riccardo's, Rita put a hand on Ann's shoulder and said, "You're a terrific reporter. I love reading your stories. They're interesting, evocative, moving. What more can a newspaper reader ask for?"

"Well, yeah, I'm a pretty good writer, but I'm a chicken when it comes to grilling my subjects. Harris wants me to dig deeper, cozy up to the mayor's people, get them to spill something nasty about their boss."

"Dirtbag."

"First in the Byrne administration, now in Washington's, Harris isn't happy unless I can find something sordid or criminal that's going to scoop the Sun-Times or Trib. The problem is I really like the mayor. He's courageous, fair, and takes a lot of abuse, not only from racists who call him the n-word to his face, but from his own City Council."

"Yeah, Beirut on the Lake, that's what they call us," Rita said, shaking her head.

Ann continued, "I watch the other City Hall reporters, Bob Crawford, Bill Cameron, Gary Washington, Bob Davis. They're not afraid to ask hard-hitting questions at the mayor's press conferences or ground breakings."

"They're all guys," Rita said. "What do you expect?"

"What about Fran Spielman of the Sun-Times? Pam Zeckman? Lynn Sweet? They're women, as tough as the male reporters. Why can't I be more like them?"

"You're a lover, not a fighter. Remember?" Rita said. She placed her martini on a cocktail napkin, and then twisted to view the crowd.

With Rita's attention elsewhere, Ann sipped her drink, stared at the murals, and thought about her job at the Ledger. From that very first day, when she had flopped into her chair and drank in the tumult around her, and when she was introduced to byline names who were now flesh and blood, and when the published edition confirmed she was in the thick of the city's action, Ann believed she was the luckiest woman alive.

That feeling of euphoria never left her, especially when her very own byline began to appear under several stories. She recalled her first feature; it was about Mayor Washington's summer youth employment program that created a lottery to ensure fairness in awarding coveted jobs. As she stood in a crowd of other journalists, clutching a 4-inch by 8-inch Reporter's Notebook and a ballpoint pen, she scanned the news release given to her by the mayor's press secretary, Grayson Mitchell. Then she focused on Mayor Washington. When he left the podium, Ann approached one of the young people who stood to benefit from a summer job. She shook the teenager's hand; introduced herself, and proceeded to conduct an interview while hoping she didn't betray her nervousness or inexperience.

When she returned to the newsroom, it took her three hours to write the piece that a more experienced reporter could've knocked out in thirty minutes. She recalled her fear when she looked at the clock and realized the deadline was approaching. Harris had already circled her desk once and raised his hands in a *so, where is it*? gesture, but she was still trying to get the lead exactly right. Ann wanted the kid's personality to pop out.

She wanted his desire for a job, his glee if he were selected, and his relief to have won an alternative to the gangs and the streets to be clear, to be palpable. She continuously rewrote her lead, determined to yank the reader in by his shirt collar and hold onto him until he got to the end.

Ann was smiling at her recollections now. If anyone saw her at the bar with that goofy look on her face, they'd surely think she had one too many. But that wasn't it; she was recalling the morning when her first bylined story appeared. She had left her apartment at 5 a.m. to await the Chicago Ledger's delivery truck. First she waved at the transvestite prostitute who daily trolled Ann's block for predawn customers. Then Ann took her own spot at the newspaper box. As soon as the driver deposited his stack and slammed the door shut, Ann dropped in a coin, grabbed a paper from the top of the pile, and with her heart racing, licked her finger to quickly turn pages.

Yes, she had shouted when she saw **Chicago Teen Says Summer Job Beats Gangs** By Ann Robins, Chicago Ledger Reporter. It had landed on a decent page 19. When she read and reread the story, and confirmed the majority of her words were intact, she nearly cried. As other people came to the newspaper box to pay for and pluck their paper, Ann stepped aside. But before each one walked away, she couldn't resist, "Catch the story on page nineteen; I wrote it!

"That's me, Ann Robins." She pointed to the two-column piece, and then to her chest.

Most of the people smiled, some looked at her as if she was kooky, and others (mostly women, probably mothers) stayed to read it right then and there. "Congratulations," they'd said. "You must be very proud."

The morning the story appeared, Ann bought half a dozen copies so she could rush back to her loft, clip her bylined piece, and mail each one off to Audrey and Jessie, Sylvia, and who else? Joel? Part of her had wanted to share the moment with her separated spouse; but the other part wasn't sure what her mailing would've conveyed.

Would he take it as a sign she wanted him back? Would he even read it? Since Ann wasn't sure of her motivation, and she also feared she'd never receive the response she desired, *Terrific, sugar, I'm so proud of you,* she decided to scrap the idea. She'd just file away the extra newspapers, somewhere.

❧

Ann's barroom musings got stuck on her estranged spouse. Despite being separated for nearly two years, Ann and Joel kept in touch and were even friendly towards one another. Any anger or hurt she initially felt dissolved with each of her successful steps toward self-sufficiency. And to be honest, she often felt happier in her single state, when she could eat pizza on the living room couch or go to bed as early as 8 p.m., without being chastised by a husband who frowned on those behaviors.

She remembered Rita's question when Ann first told her about Joel's new love for an old flame. It was during one of their first visits to Riccardo's and they were seated on the very same stools as tonight. "You don't hate him?" she had asked.

"I may be many things," Ann told her, "but I'm not a hypocrite. How can I hate Joel for having one lousy affair when I had three? Well, really two-and-a-half."

"But you didn't bolt," Rita said.

"I'm not sure that's praiseworthy," Ann said. "I knew things between us had soured. I should've insisted on couples therapy before it was too late."

"No guilt trips, please," Rita had said. "So, are you dating up a storm?" Her eyes widened at the prospect of more juicy stories. "Now that you're free, how many guys have you fucked?"

Ann had hesitated, took a sip of her drink, then replaced it carefully on the napkin. "Several dates, fix-ups, all in the under five-seven height category. Sex, zero."

Rita twisted on her bar stool to put a hand on Ann's arm. "*Bubbalah*," she crooned, "I'm so sorry. Maybe your, well, attitude needs some adjusting. A new hairdo, maybe? Some highlights." Then she used her fingers to poke through Ann's hair.

"No, no," Ann said. She lifted Rita's hand and dropped it back on the bar. "I've had offers, persuasions, begging. But I'm just not interested.

"None of my dates turned me on. None made me feel like tearing off my clothes, and then theirs. Actually, I couldn't wait for each one to leave so I could return to my comfy, uncomplicated single life."

"To each her own," Rita had said, using her free hand to signal a martini from the bartender.

"Hey ladies, fancy meeting you here." It was David Harris, who just entered Riccardo's. Her boss' voice woke Ann from her musings. He had threaded his way through the crowd and took a position behind Ann and Rita. "Can I buy you sweet young things a drink?"

"You're a writer, Dave. Surely you can come up with better opening lines," Rita said, turning to face him.

"Give me a break," he said, "it's Friday." Then he kissed the cheek Rita offered him.

From the look on his and her face, Ann wondered if the two of them had ever been, or still were, an item. Rita never included Harris in her roster of former or current lovers, but maybe this guy was special. A secret? She'd have to pry later.

"What about you Robins?" Harris asked. "You gonna give me grief, too?"

He stretched to reach Ann's cheek and she was so thrown by this gesture—so unlike his treatment of her in the office—that she returned his kiss. Face to face now, with background music playing in her ears, and encouraged by her scotch, plus Harris' bear-like body, she planted a second kiss on his lips.

It was a quick kiss, didn't last more than a second, but it was enough for Rita to say, "Whoa. Hey Dave, take my seat. I see some pals at that table I've got to make nice to. You guys have a lovely evening." Then, she took her martini and cocktail napkin off the bar, and before hopping off the stool, looked at Ann with raised eyebrows. *Call me later,* Rita mouthed, and used her left hand to bring an imaginary phone to her ear.

❧

"No, nothing, never," Harris said when Ann asked if there was anything between him and Rita. "I think she's a great broad, and we tease each other, but I'm not her type.

"She likes tall, dark, and handsome. I'm more short, hairy, and cuddly." Then he stared at his drink and his face seemed to change from humor to regret.

Ann had accepted his suggestion to move from the bar to a table for two. She switched from her scotch, and Harris from his vodka, to the first of several bottles of wine.

Away from the office, and perhaps softened by the alcohol, his growling was gone and replaced by a low voice Ann could appreciate even though the bar's noise and music tried to drown him out.

Close up, his smile was charming. Even his wardrobe, in the dimmed light, looked bohemian rather than wrinkled. Why had she never noticed his hands and arms before this night; his shirtsleeves were always rolled up from wrist to elbow?

Why now, when his arm was touching hers, did she just notice the hairy limb, its warmth, its feeling of strength and protection. Why now was her body stirring as if it was Larry, Neal, or John leaning into her? This arm belonged to her boss, for God's sake. She had enough brain cells untouched by booze to warn her she was entering dangerous territory. Her job could be at risk. The job she loved, adored, and thanked God for. And yet, she had that feeling—she called it her *train has left the station* feeling—that it was too late. She had climbed aboard and was willing to travel to wherever the locomotive was headed.

They were climbing into his Honda to drive to his place, where he kept his stash. Harris entered on the driver's side, while Ann opened the door to the passenger's side. "Just throw that shit in the back," Harris said. Ann stood and stared at the pile of debris on her seat. "Didn't know I'd be having company."

She grabbed as much as she could—some slipped onto the floor mats—then she kneeled on the seat to heave the pile onto the backseat where it joined empty cans of Coke, crushed packages of smokes, and yellowed newspapers. *Oy vey*, Ann thought. She said, "Okay."

She didn't attempt conversation because the moment he turned on the car's ignition, Harris lit a small cigar, used his left hand to steer, and his right to make a call on his portable phone. Ann was afraid to add yet another distraction to this driver whose speedometer displayed an alarming 70.

She shouldn't have been surprised when she saw his apartment, which resembled his car. He was single, she knew that much; but did he have to be so messy? Stuff was everywhere: dishes piled beside the kitchen sink, stacks of newspapers and magazines falling onto the living room floor, pieces of clothing dropped in a path from bedroom to bathroom to front door.

As Harris went to fetch a baggie from his hiding place, Ann searched for a clear spot to shed her coat. She found a dining room chair, hung her London Fog on its back, and then straightened the raincoat's shoulders. Dressed thusly, the chair—with the table's dried flower centerpiece mimicking a lady's hat—appeared to be another person in the room. Someone more sober, upright, wiser, who thought it best to face the windows, rather than the drama likely to unfold behind her back.

Twenty-Four

It was noon on Saturday; Ann and Rita were at their usual table at Bon Ton's, their favorite North State Street luncheonette, when Rita blurted out, "So, tell me already; I can't wait any longer." Then, she took a bite of her poached chicken sandwich.

"Well, we went to his place..."

"Did you sleep with him? I have to know that first," Rita said.

"Let me tell it my way," Ann insisted. She wanted to relive every moment of the previous night.

Rita returned her sandwich to her plate, leaned back in her chair, crossed her arms in front of her, and said, "I'm all ears."

A pair of women at the next table paused in the middle of their conversation. With forks held aloft, and heads slightly turned towards Ann, they waited for her next words.

She needed sustenance before continuing so she bit into her sandwich, chewed, swallowed. "We polished off two bottles of wine at Riccardo's, talked about everything, our marriages—his two, my one—, kids, parents, favorite books, philosophy of life..."

"Will you hurry and get to the good parts," Rita said, returning to her food. "A person could die of starvation while you increase your word count." The two women at the other table remained wordless but nodded in agreement.

"All that background is important," Ann said, "because I saw the other David, the one who's a lovely, caring person, not my boss."

She spoke loud enough to include the eavesdroppers. Ann suddenly enjoyed being the center of attention, especially since it involved her and a new man. She wished she could've announced it to the whole restaurant.

"So it's *David* now," Rita said. "After one evening."

"I'm afraid so."

"Did you say you went to *his* place?" Rita asked, her eyes widening. She quickly took another bite of her sandwich, perhaps realizing her question might have revealed something.

Ann paused. Now it was time to dump her eavesdroppers. The rest of the conversation might be something neither she nor Rita wanted to broadcast. Ann leaned across the table and whispered, "Okay, time to fess up. Did you and David ever get together?" She hoped the answer was one she could live with, one that wouldn't affect her long relationship with Rita, or the one just budding with David.

"Once, I swear it was only once," Rita said. "It started out the same as your story, two bottles of wine. But he's definitely not my type. I was so wasted; I thought *what the hell.* But after I got a look at his place, the chaos, I knew it would only be just that one time.

"I mean, he's adorable and all that, and a great lover; which it looks like I don't have to tell you. But I just couldn't get his messy apartment out of my head. Oh, and he never called for a second date." She added that, perhaps trying to escape from her own trap. But then muttered, "Maybe he could tell how disgusted I was..."

Ann's face grew darker, so Rita stopped and shifted gears. "You know me, sweetie," she said putting her hand on her friend's arm.

"I'm compulsively neat. I probably got the best fucking of my life, and there are those other qualities you've uncovered. I know it's shallow to judge a guy on how he folds his clothes; but that's me. It says more about Rita Diamond than David Harris."

"So you have no feelings for him?" Ann asked. The other question, did David long for Rita, would have to be answered by him. Later.

"No, none, you have all-clear from me. Go forth with my blessings. Just control yourself at work. You wouldn't be the first female fired while her boyfriend lives on to write another column."

By their third night together, Ann and David had become a pair. "No seeing other people?" she asked. They were lying in bed; he was finishing a Tiparillo; she was waving away the smoke. "Agreed," he promised.

Ann took him at his word. But she couldn't stop herself from keeping an eye on him at the office. Why hadn't she noticed his habit of touching whomever he was engaged in conversation with? When he was just Harris, and not her David, it must've slipped her notice. He was definitely a touchy-feely kind of guy; couldn't seem to talk without one of his hands somewhere on the person's body—perhaps a shoulder, elbow, or wrist. She studied the women on the other end of his touch. Did they smile? Return his touch with one of their own? Or hopefully, back away, out of his reach.

She didn't think she was a jealous person. But now, she recognized feelings that first surfaced when she saw Joel on stage with a young, attractive actress. And then there was the big blast when she learned about Lois Golden. But that was *hurt*, rather than jealousy. Or were they really the same thing?

Ann tried to dismiss these feeling in her new romance, deciding instead to enjoy being coupled again. Mostly, she was happier than she had been in a long time, and eager to share her cheery feelings with her daughters.

"I've met someone," she told them. She envisioned Audrey and Jessie on the other end of the line sharing the phone's receiver. Ann had timed her call for the hour before rehearsal, when the girls could take a few minutes away from their latest production to chat. Two o'clock in Chicago, three in New York where the sisters operated a very far off-Broadway theatre company called The Robins' Nest.

"Terrific, Mom," they chorused at Ann's bulletin. They wanted details and she provided as much as possible during the expensive long-distance minutes. More would come later, she promised, but knew she wouldn't share her worry about her employee-boss status. And she definitely would hide anything that hinted at jealousy or insecurity.

She had been proud of the way her daughters adapted to their parents' continuing separation. They were always cordial to Lois Golden, and encouraged Ann "to date and find someone who'll make you happy."

And why shouldn't they wish her bliss? *Their* lives had been high flying.

After spending four years at Indiana University (Audrey) and the University of Wisconsin (Jessie), where they engaged in the typical first-time-away-from-home behavior of beer, pot, and boyfriends; as well as the uniquely Robins' experiences of drama and musical troupes, Ann's daughters returned to Chicago. In a small theatre on the north side, the Robins sisters teamed up to write and produce a hilarious spoof and several off-color musicals that garnered notoriety and press clippings. And it was those shows that eventually moved Audrey and Jessie to New York where they continued to produce their original wacky shows.

Now that she had her daughters' blessings (she may have proceeded without them, as there was that train ride she couldn't alight), Ann went full throttle into her romance. At times, she had to put on the brakes, just as Rita had urged. In the office, she and David were careful to keep to their usual routine: he was *Harris*, she *Robins*, and they played their roles of grumpy boss and put-upon reporter like actors in a B-movie.

Whenever possible, she would find a way to initiate a touch. She'd place her hand on his arm, as if to ask a question, but then linger. Or he might bump into her and hold the contact for an extra minute. Those physical contacts were silly, she knew, but it only made her hungrier for him when they met again in the evening.

It was always at Ann's place. "It's easier," she had said when they first started planning their get-togethers. (Easier and cleaner, but that was left unsaid.) "I'm closer to the office, and no one we know lives in this neighborhood," she explained. The only nights David slept over in her apartment were Fridays and Saturdays, because any extended lovemaking weekdays would've made her in no shape to rise early for work.

"We'll have to keep to Happy Hour," David suggested. "Otherwise, everyone will wonder why we both disappeared."

So on Fridays after work, Ann and Rita would spend their usual hour at Riccardo's, David would sidle up to buy each of them a drink, then he would fade into the crowd. (Of course, David knew Rita was privy to the romance. "She's my best friend," Ann told him. "Besides, she was there at the very beginning."

"It's okay, babe," he had said. His easy acceptance of Rita into their secret, plus the smile on his face when Ann told him, made her wonder if he was glad to have Rita in on it.)

On the Friday evenings following Riccardo's, he'd let himself into Ann's place with the key she had made for him. She'd usually arrive first, rarely David. When he didn't appear at her loft until an hour or so after her, his excuses varied. *Got into a debate*, or *pressured to stay another round*, or *it was so-and-so's birthday*. She never protested.

❧

Naturally, David overtook Joel as the main character during Ann's weekly sessions with Maria Palmero. Although couples counseling hadn't saved her marriage, Ann continued therapy on her own. She felt lucky her health insurance covered the fees, because she believed Maria's support would help Ann continue her growth as a strong, independent woman.

"You look different today," Maria had said on the Tuesday following Ann's first date with David. "In a good way," she continued. She seemed to be treading carefully. Her sly smile may have indicated she knew the cause of Ann's upbeat appearance.

"You've got a grin on your face; your eyes look as bright as when you moved into your loft, and when you got your job at the Ledger. It's that top-of-the-world-look. What's up?"

"I've met someone," Ann said. "He's brilliant, talented, a wonderful lover." She was glowing as if she was a cheerleader who had just snagged the team quarterback.

"Sounds wonderful," Maria said.

"The only problem," Ann said, in a voice more boastful than anxious, "he's my boss at the Ledger."

"That's definitely a complication."

❧

As the affair continued, Ann introduced new questions she wanted to explore with her therapist. "He and Joel are like night and day," she told Maria. "I wonder how I could be married to someone for so long, and then fall in love with his opposite?"

"Tell me how they're different," Maria said. She was using her leaning-forward-arms-crossed-on-the-knees-I'm-all-yours pose.

"Well, for one thing, Joel is fixated on his appearance, especially after he got into acting. He goes to the Y several times a week, and I doubt if his body has an ounce of fat. And the minute his favorite European-style clothing goes on sale, he races to the Oak Street boutique that carries the line."

"And David?"

Ann laughed. She thought about the rolls of fat that layered David, a roly-poly figure that made it tricky to get her arms around him. (Like Gene, her dad.)

In her mind's eye, she saw David's clothing, the identical white shirts purchased half a dozen at a time, each one eventually dotted with mustard or ketchup stains, and never placed on a hanger except at the drycleaner's. "Let's just say David feels differently about his outward image."

"Anything else?"

"Well, David's got this whole rebel thing going. No seatbelt, smoking pot, profanity, his whole devil-may-care attitude about life."

"And you find that attractive?" Maria asked. Her expression seemed to shift to one of concern.

"I guess I do; sort of like falling for the high school bad boy. You know, the one with the ducktail haircut and a pack of smokes tucked into the cuff of his tee shirt."

"Hmmm," Maria said. "I find it interesting you didn't see Joel's rebellious side when he gave up law for the stage. And didn't you tell me he refused to go into the family business, even after his father promised him the world?"

"Yes, yes, I'll give that to Joel. But you see, David's wild side extends into the bedroom."

"Oh," Maria said with a raise of her dark eyebrows.

Twenty-Five

Ann was fast asleep when she was awakened by a loud noise. That was one thing she didn't like about her loft: the racket outside her window. When she first moved in, she had thought it hip and brave to live in a commercial district with food manufacturers and light industry as neighbors. But she hadn't counted on the early hours these businesses kept. She looked at the bedside clock; it was three a.m. Truck deliveries and garbage pickups were likely responsible for rousting her from sleep. But this noise was different, more like a slow moving train. And besides, as soon as her head cleared, she remembered it was Sunday and work on the streets would be stopped for the weekend. Of course, the sound that woke her from her dream was David. Snoring.

"Turn over," she said, giving his hefty shoulder a push.

"Wha?" he garbled. Then, obediently rolled over and turned his back to her.

She knew it was hopeless to try and fall back asleep for David would invariably return to his original position and the tumult would resume. So she slipped out of bed and left the room. After she quietly closed the door, pulling the handle towards her inch by inch until she heard it click, she stepped into the large open space that served as both living and dining rooms and kitchen. Her eyes confirmed it was indeed the weekend. Signs of David's two-night sleepovers were everywhere.

Surely the architects who designed this modern space to be serene and free of clutter would be aghast to see what happened to Ann's loft when her lover inhabited it.

Empty bottles of wine stood on kitchen counter tops. Ashtrays full to the brim were also on the kitchen counters, as well as the bathroom's, and replicated on the living room's coffee table. The smell of smoke rose from the crushed butts, drifted freely in the open space and high ceilings, bounced off the exposed brick walls, and lingered in the air.

Jackets (one was hers; she was picking up some of his habits) were draped on dining room chairs. Shoes, with socks stuffed inside, lay abandoned at the base of the couch.

The dining room table held its own detritus: empty cartons of Chinese takeout, paper plates with spoonfuls of leftover soy sauce, plastic eating utensils, and a small stack of napkins bearing Spicy Rice's imprint.

Instead of tending to her cleanup, Ann poured whole milk in a juice glass (nonfat was banished once David voiced his preference), and then settled on the couch. As she surveyed the scene, she wondered what had happened to her. For the first six months of their affair, the question never entered Ann's mind. Oh, it wasn't that she didn't notice his faults, or worse, worry about losing her job. (It would never be David Harris fired for violating a non-fraternization rule; always the subordinate.) But during those giddy days of early romance, she preferred to feel lighthearted and happy, and balked at any mood-dampening thoughts. But now, here was her loft, in shambles.

Sometimes, she thought her life had deteriorated as badly as her apartment. She worried that all of her hard work to make herself strong, independent, and self-sufficient was buried under the debris strewn about her loft. But then she thought about the good times she and David had together. That's when her view of him, and herself, mellowed.

Yes, he could be a slob, a flirt, reckless; but he was also incredibly bright, passionate about the same liberal issues as her, fun loving, and of course, a wonderful lover.

And, she was drawn to David's family. She remembered the first Sunday night dinner at his widowed mother's house when Ann was introduced to his brother and sister and their families. They had welcomed Ann with open arms, perhaps relieved to see David finally paired with a Jewish girl, as opposed to the two *shiksa* ex-wives.

Those evenings—filled with rich Jewish dishes and equally Jewish hot-blooded debates, reminded her of family get-togethers in her childhood. Unlike Joel's wealthy parents, David's "didn't have a pot to piss in," he had told her. But she could see there was plenty of love, and lust for life in the Harris clan to make up any financial deficits.

As Ann sat on the couch, musing about the positive and negative parts of her relationship with David, she decided she needed something sweet to help her fall back asleep. She left her seat to search for a chocolate covered donut in the box David had brought with him. But then she stopped and remembered her conversation with Rita just a few days ago.

They had met for lunch at the Greek diner near their office, when Rita said, "Have some fries." Then, she pushed her plate towards Ann.

"No, thanks," Ann said. She slid the plate back across the table. "Look at me." She stood up and used two hands to pull away rolls of fat that were spilling over each side of her waistband. "I must've gained ten pounds since I've been with David. Polish sausage, fried matzo, ice cream sundaes with hot fudge. You name it; we eat it."

"Who says you have to keep up with him?" Rita said.

Ann ignored Rita's question. "All my good work in getting myself into shape, losing the pounds my mother and Joel used to tease me about. Out the window."

"Do I hear some tarnish on the golden boy?" Rita had asked.

"No, no," Ann said. Then, she reached across the table to take a handful of fries.

Ann finished her milk (without the donut), but still didn't feel drowsy. She took the glass to the sink, trying to find a place for it among the collection of dirty dishes. On her way back to the couch, she spotted the letter from Leah that was on the dining room table, nearly covered over by last night's remainders. The one page was out of its envelope, unfolded, and left there for Ann to re-read. She could hardly believe its contents.

Of course, that's it, she said to herself. My dream, Leah's letter, that's the connection. Then it all came back to her, the dream that was interrupted by the loud rumbling from the body next to her. It was one of her recurring dreams; and each time it appeared, all of the details were exactly the same.

"We've got plenty of room," the Ann in the dream would say to a visitor in her house.

"Come on, I'll show you." Then she'd lead the person up the stairs, first to a second floor and then to a third. On every level, there'd be a series of bedrooms, each containing one or two beds. Her delight in showing off the sleeping quarters was always dampened by the condition of the linens. Room after room, sheets and pillowcases were covered in dust.

She always woke from that dream with a sense of disappointment. Why had she neglected those rooms? After all, they were in her house. Why hadn't she tended to them?

In real life, Leah was coming to Chicago and expecting to stay at Ann's place. "You'll never believe it," the letter read. "While Ken was gone on one of his trips, I met someone. His name is Jacques Dupres, and he's a professor at a small university in Paris. We're in love. But he's married, too, and neither of us wants to break up our families. Of course, Ken doesn't know, and certainly not the boys. I haven't told another soul, but I thought somehow you'd understand. I need to get away to think things through, and there's no one else I'd rather be with than you. Here's the date I'll be arriving." And then Ann read the date one more time: one week from today.

She was excited to see Leah in person after all these years. Although they had kept up a steady correspondence—about their children's doings, Ann's broken marriage (she had to tell Leah about it once the separation continued on through the years), Ken's travels, and Leah's volunteer activities—their visits had been infrequent, short, and accompanied by family. "This will be a great chance to have a heart-to-heart," Leah wrote. "I can't wait to see you!"

Ann's eyes traveled her apartment. Where would Leah sleep? She certainly couldn't suggest her oldest friend book a hotel, not with the girl-talk Leah's news demanded. Sharing the space with David wasn't an option either. Ann and David would have to take a break from each other; that was the only solution. Surely she could handle his absence from her bed for a week; and David would survive, too.

Ann wished she really did live in that generous house of her dreams, the one with all of those bedrooms, with space for every guest.

But she'd be sure to wash each and every sheet and pillowcase. And, she'd open windows to let in fresh air. Although, she couldn't recall seeing any windows. How in the world did the dream Ann breathe?

Twenty-Six

What a sweetheart. Despite being booted out of Ann's bed for one week, David agreed to accompany her to O'Hare to meet Leah's plane. "No problem," he said. "It'll give us more time to be together. And I'll finally get to meet your Leah in person."

Ann wasn't looking forward to her separation from David. It was their last Saturday night sleepover before she'd relinquish the bedroom to Leah and bunk on the pullout couch. She and David were enjoying their post-coital cigarette—she never smoked on her own, but kept a pack of Marlboro's in the dresser drawer for these occasions—when she reached across David's belly to flick ashes into the saucer he kept at his side of the bed. As her head neared David, he patted it as if she were a favored pet, and said, "You sure you can't sneak away for one night? Send her off to visit old friends?"

"No," Ann said, "not possible. We'll just have to tough it out." She nestled against his body and wrapped his right arm around her shoulders, like an afghan warding off a chill. She'd miss David's presence in her life, for not only were they going to abandon evenings together, but she'd also be using Leah's visit as her vacation week. That meant no seeing David at the office either.

"He's adorable," Leah said, as she watched David lug her suitcases into Ann's loft. The two women were seated on the couch, where they had been awaiting his final task before he left the old friends to themselves.

"Yeah, he's a cutie pie," Ann agreed, as David hoisted the suitcases onto Ann's bed. Leah's luggage was a French brand, buttery brown leather edged in a gold color. They were of a quality that would make Ann worry about someone snatching them from a luggage carousel. When Ann traveled, she used her black Samsonite, a bag she had owned since her honeymoon with Joel.

That worn and battered suitcase would never catch a thief's eye.

"So tell me, is marriage with cutie-pie in the picture?" Leah whispered, keeping an eye on David and her belongings. She watched as each suitcase bounced on the bed, then sank into the spaces previously occupied by Ann and her lover.

"David has two ex-wives," Ann said. Her eyes remained on the bed that would soon be absent of him. "He isn't eager to tie the knot again. Not that he's asked." The idea of David proposing was so far-fetched that Ann never seriously considered it. Sometimes, though, especially at those Sunday dinners with his family, she could picture herself being a legitimate member of the clan. (In those images, Ann was stout, just like David and his relatives.)

"Speaking of ex-wives, how's your Joel?" Leah asked. "Bring me up to date. I still feel guilty we haven't kept in touch with him. After all, Ken and I were friends with Joel, too. But we've always felt we had to choose sides."

"That's not necessary," Ann said. She turned away from her view of David to face Leah, as if it were necessary to clear the image of one mate before taking on another. "Joel and I are still friends. We talk a few times a month, and when the girls are in town, we go out to dinner, just the four of us, without Lois or

David. It's weird sometimes; Joel's so familiar, as if nothing had changed between us."

"Is he making a living?" Leah asked, her tone caring, now that Ann had given her permission.

Ann smiled as she thought about the comp tickets Joel regularly sent her whenever one of his shows was staged in Chicago. "Oh, dinner theater, touring companies, voiceovers, commercials. I doubt if he's making big bucks, but he seems happy."

"How does he look?" Leah asked. "Does he still have that Gary Cooper thing going?"

"Yeah, he has to if he wants to get work. I wish I could tell you he fell apart and let himself go after the separation. But it just didn't happen."

"Speaking of separation," Leah said, "how long are you two going to keep that going? What is it, four years now?"

"Five." Ann said. She reached for a Kleenex she had tucked into her pocket.

"Are you crying?" Leah asked, searching Ann's face for a clue.

"I guess that's your answer," Ann sniffed. "Even if David did propose, whenever I think about the D word—divorce, not David—I start to cry. Evidently I'm not ready to cut the cord. I'd rather wallow in ambivalence."

"What about Joel? Isn't he anxious to marry his heiress girlfriend?"

"No, he seems comfortable with our arrangement. He tells me Lois keeps bringing it up, but somehow he manages to deflect her."

"Must be that acting talent you just told me about," Leah said. "And his Southern charm."

❧

"That's it, girls," David said, as he wiped his hands on his trousers. "You're all set. Now how 'bout a goodbye kiss from my sweetheart, and her best friend?"

Ann smiled and rose from the couch. She was glad Leah had this chance to meet David, to see his helpful and friendly side. But instead of approaching Ann, David targeted Leah for the first smooch. The moment she was upright, David put both arms around Leah's waist and drew her close, so close Ann doubted a credit card could pass between the couple. While his hands rubbed her back, Leah's stuck out straight behind him, looking as if she were a mannequin about to be hoisted to a window display. Even her face, which was still as beautiful as when she was Ann's college friend, looked as wide-eyed and startled as a porcelain model.

"Help," Leah mouthed. She was trying to pull away, but David's grip was strong and not eager to be released.

"May I cut in?" Ann asked. She tapped David on the shoulder and tried to sound as if the three of them were in on a private joke. But if this embrace were to last any longer, she'd once again have to reach for her tissue.

David gave one more squeeze, and before unwrapping his arms, kissed Leah. A pure red shade, popular on the lips of Parisian women, was now imprinted on David's mouth. "Any friend of my sweetheart is a friend of mine," he said stepping away. Then he turned to Ann, gave her a hug that didn't match his previous one, and a quick kiss that transferred Leah's stain to her cheek. He was on his way out the door. "Talk to you later, babe," he said, already in the hallway.

Leah used her manicured fingernails to brush her long hair—still blonde and glamorous—away from her face. She tucked her classic white blouse, which had been disturbed during David's clutch, back into her skirt's waistband. "What was that?" Leah asked, her expression a mix of fear and embarrassment.

"What can I say," Ann said. "He's a flirt. He loves the ladies." But her voice wasn't cheery, or humorous, just flat.

Despite the years and miles since they were last together, Ann and Leah reconnected as if there'd been no distance or time whatsoever. "I miss this city!" Leah said as they rode the escalator up from Marshall Field's first floor to its seventh. The Walnut Room was at the top of Leah's list, and once they were seated and ordered their entrees, she voiced the subject that brought her to Chicago.

"I'm so confused, Ann." She reached across the table to take her friend's hand. "Part of me wants to throw caution to the wind and run away with Jacques. Just accept the fact that Ken and the boys will hate me for the rest of their lives."

"And the other part?"

"That Jacques will wind up hating *me* for breaking up his family. That our idyllic romance will become something shameful he'll wish he never got into."

"I'm sorry I can't tell you what to do," Ann said. "But as you can see, I'm hardly the one to make decisions, or offer advice on love, marriage, separation, or any of that stuff."

This was an odd role for Ann, to be seen as a person of wisdom in Leah's eyes. For most of their friendship, Ann had felt Leah's judgment. She believed she could never be as righteous, as Jewish, as morally upright at Leah. Now, the tables were turned. Well, not turned exactly, as Ann hadn't moved from her liberal, live-and-let-live attitude. But Leah had certainly made a shift in a world she once saw strictly in black-and-white.

"Remember back in college when Joel left Lois for you?" Leah asked. "Remember how all our friends hated you? That's what I fear, being despised by everyone I know."

"Not only our friends were angry at me, but my mother, too."

"How *is* Sylvia? The last thing you wrote was that she had moved to Hawaii to be with your brother."

"Living the life of Riley. She's even got a boyfriend."

"Single, I hope," Leah said. She used her left-handed fork to pierce the tomato that topped her salad and watched as the red seeds and pulp drained on the lettuce leaves below.

"Single, rich, five years younger than her. And Jewish!"

"That's my Sylvia," Leah said. "How has she taken your separation from Joel? If I remember, she was never very keen on him."

"Well, she never actually said 'I told you so,' but she was hardly heartbroken when I gave her the news. But we're supposed to be discussing your heart, not my mother's. Where do you stand now?"

"You mean this minute; because my feelings switch on the hour. I called Ken as soon as I landed. 'Have a great time, honey,' he said. 'Give Ann a big kiss for me.'"

Then Leah put her right hand to her lips and waved the harmless kiss across the table. There was a moment of silence while both woman recalled the other kiss, the one pressed on a startled Leah.

"Ken has no clue," Leah continued. "'Have a great time,' he says, which of course made me feel like a snake."

"Have you ever wondered if Ken had an affair?" Ann asked. "He's out of town often enough. Maybe a babe in Brussels, a sweetie in Spain, a…"

"I wish he did," Leah interrupted. "I'd make me feel less guilty about me and Jacques."

"Speaking of, where are you this minute?" Ann said. She checked the Timex on her wrist. "It's 12:30 in Chicago. Where are you on Jacques?"

"I haven't called him yet. We agreed to stay disconnected for the week I'm here. See if we can handle not being in touch. But I'm weakening; I just want to hear his voice, his luscious French accent. Maybe that's what drew me to him. I'm a sucker for dialects."

"Tell me about it," Ann said. She recalled Joel's Southern accent and the tingle she felt when she first heard it. "You still haven't told me how you two met. I want details."

"Ever the reporter, right?" Leah said.

"And a nosey friend."

Leah put her knife and fork down, leaned back in her chair, and started to describe a scene that Ann enjoyed capturing on the other side of the table. "I had this favorite café I would go to each morning," Leah said. "It sounds so cliché, but it's true.

"Anyway, I was reading a book, Philip Roth's 'Goodbye, Columbus,' and I could feel someone's eyes on me. You know that feeling?"

"Yes," Ann said, her chin in her hand, her attention focused on Leah and her romance; her mind going all the way back to Larry Bennett.

"I look up and coming towards my table is this handsome, tall man. Grey at the temples, smoking a pipe, wearing a jacket with leather patches on the elbows. The whole bit; just like in the movies. He reaches for a chair, and in this magnificent French accent, says, 'May I sit down?'"

"'Yes,' I said, then added, 'Since you asked the question in English, I'm curious as to how you knew I wasn't French? 'The book,' he said, pointing to my paperback. 'I use it in my American literature class.' Well, he sat down, we talked some more about Roth, and one thing led to another.

"Am I terrible, Ann? Do you hate me?"

Ann hesitated before answering. Hate her? Now, she loved Leah more. She was human after all. A flesh-and-blood woman who encountered an appealing man who lured her out of a comfortable, safe, rule-driven way of life. Ann knew how that could happen.

"Of course I don't hate you," Ann said. "Listen, I never told you about some things I've done in the past. I couldn't bear the thought of shocking or disappointing you. Especially since you were the only friend who stuck by me in college. Maybe now it's time to share."

As Ann told her stories—first about Larry Bennett, then Neal Spencer, and finally John Reeves—Leah stared at Ann. Sometimes; she'd shake her head, as if Ann was recounting visits by extra terrestrials.

"Who would've believed?" Leah said. "Sweet little Ann, housewife Ann, schoolteacher Ann, community heroine Ann. You're quite the surprise. And I don't mean it judgmentally. After all, look at the mess I've gotten myself into."

"That's just it," Ann said. "Me, you, my friend Rita, some of my friends back in Berkeley Square. Good little girls fooling around. But I don't think it's so unusual; just a big secret."

"You could be right," Leah said. "But no one would believe it of us. After all, didn't we follow the ordained paths? Graduate college and become a teacher. Marry a doctor or lawyer. Quit work as soon as baby number one arrives. Wait no more than two years for baby number two. Stop at two kids unless you fail to produce one of each sex. Stay home until the brats are in school. If you decide to get a job, make sure it doesn't interfere with wifely duties. And if you don't work, sign up for a worthy charity. Do something meaningful, but don't compete with your spouse."

"Wow," Ann said. She was smiling; Leah had finally become an ally, a member of the same team. "Sounds like you've got some repressed anger there."

A week had passed and now Ann and Leah were at the departure gate, a half-hour before Leah would leave her friend and return to Paris. She was clutching her boarding pass in one hand, and used the other to stroke Ann's face. "This was wonderful," Leah said. "Just what I needed. I'll miss you."

"But I didn't help you solve anything," Ann said. She put her arm around Leah's slim waist. "My current love life and confessions only further mudded the waters."

"No, no, you were helpful," Leah said. "You've showed me life can go on. That a few missteps don't necessarily lead to damnation. Look at you, stronger and more successful than ever. And still friends with your ex. That's something to be admired."

"Please don't use me as a model," Ann said. "I'm still figuring it out."

"That's what I'm going to do on the trip back," Leah said. "Weigh the pros and cons, then probably toss them and follow my heart. Wherever that takes me."

Before leaving the airport, Ann phoned David and left a message on his answering machine: "I'll be home, alone, it's still early enough we can have dinner together. And *dessert*, which I've missed. Give us a chance to catch up. Call me when you get in."

By 7 p.m. when she still hadn't heard from him, Ann decided to pull together a meal for herself. There was *frommage* and crackers, part of the French delicacies Ann tried to stock for Leah, cold chicken leftover from their dinner at Marché—the restaurant Leah said looked similar to Parisian markets, but lacked the snobbery —, just enough Chardonnay to fill one glass, and from the countertop a chunk of French bread that Leah first laughed at. "I appreciate the gesture," she had said, lifting the loaf in the air. "But in Paris we'd toss this to the pigeons."

Ann placed each item on a tray and took it to the couch. She clicked on the remote and tried to divert her attention from the silent telephone. But she couldn't stop herself from wondering where David was, whom he was with, and why he hadn't returned her call.

The sitcom with its laugh track occasionally caught her eye, but as soon as a commercial appeared, her gaze returned to the stubbornly quiet phone.

She put the tray on the coffee table and studied her apartment. It was clean; smoke free, a state unseen since David entered her life. There were no signs of him anywhere. She had purged all of his leftovers before Leah's arrival, and hadn't yet returned them to their former places. The ashtrays, spotless now, would remain in the kitchen cabinets until David reached up to retrieve them. The half-filled pack of Marlboros would stay inside the dresser drawer. The cable knit sweater David kept at her place in case of a sudden drop in temperature was on a padded hanger in the hall closet, instead of its usual place on a kitchen chair. Ann's loft looked like it did when she first moved in.

She leaned back and let her head fall comfortably into the cushion. She wrapped her arms around herself and sighed. She pulled the coffee table closer to her so she could stretch her legs out in front of her. Her heartbeats slowed to a steady rhythm. If she were to take her pulse, she was sure it would be on the low end.

The absence of David's tumult, smoke, and chaos brought Ann a sense of calm, peace, and satisfaction. She knew the feelings would disappear once David re-entered her apartment, her life. Ann wondered why she couldn't have both—her lover and her serenity—but she understood that was impossible. If she were forced to give one up, she had no idea which one she'd choose.

Twenty-Seven

Rita tried to warn her. Instead of the telephone bringing David's voice on the evening of Leah's departure, it was Rita's. "Be prepared," she said. "I hate to be the one telling you this, but as your friend, I thought it my duty."

"What's up?" Ann asked. Her heart started to pound. Was it the Chardonnay causing the rapid beats? The rich foods she had just consumed? Or did she instinctively know the content of Rita's call?

"While you were home, on your week off with Leah, David got cozy with that Julie who you took under your wing," Rita said. "You know she's the publisher's niece."

"Did not know that," Ann said.

Ann's mind shot to her last conversation with Julie. They were discussing Ann's daughters because Julie was always eager for an update on young women who strayed from the norm. "I couldn't be prouder of them," Ann had told her. "It took years for their father and me to break away from society's expectations. We're both delighted they didn't wait that long before they spread their wings."

She always enjoyed her motherly sessions with Julie because they helped fill the void left by her out-of-state daughters. And Julie reminded Ann of a younger version of herself. She was a recent journalism grad from Medill and about the same height as Ann. And like Ann, Julie had red hair, but her locks were still bright and shiny while Ann's required chemical assistance every six weeks.

Aside from Julie's WASP background and Ann's Jewish one, and their age, another big difference was Julie was tenacious as a terrier. For example, when Ann balked at interviewing the parents of a slain teenager, Julie strode right up to the pair at the coffin and asked the irritating: *How does it feel?* Ann could never utter those words, in that setting, even if her career depended on it.

"Go ahead," Ann said to Rita, "tell me what happened." The picture of Julie, the little bitch, was now inked into the scene.

"At first, Julie was at that desk usually reserved for interns and cub reporters," Rita said. "But as the week went by, she inched closer and closer to yours. By Friday, she was sitting in your chair—like Anne Baxter in 'All About Eve.' As soon as I saw your precious shit head, I said to him, 'Hey, Harris, what's going on?'

"'Oh' he says to me, 'we're just testing her out on some of the stories Ann usually covers. Julie here's got a reputation for being really hard-hitting.'"

"'What does this mean for Ann?' I asked him. He looks me right in the face, and says, 'Nothing, no, nothing different for Ann.' But that evening, at Happy Hour, guess who's buying cocktails for Little Miss Brenda Starr? Or should I say, Eve Harrington? I didn't even think she was legal age."

There was silence on Ann's end, which prompted Rita to ask, "Honey, are you okay? Say something."

So David made the decision for her. Ann didn't have to choose between serenity and her lover after all. And, he had already chosen her replacement. She couldn't stop the tears that were starting to fill her eyes. No matter his faults, or the dishevel he had brought to her life, to her home, she'd miss the bastard. She'd miss his family, the warm-hearted Sunday night dinners at his mom's place. She'd miss his bear hugs and their feelings of protection and comfort. Mostly, though, she'd miss the love-making—passionate, uninhibited, and fun. But she stopped crying, refusing to be pathetic, to be a victim.

"I'm not surprised," Ann said. She tried to sound tough while using the back of her hand to wipe away leftover tears. She was grateful Rita was on the other end of the phone line rather than facing her for she didn't want her friend witnessing a simpering, weak side of Ann.

"I saw it coming. I knew he was losing interest in me. There were enough signs. [His late arrivals from Riccardo's, his eager smooch with Leah, his roving eyes at the office. They were all there, but Ann couldn't admit to them until now.] You didn't need to be a bloodhound to pick up the clues. I'll get over David; I just hope I still have a job. I'd miss that more than the asshole."

❧

There was no sign of David when Ann returned to work that Monday morning. She peeked into his office, no David. Just as she was about to approach her desk, the one where Julie was now sitting with Ann's telephone cradled in her right shoulder and her fingers on Ann's computer, she heard someone call her name.

"Robins, over here." It was Darin Cox, David's boss. He was standing outside his corner office, waving her over.

In the time Ann had been at the Ledger, she doubted if Cox had spoken more than two words to her. Maybe one, "welcome," when she first arrived. Now he was calling her into his private office. This can't be good news, she thought.

"Take a seat," he said. He closed the door behind him and pointed to a chair facing his desk. As he settled himself in his high-backed leather chair, Ann studied the framed pictures on the wall: photographs of Cox with Mayor Richard M. Daley, with Illinois governor James R. Thompson, with President Ronald Regan; framed copies of the Ledger's award-winning headlined stories; plaques announcing the newspaper's first-place standing in various competitions.

"This is never easy," Cox said. He clasped his hands together on the desk. "You've done great work here at the Ledger, but we've got to let you go."

"If my work has been great, why am I being fired?" Ann asked. She mustn't cry, for that would only give more credence to the view she was a softie, a disastrous trait for a newswoman.

"I don't want to go into specifics," Cox said. He was wringing his hands now, likely trying to demonstrate how difficult the rest of the conversation was going to be.

She was unsympathetic to his task, for all of that sentiment should go to Ann Robins, who was losing her dream job. She had to hold it together, must not think of the newsroom atmosphere that jazzed her like a shot of vitamin B-12. Must erase the memory of compatriots who shared the same journalistic lingo. Must avoid remembering the rush when words flowed quickly and landed exactly in order. Must forget the absolute joy in seeing her name, her byline, in print. No, she had zero sympathy for Cox.

"You are aware of our non-fraternization policy here at the Ledger," Cox continued.

"Whom supposedly have I been fraternizing with?" Ann asked. Her eyes were wide and innocent, but her heart was beating loud enough to betray her. If her chair had arms, like the big boss', she could've gripped them for support. But her seat bore no such attachments, so she was left to teeter on its ledge.

"A photo was dropped on my desk showing you and Dave Harris kissing," Cox said. Then he reached into a file folder that lay between them and pulled out a 4-by-6-color snapshot.

"When I asked Harris about this, he told me the truth." Cox held the evidence between two fingers as if it reeked.

"May I see the photo?" Ann asked. She reached across the desk to snatch it from Cox. "Wonder how you got this?" She knew the answer without Cox's admission; it was a picture of her and David on a Ferris wheel. They were at a neighborhood carnival, and a photographer offered to capture the two of them strapped into the ride. "Only five dollars," he had said, "let's see a kiss." She and David obliged. By the time their locked-in chair had made a circle—pausing first at the very top where David swung back and forth to further weaken Ann's stomach—their picture was ready.

"I want it," David said, exchanging a five-dollar bill for the photo. Then Ann watched, her heart happy as a puppy, as he tucked the picture into a plastic sleeve of his wallet.

"Of course Dave is too valuable to us," Cox said. "I'm sure you understand. You'll have severance pay, an excellent recommendation, and anything else you need."

Then he rose from his chair, extended a palm to Ann, and said, "Just go up to Human Resources and they'll handle everything."

Before heading for the elevator, Ann went to her former desk. Julie had already sneaked away, but someone had packed and left for her a cardboard carton containing her possessions. Maybe it was Rita? She plucked the items out one by one, their memories trailing along with each: a framed photo of her, Mayor Washington, and the teenager she had profiled in her first feature. The Mayor wanted to thank her personally for calling attention to the program, and thus the signed memento.

Also in the box, a yellowed clipping from a newspaper that showed her daughters and Joel in the Berkeley Square production of "Carousel." Another framed photo, this one of her brother Danny, bare-chested and muscled on the deck of his boat *Making Happy*. A sarong-clothed Sylvia was at the captain's wheel and two blonde, bikini-clad women were smiling on either side of Danny. "Wish you were here," was his inscription.

Another old clipping, this one from the Village Voice announcing the opening of The Robins Nest, "a new small theatre showcasing the works of the zany Robins sisters." Ann's favorite fountain pens and pencils, half-used reporters notebooks, opened packages of low-cal snacks; all stuffed into one carton. No telltale photos of her and David, of course. All of those were on display in her loft. And once she and her box of precious possessions would arrive home, any remnants of David Harris would be tossed in the trash.

She replaced the items and cradled the box in her arms, which almost obstructed her view ahead, but she was just tall enough to witness Harris walking swiftly into his office and closing the door behind him.

"Motherfucker," she said. She thought she cursed quietly, but the quick turning of heads told her otherwise.

Twenty-Eight

"Remember, we're just looking," Ann said to her daughters as they toured Chicago's annual dog show at McCormick Place.

"I know, I know, Mom," Jessie said. "But Audrey and I think it'd be good for you to have a dog. For companionship, for safety."

"Not only that," Audrey said, "but now that you're home all day, you'll be around to take care of a pet. You wouldn't have to crate her, or worry about her being alone."

"True," Ann said. The girls had flown in to help Ann celebrate her 50th birthday, and decided along with their visit — which Ann swore, "is the best present of all"—a dog would be the perfect gift.

"You just want me to have something else to dote on," Ann said. She knew her daughters were right; it was time she got her dog. Ann had loved dogs as long as she could remember. In childhood, Sylvia nixed them. And in marriage, she never pressed for one because Joel was allergic to animals. When he first left, she thought it best to keep her place pet free, just in case. Then, her full-time job at the Ledger made ownership unwise. Now, with all those excuses behind her, she had no reason to bar a dog from her life.

As she strolled the exhibit hall, with the dueling scents of dog fur and deodorizers leading the way, Ann linked her arms into each one of her daughters. "You think if I have a puppy in my life, I wouldn't call you so often, or worry about you so much," she said.

"No, no, you're wrong. We love you, little mama," Audrey said. "We love your phone calls." But her attention was elsewhere. She was standing at a booth marked Clara's Collars and held up a red cloth circle with *Bitch of the House* stitched in black.

"Look, sort of funny and sort of gross," she said. Then she unlocked the collar's latch and attempted to place it around her own slim neck. "Whadda ya think?" she asked. "Edgy, right?"

"Take that off," Ann said. She snatched it away and returned it to the vendor's counter. "I know that's what they call female dogs," she said to a startled Audrey, "but the label doesn't suit you, sweetheart."

"I think we should look at the dogs before we check out their accessories," Jessie said, pulling on Ann's arm to lead her to the hall marked Breeders.

"Oh, look, Toy Poodle," Audrey said. She reached through a metal crate to touch the dog's fur. "She's like a doll. You could carry her around, put a ribbon in her hair..."

"Too small," Ann interrupted. "If I get a dog, I want a big one, with a loud bark, something scary enough to chase away the bad guys."

"How about a German Shepherd?" Jessie asked, pointing to the Large Breed section.

"One German brand in the family is my limit," Ann said.

"The Volkswagen?" her daughters asked.

"Yeah," Ann said. Then, her thoughts went back to the beige VW Beetle that took a young officer and his pregnant wife from Chicago to Fort Maxwell. "Audrey, did I ever tell you it was during our ride to the Army base when I knew I was pregnant with you?" she asked.

"Yes, Momma, you told me," Audrey said patiently, as if she were the adult and Ann the child. Then she stroked her mother's hair as lovingly as she done with the puppy. "You tried for a whole year to get pregnant, and here I was, growing inside you on the way to Massachusetts." Then Audrey knelt down and put an ear to Ann's tummy. (Her pose reminded Ann of those parts in movie where the husband first learns they're having a baby.)

Audrey ignored the wide-eyed and open-mouthed strangers who were gaping at her performance. Now, she was cooing to Ann's stomach (nearly flat now, but Ann *could* remember when it was big as a beach ball, when her daughter actually inhabited it).

"Come out little baby, it's time to come out. And then, miracle of miracles, out I popped!" With that, Audrey sprung up on her feet, full-grown and cheeky.

Ann laughed; that was one thing she loved and admired about her daughters: their ability to disregard others' views. Not only in this small scene, but also in the way they lived their lives. She was always happy for any opportunity to describe their unorthodox paths: a seedy New York theatre instead of a corporate office or schoolroom; lovers in a variety of shades, ethnicities, and sexuality, rather than a doctor or lawyer husband; a Greenwich Village walk-up in place of a Highland Park two-story.

She was proud of their bravery, their self-confidence, and she wondered if in any way they identified with their mother. Perhaps they had witnessed Ann's movement through life, with its changes in directions and reversals. She hoped they admired their mother's survival. Perhaps her trajectory—unorthodox in some ways—gave her daughters the encouragement to be different, to take risks, and to thumb their nose at society.

She liked to think that was the case.

As Ann and her daughters strolled the aisles, she lagged behind at a booth marked English Bulldogs. She read from the poster, "Although Bulldogs have comparatively small statures, they are stout, exceptionally sturdy, and widely built. They have round dark eyes..." She stared at the dog on display, his white and brown coat wrinkled into folds near his big head. David Harris. In those comic comparisons of dogs and owners, Harris and this Bulldog could be a pair.

As Ann stared at the animal, she remembered Harris' phone call after she was booted from the Ledger. He had admitted his treachery, acknowledged he was weak when it came to attractive, young women (did he have to add that?), and apologized for his gutless behavior. But, he never asked for a second chance and Ann was proud to say she never offered him one.

For a few weeks after his call, she'd get weepy if she saw something that reminded her of him. But without daily office sightings, without Friday nights at Riccardo's (no longer a Ledger reporter, she worried she'd feel out-of-place at the bar); eventually, he faded from her mind. She was optimistic there could one day be a new man in her life. And if not, well, she'd have her daughters, her mother and brother, her friendship with Joel, her women friends, her freelance writing career; and perhaps now, a never-straying, warm-bodied pet for company.

"Okay, this is it," Jessie said. She was standing before a booth marked Golden Retrievers. Instead of being restrained in a crate, the dog here was sitting on his haunches on a square of fake grass. His face wore a big grin and his long tongue stretched out like a ribbon.

His breathing was fast and loud, as if the young woman standing in front of him was his long-lost owner. A red bandana circled his neck, which seemed appropriate for a dog whose tag read, Cowboy.

Cowboy rose on his hind legs, put both front paws on Jessie's shoulders and licked her face. "You've made a pal, young lady," said the woman who was tending the booth. "Down boy." The dog immediately obeyed.

Jessie used a sleeve to wipe her face, and then turned to Ann and read from a flyer she had lifted from a stack next to Cowboy, "Golden Retrievers are known to be friendly, protective, and loyal to their owners. Perfect."

"Loyalty would be nice," Ann agreed. She reached over to pet the dog's copper-colored head, and then said to the woman tending the booth, "I was thinking more of a puppy. Will you be having a litter available soon?"

"He's our champion stud," the woman said. "Just look at his certificates and ribbons."

Then she opened a three-ring binder and flipped through pages of photographs, documents, and show ribbons preserved in see-through protective pages.

"We'll have some pups in a few weeks, just add your name to this here list. We'll call you when they're born, and then six weeks later you can pick out your male or female."

"No, Mommy, no," Audrey said. "You don't want a purebred puppy. You want to adopt a dog from a shelter. Thousands of dogs are waiting to be rescued. That's what it says here in this brochure." Audrey was reading from a three-paneled folder she had plucked from a tote bag filled with descriptions of boarding kennels, veterinarians, and obedience trainers.

"Well, that certainly would be one way to go," the woman sneered. She turned quickly from the three Robins women to attend to a family eyeing Cowboy's lineage. Then she tossed out, "If you adopt, you can never be sure of what you're getting. After all, abandoned dogs are usually older; they may have personality issues or temperament problems. With a purebred, you know what you're buying."

"Abandoned?" Ann asked. "Those dogs over there at the Golden Rescue booth have been abandoned? Let's check them out, girls," she said. She turned her back on the breeder.

Three dogs were in this booth; one a puppy, and the other two medium-sized. Each had the gleeful face of Cowboy. "See,

Mommy, you can still get a puppy," Jessie said, as she lifted the tawny ball of fluff and cradled it in her arms.

"If you're considering adoption, I'd recommend this one," said the woman standing next to the dogs. "Her name is Sadie and she's older, 18 months, housebroken, fixed, and ready for a new home."

"Hi, Sadie," Audrey said. Then she turned to the woman and asked, "Why was she given up?"

The woman stroked Sadie's carrot-colored fur, gave her a kiss on the top of her head, and said, "Can you believe it? This is the sweetest, gentlest dog I've seen in a long time. Her owners got a new baby and decided they no longer had the time or interest in caring for their pet. Dropped Sadie off with us; just like that. As if you couldn't break a dog's heart."

Ann reached to pet the dog named Sadie. "Sweetie," she said. "Want to come home with me?"

Twenty-Nine

Ann was grateful it was a graveside service, for it meant there'd be fewer mourners to spot her. She didn't want anyone's stares or sympathies be directed towards her. All expressions of concern should go to Pearl, Manny's widow, rather than to Ann, the estranged, and out-of-place daughter-in-law.

"Will you be okay back here, Mom?" Audrey asked, as she stood with her mother. "You know we have to sit up front." She collapsed the umbrella she used to escort her mother from car to tent, and then gave it a small shake to release its droplets to the carpeted ground.

"No, no, I'm fine, you go ahead. Be with your dad and grandmother," Ann said.

"I'm not sitting next to *her*," Jessie said. She leaned her head in the direction of Lois Golden, who was walking in on the arm of Joel.

"Go sit next to Clair and Ted," Ann said, nodding towards Joel's sister and brother-in-law. She could feel her high heels sinking into the carpet that had been hastily laid on the wet grass when the gravediggers saw the sky open up. Feeling rocky on the uneven floor, Ann grabbed onto the back of a chair in the last row of mourners.

"We *should* be next to Dad," Audrey said. "Come on Jessie, we don't have to talk to her; but Dad will want us to be with him in the front row."

"Go, go, girls," Ann said. "Don't worry about me."

Manny's death and funeral had occurred the same week his granddaughters were in town for Ann's birthday. A perfect metaphor for life, Ann thought: celebration and grief in the same seven-day period. The girls had been asleep in Ann's bedroom when Joel called with the news. (They had offered to use the pullout couch in the living room, but she declined because her early morning coffee grinding and computer noises would surely wake them.)

"Daddy passed away last night," Joel had said, without introduction. Of course, there was no need to give his name. She could recognize his voice no matter how many years they'd been apart. And now that sorrow had rekindled his Southern accent, there was no doubt as to her caller's identity.

Her voice, on the other hand, could often be confused with his daughters'. But considering the early hour, Joel knew instantly the person answering the phone would be his once-wife. First wife, ex-wife, separated wife? (She ran through the possible titles.) She was trying to figure out a label for her murky marital status.

Ann often wondered what designation Joel used to introduce Lois to others. *Girlfriend* sounded silly for people their age, *partner* was either too corporate or reserved for couples of the same sex, and *significant other* was a mouthful. Evidently though, Lois' rank didn't prevent her from occupying the wooden folding chair next to Joel in the mourners' row.

"Oh, I'm so sorry, honey," Ann had said to Joel on the phone. "What happened?"

"Mama and Daddy were in Florida about to step onto their cruise ship—Greek Islands, I think—when he took ill.

"The cruise people called an ambulance, rushed him to the hospital, but it was too late. Massive heart attack. The funeral's Sunday. Please be sure the girls are there. You, too, Ann, okay?"

"Of course, honey," Ann answered.

Honey was another tongue twister Ann encountered whenever she spoke to Joel. She just couldn't get out of the habit of using that term of endearment. But it seemed Joel didn't have a problem letting *Sugar* dissolve and replacing it with her given name.

❧

"Can you believe I still called him *Honey*?" she said to Rita after updating her with Joel's news. "I suppose it's because I don't hate him. After all, that's what we called each other for 23 years; we never used first names. And when the kids were around, we used *Mommy* and *Daddy*. How pathetic is that?"

"Listen, I'm not criticizing," Rita said. "I think it's sweet; just a bit odd for someone who's separated, and whose spouse is living with another woman, and by all rights, should hate his guts."

❧

As she stood in the back row of Manny's funeral, Ann studied the wardrobes her daughters had gleaned from her closet. "Thank God you wear so much black," Jessie had said while tossing to the bed handfuls of hangers bearing black tee shirts.

"No suits, Mom?" Audrey asked. She moved each garment along the closet pole as if she was in a dry cleaning store trying to match a customer's ticket stub.

"Not since I left gainful employment," Ann said. "As an author I'm permitted to wear clothing more suited to creative types." (She hadn't published anything but freelance articles, but figured if she called herself *author* often enough it might one day appear under a book's title.)

"Okay, how's this?" Jessie asked, one hand holding up to her chest a long-sleeved black shirt and the other covering her lower half with a peasant skirt.

"My ethnic look," Ann laughed, "it'll work."

As for Audrey, she selected a short-sleeved black top and layered it over her own tee shirt that bore The Robins Nest Theatre name and logo (two birds fluttering above an about-to-be-hatched egg). She paired that with her own black slacks.

Her daughters were appropriately dressed for this somber occasion. As for herself, Ann was also clad in black, her only jewelry the gold band she still wore on her left hand; a habit as hard to break as the pet name she called Joel. She wore no necklace or broach, and her blouse would remain empty of the torn black ribbon worn by the deceased's immediate family.

Ann turned her attention to the rabbi who was intoning Manny's virtues: "a wonderful husband and provider to his wife, a hard-working and loving father to his children, a caring grandpa to his granddaughters." Ann smiled at the rabbi's use of *grandpa* rather than *zadie.*

In her world of Ashkenazi Jews, the Yiddish tag was universal. But because Manny and Pearl had settled in South Carolina rather than the ghettos of Chicago or New York, they tended to leave behind much of the *schtetl* dialect and customs that clung to Ann's family like chicken fat.

Truthfully, she couldn't imagine her daughters calling Joel's father *Zadie.*

They certainly loved Manny, and he was appropriately crowing and affectionate whenever he saw them; it was simply a case of distance. Often, when Audrey and Jessie came to Chicago, their grandparents were on a trip somewhere. And Manny refused to visit New York, calling it "a god-awful sewer of a place." Still, his granddaughters were shocked and upset when they learned of his death.

Ann had waited until the girls woke before giving them Joel's news. At first, she thought she should rouse them from sleep and let Joel tell them himself. But since he didn't suggest it, Ann decided to postpone the sad announcement. Besides, she wanted to absorb every happy moment of her daughters' homecoming before ruining the morning.

She listened for their voices on the other side of the bedroom door. "You up?" one of them asked. Their voices sounded so much alike, it was often difficult to identify the speaker. "No, let me sleep," the other begged.

"I heard a phone ring. Maybe it was from the theatre."

"Okay, okay, I'm up."

Then, they both appeared in the living room. Ann wished she took a photo to capture this favorite view of her daughters: faces still childish and sleepy, long hair messy and half in their eyes, faded t-shirts and men's boxers as pajamas. Could there be any sight more beautiful? If only she could keep them there forever. Lock them inside her apartment and refuse to let them out. Impossible, she knew, but a frequent wish.

"Sit," Ann said. "I've got some bad news." She repeated Joel's explanation of what happened and watched her daughters sink into the couch.

"Poor grandpa," Jessie said.

"Poor grandma," from Audrey. "How will she manage without him? Should we call Daddy with condolences?"

"That would be nice," Ann said.

"We'd better call the theatre and let everyone know we'll be gone a few more days," Jessie said.

Ann was glad her daughters didn't hesitate in deciding they would stay in town for the funeral. She'd have them to herself for a bit more time. Well, perhaps not to herself, she'd have to share them with Joel, with Pearl. She supposed she could be big enough to handle that.

As the rabbi went on with his eulogy, Ann's mind replayed scenes starring Manny, as if she were a projectionist in a small movie house. Through the ray of dust motes that glistened in the light from the imaginary machine, she saw Manny proudly inspecting the first house she and Joel owned, the one in Spring Grove that Manny's loan had enabled. (Did they ever repay the money? Ann couldn't remember.) "Y'all got yourself a good place," Manny had said as he knocked on drywall, then tilted his eyeglasses upwards to get a closer look at the nails that had been pounded into the wooden doorframe. Did he really believe that cheap lumber was a quality product, or was he fibbing for his son's benefit? Either way, he had been kind with his assessment.

At the graveside, when Ann stood on tiptoe to get a better look at the first row of mourners, she could just about see Joel put his right arm around Pearl. She waited to see where his left would go. Would it encircle Lois? That might be hard to take. Perhaps in deference to his daughters who were in the same row, as his separated (but still friendly) spouse standing in the back, he kept that arm on his own lap. Ann couldn't see Lois' hands, but she likely placed a sympathetic one on Joel's knee.

Ann recalled Lois' surprise phone call soon after Joel's departure: "Ann, I hope you can forgive me," she had said. "I never meant to hurt you, and it was certainly not retaliation. Joel and I fell in love, and this time as grown ups, rather than the foolish kids we were back in college."

Ann had paused before answering, and then finally said, "I'm not angry at you, or at Joel. I know this wasn't deliberate. I understand how these sorts of things can happen. [Did she ever.] I wish you the best." Then, that was it. Any further contact between the two women was cordial—certainly not like their long-ago friendship, but good enough, considering the circumstances.

❧

"Manny Robins was a Jew and a Southerner," the rabbi said, "and these two identities made him the compassionate and courteous human being we all knew and loved."

Again, the rabbi's remarks elicited a smile on Ann's face.

She was usually irked when during a eulogy, a rabbi claimed knowledge of the deceased; for generally, all of his information would've been collected the day before, when relatives listed virtues for the note-taking rabbi. Ann had been at funerals where the rabbi screwed up—mispronounced the name of the beloved wife, or embellished ethics known to be false—but this wasn't the case for Manny. Compassionate and courteous were his legitimate trademarks.

Ann thought about his phone call to her years ago, soon after Ann had moved into her loft. "How's the prettiest gal living in the sorriest part of town doing?" he had asked.

"Hi, Dad," Ann answered. She hadn't had time to figure out the proper title for an in-law whose son was now attached to someone else. It would've been disrespectful to use *Manny,* and the only time he had been *Mr. Robins* was at their very first introduction when a nervous Joel brought Ann home to meet his parents.

"You know Joel's momma and me are still torn up 'bout this separation thing," he said.

"I know, I know." She was trying to hold back tears that surprisingly escaped whenever the topic arose.

"Now we're not taking sides; you know we love you both. But it seems to me you could apologize to our boy and get back together."

Didn't Joel's parents know about Lois? Their son was an actor, true, but hiding that information must've taken some emoting.

"My bull-headed son spilled the whole story. Naturally, I was thunderstruck when he told me about your, how do I put this politely, your mistake.

"I sure thought you had enough brains to avoid that sort of thing. 'Forgive the girl,' I told my son. 'One slip-up shouldn't wreck a marriage.'"

Ann didn't have the heart to tell Manny about his son's part in the split. If he didn't know about Lois, and her Highland Park lovers' nest, Ann wasn't going to be the one to blab. You could call Ann a lot of things, but *snitch* wasn't one of them.

"My boy told me about the place you've been living in, gave me your phone number, too. 'How could you let your little-bitty wife live in that part of town?' I asked him. 'Don't you have any pride left?' That's what I said, and I don't take back a word of it."

"Dad, I'm grateful for your concern, but I'm fine. My neighborhood has come a long way from Skid Row. Today it's quite the trendy place to live."

"Right," Manny said with unusual sarcasm. "Listen here, y'all belong in the suburbs. All this nonsense started when you left, what was the name of that place? Spring Grove, that's it; that's where you should've stayed. Moving to the city, to that godforsaken *integrated* place; that's where all your trouble began. Why, I could hardly believe my ears when Joel told me about your, your...Nope, can't even say it."

"Dad, I'd rather not talk about that with you," Ann said. "I appreciate your concern, but it's really between Joel and me."

"What about my grandbabies? How do you think your foolishness affects them?"

"Well, your grandbabies are grown women," Ann said, "and they seem to be handling everything quite well." (Ann and Joel were sticking to the "we've grown apart" script with their daughters. If the girls placed any blame on Joel and his affair with Lois, Ann didn't dissuade them. Perhaps later in life, after her daughters had made their own messes, she'd tell them of her role in the family soap opera.)

"Those girls put on a good face," Manny said. "Y'all are professionals at that sort of thing. All that playacting you let your husband and daughters get into. You should've put your foot down, insist he stay in lawyering, make those girls of yours find Jewish husbands, or at least get some sensible careers."

Ann kept silent and let Manny continue, for she knew he was broken-hearted and felt helpless not being able to repair things. For a man who had always been in charge—in his marriage and work life—this episode must've been as puzzling as a Yankee's accent.

One thing he wasn't conflicted about was his pride in Ann's writing. Whenever her byline appeared, Manny would phone her and repeat his latest golf course conversation. "'That's my daughter-in-law,' I told the boys. Took that Ledger 'round to my foursome, pointed to your name under the headline, and crowed like the loudest rooster. My pals are getting sick of me pushing your stories in their faces." Evidently, Manny hadn't told his friends about his son's split. That's what we call *burying the lede*, Ann thought.

Of course, Joel couldn't hide Lois and his living arrangement from his parents forever. Ann couldn't remember the occasion; perhaps it was some traditional or Jewish holiday when Joel would be joining his parents for dinner and thought it a good setting for the introduction.

Manny had described the scene to Ann in one of his phone calls: "Well, your mother-in-law and I nearly bust a gut when Joel walked into the house with her.

"I'm not sure y'all remember, but Joel and Lois used to be sweethearts before you came into the picture," he said. Remember? How could she ever forget that bit of irony? "She was as pretty as ever," Manny said, but then caught himself, "of course, older and maybe some pounds heavier." Could he be any kinder?

"Our Pearl was sort of speechless, just took a seat on the couch and listened to her son work his way out of the bramble bush. But I didn't beat around that bush. 'Son,' I said, 'what's going on?'"

Ann closed her eyes trying to conjure the Winnetka living room, the upholstered couch with its pattern of cabbage roses, the vestibule where Joel and Lois awkwardly stood, and the baby grand where Audrey played her latest composition for her grandparents. (Had they removed the old framed photos of bride and groom that stood on the piano? If not, one of those polite Southerners surely would walk briskly to the spot and place the picture facedown.)

"'Momma, Daddy,' Joel says to us, 'Lois and I are a couple. We're living together, I've moved into her house.' That's it; then the two of them take seats on the couch next to my open-mouthed Pearl. 'Hell, son,' I said, 'you're not even divorced; or did your momma and I miss that bit of news?' Then Joel straightens up his shoulders as if he's being questioned by Union soldiers, and says to me, 'I know, Daddy, I know I'm not divorced, but Lois is willing to wait until that happens.' Then he looks at Lois, who's as embarrassed as she could be, and wraps his arm around her, protecting the poor girl from the likes of me.

"Well of course Pearl and I behaved ourselves throughout dinner, asking polite questions about Lois' kids, her hobbies, that sort of stuff.

"But when I got my son by himself, I told him, 'Joel, don't you go and rush into anything. You know how I feel about Ann; it would break my heart to see you divorce my best girl. Promise me you'll take your time. And that's what he did, promised me he wouldn't do anything hasty."

When the graveside service ended, Audrey and Jessie returned to escort Ann to her car. First she stopped to hug a weeping Pearl and offer condolences, and then reached up to kiss Joel on his cheek. "He was my best pal," Ann said.

She turned to shake hands with Lois, and that's when she saw it: an emerald cut diamond on Lois' left hand, the ring finger right next to the pinkie. *Fiancée.* Finally, Joel had come up with a proper description for Ann's replacement.

Thirty

The minute Ann heard the clicks of three seat belts being attached inside her Honda Civic, she blurted, "Did you know?" She targeted the question first to Audrey who had taken the passenger's front seat. Instead of waiting for her daughter's answer, she followed up with, "Have they set a date?"

"Not a clue about any of that stuff," Audrey said. She sounded both innocent and baffled. "I saw the ring as soon as I sat down, but I didn't have a chance to ask Dad about it. And I certainly wasn't going to ask *her*."

"What about you?" Ann asked. She turned her head over her right shoulder to send her question to Jessie who was stretched out in the backseat.

"Nope, clueless as well," Jessie said. "I did ask Dad 'what's up?' but he said he'd fill me in later. I'm still waiting." Then she joined her sister in posing a question to Ann, "Are you okay, Mom?"

"It was a shock, I'll admit it; but I guess I should've expected it." Ann said. She shook her head as if to rid it of the diamond's image, and then thought, must keep my eyes on the road. It had been years since she was last at Claire's; and never this route—from cemetery to *shiva* house.

Despite a few missed turns along the way, Ann's car arrived at the same time as the other mourners. She and her daughters left their umbrellas in the car and raced to the front door to avoid the steady rain. One by one, they cleansed their hands in the bucket that was provided for the post-cemetery Jewish ritual, and then stepped into a house that felt both familiar and strange.

Joel met Ann at the door and took her by the elbow to pull her away from their daughters. "Ann, please come out in the back with me," he said. His voice was hushed, which was appropriate for the occasion, and as it turned out, for their upcoming conversation. Then he steered her to a corner of the porch, away from cigarette smokers who had been chased outside.

"I wanted to tell you before you saw the ring," he said. "But with everything going on around Daddy's passing and taking care of Momma, there just wasn't time. I'm really sorry you had to find out this way."

"Remember *my* engagement ring? From Feldman's?" Ann said, veering the conversation from his futile apology to a long ago memory. "It was sweet and small, but I really loved that ring. Then I went and left it on the bathroom sink in what's her name's house. Rosalie? Roberta? I can't remember. It must've fallen down the drain. We never found it, and we never replaced it. Remember?"

Through the porch window that looked into the dining room, Ann could see the goings on inside: men and women embracing Pearl, then walking to the buffet table to fill their plates. From one end to the other, the table was loaded with deli trays.

People dressed in black (like crows gathering at a picnic) inched along the rectangle, piling their plates with Jewish delicacies and the occasional Southern dish. Bagels and biscuits, corned beef and fried chicken—odd pairings, but something Manny would have enjoyed.

"It's time, Ann," Joel said, pulling her back to the present. "It's time. You and I have been apart for, what is it, six or seven years. Lois put her foot down. I don't blame her, do you? She told me, 'marriage or it's over.'"

Ann thought for a moment, then asked, "So, what is it, Joel? What does Lois have that I don't?" She looked up at him, at his hazel eyes now bordered by small wrinkles, at his light brown hair now touched by grey. He was still a good 12 inches taller than her, so she had to stretch upwards to take him in. And for a moment, she stood in a pose she hadn't taken for three decades. It was the same stance the photographer had captured for their wedding album. In that long ago picture, on a day that broke sunny and warm, she was the adoring young bride and he her earnest groom. But on this day, everything was different, including the couple's dark wardrobes and the rainy weather.

"She needs me," Joel answered, and then he turned away to place his hands on the porch railing. Hidden from Ann's direct stare, he seemed to grow bolder.

"You never seemed to have needed me. You were always so independent, so competent. Even from the very beginning, when you were just my wife and then the mother of my children, I never felt *needed*. Some mornings, when I went off to work, I'd think, if I disappear Ann would just roll up her sleeves and continue on, managing quite well."

"I'd cry," Ann said, her voice sounding flat and defeated.

"Yes, you probably would cry," Joel agreed. He was still speaking towards the damp air in front of him. "But after drying your tears, you'd make a note on the grocery list to buy another box of Kleenex, and then go on as usual. Hardly skipping a beat."

"So now I get demerits for being organized, capable?" Ann asked. "I thought you appreciated my competence. You didn't seem to mind, back then, my handling of all of that stuff."

"You know what I mean," Joel said. "With Lois, she wants to know where I'm going when I leave the house, when I'll be home; as if her day had no meaning unless I was in it. And at night, when we watch TV together, she's at my side, not going up to bed an hour before me."

"And you like that?" Ann asked. "You don't find it stifling, all that togetherness, all that neediness?"

"I love it," Joel said. He turned to face her. "I love it." Then he walked back inside the house and left Ann out there on her own.

She waited a few minutes before reaching for the door handle. Her hands were still damp from their dip in the water at the doorstep, so she shook them a few times. When she was certain none of the smokers could see her next move, she gave her hands a final swipe on the back of her slacks. Dry and clean now, she removed the gold band from her left hand, and used the right to tuck the ring deep inside her pocket.

Compared to the length of their marriage and separation, the divorce itself was over in a blink. Ann saw no reason to protest or fight. She realized Joel was happier with Lois; and as for herself, she had to admit she was content with Sadie as companion. Without a spouse or boyfriend to make demands, Ann was free to rise as early as she wished, write as long as inspired, pamper the dog as much as she chose, and retire to bed at her preferred hour. If she hungered for male companionship, she could always count on a friend to find a single (usually short) guy for a fix-up. But inevitably, Ann would spend most of those dates peeking at her wristwatch and wishing she were back home with Sadie.

With minimal attorney interference (Joel served as his own counsel, and Ann turned to a woman Rita had used in one of her settlements), they agreed to split any remaining assets and relieve each other of future obligations. Then, with the judge and lawyer hustling out of the small, empty courtroom, Ann and Joel kissed each other's cheek, held a hug longer than most divorcing couples, and that was it; their marriage was officially over.

Before they left to go their separate ways, Ann noticed that Joel's eyes were misted with tears, just like hers. She suspected their feelings for each other would remain conflicted for years. They'd recall their early happy marriage, the immediate joys of parenthood, their tenuous support as each strained convention, their pride in daughters who inherited best traits of each, and ultimately, their sadness as they pulled away from one another.

Instead of going straight home, Ann decided to walk to the Art Institute where she strolled through the galleries. "It helped me see the larger world out there," she explained to Rita on the phone that evening. "Art, creativity, life, suffering, all there in the museum. My little story is just a speck in the universe, uninteresting, unimportant. The world goes on."

"Shall I cue the violins?" Rita said. "Sorry, I don't mean to be flip, but your lack of anger, your stoicism, is freaking me out. Tell me you're okay, that you're not masking a breakdown."

"I'm okay," Ann said.

As it turned out, Joel's engagement wasn't the only nuptial surprise Ann received that month. "I've got the best news!" Sylvia gushed over the phone. "Marty proposed and we're getting married soon. 'No sense waiting,' he said. 'We're not getting any younger.' So of course, I said 'yes,' and I need you and the girls to be here. It's going to be very informal, with the ceremony on the beach, and the party in the Aloha Gardens."

"On the beach?" Ann said, "how wonderful, how very Hawaiian."

"No shoes!" Sylvia said. "Barefoot! Can you imagine? Promise me you'll come."

"Of course I'll be there, Mom, I wouldn't miss it for the world. But I can't speak for the girls. I'm sure if their schedule permits, they'll be there, too."

"Danny's going to be the best man. You'll be my maid, or is it matron of honor, okay?"

"Whichever," Ann said. "I'll be she." After she hung up the phone, Ann went into her bedroom and lifted off the nightstand the framed wedding portrait of her parents. She used her sleeve to wipe away dust and studied the sepia picture. The bridal couple appeared serene and elegant: Sylvia in a long white gown with a lace train that rippled out at least two feet in front of her. She clutched a bouquet of roses and lilies-of-the-valley that was so big it nearly obscured the upper part of her body. Although the photo was not in color, Sylvia's eyes were bright, her lips dark. Ann could imagine the blue and red popping out in real life. She looked stunning.

Gene was dressed in a black tuxedo and stiff-looking white shirt. His lapel held the same lily-of-the-valley as his young wife (19!). His black hair was slicked back and his boyish face (he was 25) wore a slight smile, as if he knew he had won the town beauty and tried not to gloat.

That photo was in every house Ann ever lived in. It wasn't until she was out of childhood that she realized the backdrop was painted scenery, somewhere in a photographer's studio. Everything was phony, the French doors leading to a balcony, the lush draperies hanging on either side of the doors, the staircase, and the mural depicting a landscape. All illusion.

Poor Sylvia. In her first marriage, she held no love for her husband. In her second, she took on an aged and ailing cheapskate. You'd think she had had enough of the whole marriage business. But here she was, about to make a third leap. Well, bully for her.

❧

Several months after Sylvia's announcement, Ann was in her loft apartment with a CD of Carmen McRae playing in the background. She turned to her dog lying flat at her feet, and asked, "So, what do you think? Which one should I open first, right or left?" In each hand Ann held a large, square white envelope. At first, Sadie remained perfectly still, and then realizing her mistress was talking to her, energetically thumped her thick tail on the wooden floor.

Ann decided to first attack the envelope bearing the return address of Lois Golden. She used a knife to slice open the flap, then, after reading the "who, what, where, and when," placed the wedding invitation face down on the table. Next, she opened the floral-scented envelope that held an invitation from Sylvia Fisher Simon and Martin Henry Guthman requesting Ann's presence in far off Hawaii. And guess what?

"Can you believe it?" she asked Sadie. "The very same day!" The dog rose from her horizontal position to place her head on her mistress' knees. She looked up at Ann; her dark brown eyes pleading for an end to the conversation and a stroll outside followed by a game of fetch.

By now, Ann was certain she could interpret Sadie's gestures, even though others scoffed at the idea. "You're full of it," Rita had once said as she listened to Ann describe Sadie's body language.

"No, really, she gets depressed if I ignore her for too long." Ann said. "Attention must be paid. My dog is very needy. Like today for instance, when I left the house to meet you for lunch, Sadie dug her teeth into my sleeve trying to drag me back inside."

"Doesn't that bother you?" Rita said. "You can't go anywhere without worrying about your dog getting blue because you've left her side. That would make me crazy."

"No," Ann said, "I sort of like it."

"Guess what came in the mail today?" It was Audrey, calling from New York. "Hmm? " Ann teased, "two wedding invitations?"

"You got Grandma's? *And* Dad's?" Audrey asked.

"Yes, isn't that sweet?"

"Are you going to Dad's?"

"Fortunately, your grandmother bailed me out. Did you notice the date of the dual nuptials? They're exactly the same, Sunday, June 17, 1990? Your dear *Bubbie* gave me the best excuse in the world."

"Hey, Mom." It was Jessie, grabbing the phone's receiver from her sister. "Are you okay? I overheard you got Dad's invitation, too."

"I'm okay, Jessie," Ann said. "Honest, I'm perfectly okay. So what are you two going to do about the conflict in wedding dates?"

"Well," Audrey said," I hope you and Grandma understand, but we'll have to go to Dad's wedding."

"I understand. I'll miss you, so will my mom. This will give her one more thing to be angry at your dad about, keeping her granddaughters from attending her wedding."

"No love lost there?" Audrey asked.

"Not from day one," Ann said. "I bet my mother thinks Dad [There was that title again. Would she ever lose that habit, now that he was marrying another woman?] planned the date deliberately. But he doesn't even know she's getting married."

"Believe me, we'd rather be on a Hawaiian beach than in a Highland Park living room watching our father pledge to honor and obey another woman," Jessie said. "But we have to be there to support Dad."

Leah also had to decline Sylvia's invitation. (She wasn't on the list for the Golden-Robins nuptials because her relationship with the bride remained as fractured as it had been in college, when Leah took Ann's side in the young couple's breakup.)

"I really would've loved to attend," Leah told Ann, "but Ken and I will be in London visiting Benjy and his family, and then to Spain for Adam and his latest girlfriend. I sent Sylvia a gift of French perfume, very floral, very pricey. And some wine for the groom."

"You'll be missed," Ann assured her, but was happy to learn Leah's marriage was still surviving the past liaison with Jacques. (Leah had taken a lesson from Ann's unfortunate confession to Joel, and never told Ken about her own *affaire de cœur*.)

The ceremony was arranged to begin about fifteen minutes before sunset so the wedding photos would include that stunning (and real) Hawaiian backdrop.

Sylvia looked gorgeous in a simple white dress designed to resemble a sarong, but a bit more modest for a woman her age. Instead of carrying a bouquet, the bride wore several leis of lilacs around her neck.

Her long hair, which she had piled atop her head, was still mostly black, and the gray strands that invaded over the years, only added to her beauty. She wore a white orchid on her right ear, which would be transferred to her left after the "I Do's" were declared.

The groom was also in white, his shirt unbuttoned several inches from his neck and his slacks bore a crease that ran down to his bare feet. With his tan, Marty (he insisted on the nickname immediately after introductions) could easily pass for a native. Everyone agreed the couple looked as glamorous as movie stars from the '40s.

Ann had planned on shopping in Fields for an outfit to wear to her mother's wedding. But Sylvia insisted she'd handle the purchase. "Your choices in Chicago are going to be drab and somber," Sylvia said.

"The shops here have a gorgeous selection of brightly-colored dresses, much better suited for our tropical climate. Trust me." Ann relented and was relieved to find Sylvia's selection was a lime green frock that complemented Ann's red hair, and in a style that flattered her short, busty figure.

As Ann stood to the side of her mother and listened to the rabbi (also shoeless, but wearing a multi-colored *yarmulke*) recite the blessings, she used a Kleenex to wipe her eyes. These were tears of joy.

Following the ceremony, and the dinner that was a mixture of Hawaiian cuisine and Jewish dishes, Ann took her brother's hand to lead him to the dance floor. As they moved slowly to the music of the Aloha Gardens house band, Danny asked, "So, what about you, sister dear? Now that you're officially single, are you planning to go hunting for a mate?"

She looked at her brother, whose face resembled their dad's, and whose protective embrace also recalled Gene. She laid her head against Danny's Hawaiian shirt and thought about the heartwarming ceremony she just witnessed. For a moment, she imagined the other one taking place in another setting. But that scene quickly dissolved as she inhaled the aroma of the tropical flowers and felt on her bare arms the soothing breeze of the Pacific Ocean.

"You never know, brother dear," she said, "you never know." Then she listened as the band switched to a faster beat. Her feet caught the rhythm, and soon, she was twirling around the floor, moving easily to the happier, lighter tune.

CPSIA information can be obtained
at www.ICGtesting.com
Printed in the USA
FFOW02n2328130718
47420888-50649FF